An Unconventional Education

A Pride and Prejudice Variation

Sydney Salier

To Michael

As always, thanks

My thanks also to all those lovely
readers on FF who helped to improve this
story.

CONTENTS

Sydney Salier

Part 1

1   Prologue

Mrs Stephanie Mortimer had finished her morning's business and now the lady relaxed in her favourite parlour, overlooking the garden, with a cup of tea and reminisced.

She was the youngest daughter of Viscount Middlebrook. In her second season she had met, and fallen in love with, The Right Honourable Mr Gerald Mortimer, despite the fact that he was a widower three decades her senior, and had two grown-up sons both several years older than herself.

After an initial hesitation on his part, due to his disbelief that she could care for a contemporary of her father, they had married and been blissfully happy for twenty years.

Mr Mortimer's sons, after getting over the shock of their father's choice of bride, delighted in calling her *Mother*, when they discovered that the marriage was a love-match on both sides.

The couple's only disappointment was the fact that they remained childless, but it gave them the opportunity to focus on each other, a situation they both enjoyed.

Mr Mortimer, as a doting husband, indulged his wife by encouraging her to learn whatever she was interested in. This included estate management, so that Mrs Mortimer could look after her own interests when her husband inevitably predeceased her. This would allow Mrs Mortimer to successfully manage the small estate in Hertfordshire which her mother bequeathed to her.

He also ensured that she was exceedingly well provided. There were investments which would provide a very comfortable income indeed for his wife.

The family townhouse was to go to the oldest son, along with the main estate while the younger son inherited the smaller family estate.

Therefore, Mr Mortimer bought a townhouse in a very fashionable area for her, which she decorated according to her own taste, and where they stayed while in town.

When in society, the couple, while of enough consequence to have access to the first circles, were not interested in jockeying for position, like they observed others to engage in. As a result, and the fact that Mr Mortimer was exceedingly wealthy, they were well respected by others with the same attitude, which, in many of those cases, was because their friends' position was unassailable.

Mr and Mrs Mortimer, between themselves, delighted in poking fun at the obvious machinations of society matrons while trying to find suitable husbands for their daughters.

~~~ooo0Ooo~~~

But eventually, their time ran out. After a short illness Gerald Mortimer, beloved husband of Stephanie, died.

When she found herself bereft of her husband's company, the company of London society lost its appeal. She therefore decided to spend her mourning period at Brook Hall, her estate on the outskirts of Meryton in Hertfordshire.

She kept in sporadic contact with her stepsons and their families, who proudly informed her of the progress of her grandchildren. They even visited on the odd occasion.

After the initial period when she was too grief stricken to pay much attention to anything, she started to come out of her self-imposed seclusion and became acquainted with her neighbours.

She took a particular interest in one family. Or, to be more precise, the daughters of one family.

Although in town children were often sequestered in the nursery and only allowed to spend brief visits with their parents, in a country town the children were much more visible.

Mr and Mrs Bennet had been blessed with five daughters, but no son. Mrs Bennet felt that lack severely, since their estate was entailed to the male line. Being a silly and frivolous woman of mean understanding, she did not appreciate the gift her daughters were.
~~~

Mrs Mortimer, who was childless and but a scant decade older than Mrs Bennet, could not comprehend the woman's attitude. At least Mrs Bennet had five beautiful healthy girls.

Admittedly, Mrs Bennet doted on the oldest and the youngest girls, who at the time were eleven and four years of age respectively, she dismissed the others as inconsequential because they were not pretty enough for her liking. Her favourites were both blond and blue-eyed like herself, while the others took after their father in colouring.

It appeared that Mr Bennet did nothing to check his wife's behaviour and attitude. He also had a reputation of being an indolent master of his estate. Since Mr Bennet but rarely left his book-room, it was some months before Mrs Mortimer had a chance to meet the man and judge for herself.

As an outsider she had a clearer view of the man than his neighbours, who were used to seeing him. To her it was obvious that Mr Bennet was unwell, even though he was trying to hide his condition.

It explained his indolence and his inability to restrain his wife in her more outrageous manner, and her callous disregard of her middle three daughters.

Mrs Bennet seemed to have particular ill feelings towards her second daughter, while the two younger ones were largely ignored by her. Based on their appearance, dresses which were more appropriate for servants rather than the daughters of a gentleman, as well as hair that was inexpertly braided, it seemed that Mrs Bennet tried to disassociate them from herself.

Jane and Lydia on the other hand, always had the prettiest dresses, looked well cared for, and were always being petted by their mother. Mrs Bennet seemed intent on spoiling them in any way she could.

Mrs Mortimer noticed that the oldest girl tried her best to shield her younger sisters, particularly Elizabeth, the second oldest.

Jane seemed uncomfortable with the attention she received, while Lydia was the worst behaved child Mrs Mortimer had ever had the misfortune to see. At the age of four, Lydia Bennet had perfected the art of the tantrum and used it mercilessly to get her own way.

<div style="text-align:center">~~~ooO0Ooo~~~</div>

When in the country, Mrs Mortimer loved to go riding early in the morning. Over the months she had been at Brook Hall, she had explored the estate and the surrounding area.

One particular spot she enjoyed was Oakham Mount, which was shared by three estates, Brook Hall, Netherfield Park and Longbourn.

Since this morning it had rained, she delayed her ride until the afternoon. When she reached the top of Oakham Mount, she spied the curled-up form of a weeping child. Mrs Mortimer dismounted and tied her horse to a shrub. She quietly called out, so as not to startle the girl, 'Elizabeth.'

Lizzy immediately sat up, and, keeping her back to Mrs Mortimer, wiped her face on her sleeve, before turning to face the intruder.

Before Elizabeth could say anything, Mrs Mortimer sat down next to her, and asked quietly, 'I heard you cry. Can I help?' While holding out her arms.

The sympathy in the voice and face of this gentle lady, whom she had seen around the village, was too much for the battered spirit of Elizabeth. The tears started to flow again and she trembled.

Mrs Mortimer gathered the girl into a gentle embrace and held her while she cried.

'Why does Mama hate me so? I cannot help it that I am not a boy,' Lizzy sobbed. 'But when I show her that I am as good as any boy, by climbing trees and winning footraces, she calls me a hoyden.'

'I think your mother is a particular kind of woman, and she expects all girls to be just like her, particularly her own daughters. She cannot understand that some girls are different. Not worse, just different.'

'You also think that I am different,' accused Lizzy.

'I think that you are different from your mother. But that is not necessarily a bad thing. I used to know a girl who was very much like you.'

'You did? Did her mother hate her too?'

'Yes, I did, but no, I was lucky. My mother was more understanding. She told me that while society thinks that girls should not behave like boys, while at home and in private, she saw no reason why I should not have fun.'

Lizzy, to her credit and despite her distress, immediately noticed about whom Mrs Mortimer was speaking. 'You did all those things too?'

'Yes, I did, but only where other people could not see me. Although my brothers and our friends knew.'

'But why did your mother think it was acceptable while mine tells me it is wrong?'

'My mother and yours are also very different people. As I said, I was lucky.'

'And I am not. It is not fair. She made me a girl. I did not ask to be a girl. But she hates me for it.'

'I think your mother is frightened. I am told that your estate is entailed to the male line.'

Lizzy looked frustrated. 'Mama always carries on about a tail and how, because of that, we will end up living in the hedgerows. But she does not explain.'

'It is not a tail, like a horse's tail. The term is entail, and it means that girls cannot inherit the estate. When your father dies eventually, none of you sisters can inherit. Longbourn will then go to your father's nearest male relative. Your mother is frightened that when that happens, she and you and your sisters will lose your home.'

'Oh.' Elizabeth tears stopped and she looked thoughtful. 'I can understand that that would frighten her, but why does she have to take it out on me? It is still not my fault that I am a girl.'

'I am afraid I do not have an answer for you. But you are absolutely correct. It is not your fault.'

The two spoke a while longer until Elizabeth had calmed down enough to return home.

After having watched this situation for months, Mrs Mortimer had enough. She decided to take action.

<p style="text-align:center">~~~ooo0ooo~~~</p>

2   Actions

One Tuesday morning, when Mrs Mortimer was aware that Mrs Bennet had gone out visiting as she always did on that day, she presented herself at Longbourn and requested to see Mr Bennet.

Mrs Hill, the housekeeper knew of Mrs Mortimer through the servants' grapevine, and escorted the lady to the Master of Longbourn, who was ensconced in his book-room as was his habit.

'Mrs Mortimer to see you, Sir,' she announced.

Mr Bennet looked up in surprise at the visitor. He was seated at his desk, with Elizabeth beside him, obviously engaged in teaching his second daughter.

He rose slowly from his chair and bowed. 'Mrs Mortimer, what an unexpected pleasure,' he said sarcastically. 'I am afraid my wife has gone visiting, if you wanted to speak to her.'

'Good morning, Mr Bennet. It is not your wife I wished to speak to, but yourself.'

'I can think of no reason why you should want to speak to me.'

'In that case I will be happy to explain to you in private,' answered Mrs Mortimer. She turned to Elizabeth, who had risen and curtsied. 'Miss Elizabeth, would you be so good as to give Mr Bennet and myself a few minutes of private discussion,' she asked with a friendly smile.

Lizzy looked at her father, who nodded in agreement. 'Yes, Madam,' she said politely and left the room.

When she was seated across the desk from Mr Bennet, Mrs Mortimer broached the subject. 'Mr Bennet, you may call me interfering but I am concerned about your daughters. Particularly Elizabeth, Mary and Catherine.'

'If you are concerned about my daughters, do you not think you should speak to my wife rather than myself. After all, she is their mother,' he said caustically.

'But she does not act like one. Which is why I have come to you to offer you a proposition.'

'You came to proposition me?' he asked slyly.

Mrs Mortimer gave him a disgusted look. 'Not likely. Your health is not good enough that I would risk propositioning you. Even if I were inclined to be interested.'

Mr Bennet looked shocked at her pronouncement. 'How do you know? I have not told anyone...'

'Mr Bennet, your family and neighbours see you regularly. They are obviously not observant enough to see the slow deterioration. Not having met you until recently, the signs are clear to me.'

'I see. Since you are not interested in my diseased carcass, what other proposition do you have?'

'It concerns your daughters. Particularly your middle three. Your wife does not care for them. She publicly berates them for no real reason. In particular Miss Elizabeth. To me those girls seem to be intelligent, perfectly nice and well behaved, unlike Miss Lydia who is a spoiled termagant. While I understand that due to your health you find it difficult to check your wife's actions against the girls, I worry for them.'

He gave a mirthless chuckle, 'what would you have me do? As you discerned, I am in no position to interfere. My wife would raise such a ruckus that the strain would probably kill me sooner rather than later. At the moment I try to hang on as long as I can, so that the girls might have a chance to grow up in a decent household, if not a loving one.'

'Allow me to adopt them,' Mrs Mortimer stated concisely.

Mr Bennet stared at her. 'You wish to adopt my daughters? Why?'

'My husband of twenty years died last year. We were not blessed with children. I have this big empty house which requires children's laughter to make it a home.' Mrs Mortimer smiled. 'Also, Elizabeth reminds me of myself when I was that age...'

'What about Jane and Lydia?'

'I am willing to take them as well, but I suspect Mrs Bennet might object. Although I think Jane would welcome the change.' She chuckled. 'Lydia on the other hand would not find me so easy to manipulate and object quite vociferously.'

'You already know my family very well,' replied Mr Bennet with a sad smile. 'Part of me says that I should be offended by your officiousness, but the realistic part of me appreciates your offer. I would like to think about it for a few days, if you will allow.'

'Naturally. I understand that my offer was unexpected. Let me add, that you are of course welcome to visit with your daughters any time you choose. They will also get the education appropriate for a gentleman's daughters, plus anything else they wish to learn.'

'Anything?' Mr Bennet now grinned mischievously. 'I should warn you that Lizzy would like to learn to ride, astride of course, as well as fencing and shooting. At present she would like to become a pirate.'

'I do not know about being a pirate, but I can teach her all the other skills.' Mrs Mortimer returned the smile in kind. 'I had a very understanding mother and an indulgent husband.'

Mr Bennet laughed outright at that statement. 'I can see that you and Lizzy would do very well together.' He became more serious again. 'But I still need some time to get used to the idea.'

'Certainly, Mr Bennet. Please let me know what you decide.'

<div align="center">~~~oo0Ooo~~~</div>

After Mrs Mortimer left, Mr Bennet considered all the lady had said. He was impressed by her perceptiveness. Neither his wife nor his friends and neighbours had realised the state of his health.

She had surprised him into admitting his concerns, and he had spoken more freely to her than he thought possible. He sighed, wishing that his wife was more like this lady. She seemed intelligent and kind, and accepting of the foibles of others.

In recent months Mr Bennet had become ever more worried about his wife's behaviour towards their middle daughters. As he admitted to Mrs Mortimer, he felt incapable of tempering Mrs Bennet's actions for fear of what it would do to his own health.

Yet, he needed to live as long as possible to delay his cousin Collins from inheriting Longbourn. Mr Bennet was certain that his cousin would evict his ladies, the day he took possession of Longbourn. The man was a vicious fool and held a grudge against the Bennet family. Mr Bennet hoped that Collins' son was a better person than his father, but he was still afraid that that was a forlorn hope.

He had considered asking his brother-in-law, Edward Gardiner, to take the three girls, but Gardiner had recently married and his wife was expecting.

Much as he hated to admit it, Mrs Mortimer's suggestion seemed to offer the best hope for his daughters' security and welfare. The added advantage was that Brook Hall was only two miles away. He could still see his daughters frequently.

Although inclined to accept Mrs Mortimer's proposal, based on his own judgement of her character, he determined to make enquiries to ensure that his daughters would be safe.

~~~oo0Ooo~~~

The following afternoon when Elizabeth came for her lesson with her father, she appeared rather thoughtful to Mr Bennet.

'Is something the matter, Lizzy?' he asked.

'I was just thinking about Mama. Is there anything you can do to make her less frightened?'

'What makes you think that your mother is frightened?'

'I met the nice lady who came to see you yesterday on Oakham Mount, and she explained that Mama is frightened about the entail, which is why she is so mean to me. I thought that if you could fix it that Mama is not scared anymore, she might be nicer to us,' Elizabeth explained hopefully.

'I am sorry, my dear, there is nothing I can do about the entail. Your grandfather decided that only a man can inherit the estate, and since I do not have a son, Longbourn will have to go to my cousin Collins when I die.'

'Is your cousin a nice man? Maybe he would let Mama live here?'
~~~

'I am afraid he is not nice, and your mother is rightly worried. But I have a plan to fix things for you,' Mr Bennet tried to reassure his daughter. 'But tell me about the nice lady who explained about the entail.'

Elizabeth allowed herself to be diverted and explained about her meeting on Oakham Mount.

Mr Bennet was again favourably impressed by Mrs Mortimer as the tale unfolded. He was beginning to hope for a positive report into the investigation about Mrs Mortimer, which he had requested his brother-in-law, Mr Phillips, to undertake.

~~~ooo0Ooo~~~

The following week, a footman from Longbourn brought a note to Mrs Mortimer, requesting her to call on Mr Bennet the next day.

When she arrived, Mrs Hill was expecting her and took her straight to Mr Bennet, who was not alone in his book-room.

Mr Bennet introduced his brother-in-law, Mr Phillips, the local solicitor. When they were all seated, Mr Bennet explained with a sigh, 'Mr Phillips has prepared the papers to allow you to adopt Lizzy, Mary and Kitty. I have made enquiries and have determined that my girls will be better off with you than at Longbourn.'

'Thank you, Mr Bennet. I promise you that I will take good care of those precious girls. Have you told them yet?'

'I was about to do so, once we have signed the papers. After all, there was a chance that you had changed your mind.'

'I look forward to have them living with me. What about Jane and Lydia?'

'I would not deprive their mother of all her daughters. They will stay, but I have a request, Mrs Mortimer.'

'What can I do, Mr Bennet?'

'If something happens to me, I would like to name you primary guardian for Jane and Lydia, with my brothers in law Philips and Gardiners as a back-up in case you are unavailable, to ensure that Mrs Bennet cannot pressure either of them into a marriage for her own
~~~

convenience. I am hoping that my daughters will find greater happiness in marriage than I did.'

'Certainly, Mr Bennet. Do you also wish me to interfere if the girls choose an unsuitable man?'

'If he is poor but decent, then no. If his character is unsuitable, then by all means, do whatever you need to do to separate them.'

'Very well, that agrees with my thinking. But on a related matter. Even though Jane and Lydia will remain at Longbourn, they are welcome to share lessons with the other girls.'

Mr Phillips, who had quietly stayed in the background, smiled and nodded. 'I believe Jane will be overjoyed to be allowed lessons in becoming an accomplished lady.'

'Lydia is too young to appreciate anything other than toys and pretty clothes. I suspect as she gets older, the toys might change but not her attitude,' commented Mr Bennet.

'In that case, I will send my carriage to collect Jane for lessons three days a week, if that is agreeable to you.'

'Most agreeable, thank you.'

~~~ooO0Ooo~~~

Mrs Mortimer read through all the documents, and, finding them in order, she and Mr Bennet signed them. Mr Phillips and Mrs Hill witnessed their signatures.

Mr Phillips had prepared three copies of all the documents. He handed one set to Mrs Mortimer, gave the second set to Mr Bennet and kept a copy to store at his office. 'Just to make sure,' he commented, before leaving.

Mrs Hill, who had been told by Mr Bennet about the changes to occur, went to fetch the four oldest girls from the school-room.

When the girls entered, Mr Bennet called them to him and gave each of them a hug. Then he asked the younger three, 'how would you like to go and live with Mrs Mortimer?'

Elizabeth gave the lady a dubious look, before asking her father in a sad voice, 'do you not love us anymore either?'
~~~

'Not at all, my dear Lizzy. It is because I love you very much that I am suggesting this. I know things have been difficult for you with your mother. Mrs Mortimer likes you very much and would like you to live with her. As a matter of fact, she would like to be your new mother,' he reassured her.

'Where would we live?'

'At Brook Hall, which is about two miles from here,' Mrs Mortimer entered the conversation.

'That is not so far. What about Jane and Lydia?'

Jane had been watching this exchange with a thoughtful look. At the age of eleven she thought of herself as quite grown up, compared to her sisters. She loved all her sisters, even Lydia when she was not throwing a tantrum, and as the oldest she felt protective of them.

While Jane always tried to see the best in people, she had been aware of their mother's irrational hatred towards Elizabeth.

'Lizzy, we cannot all leave Mama. You know that she treats me differently to you. I will be well, but I think you and Mary and Kitty should accept the offer. Brook Hall is not so far. We can visit.'

Mrs Mortimer smiled at Jane. 'You are quite right, Miss Bennet. I will arrange for masters to teach your sisters, and your father has agreed that while you will continue to live at Longbourn, he will permit you to have lessons with your sisters.

When Mary heard the words masters and lessons, she piped up, 'pianoforte lessons too?'

As Mrs Mortimer answered, 'yes, Miss Mary, pianoforte lessons too,' the girl's face lit up.

Kitty looked nervously between her sisters, unsure about the proceedings.

'We will find fun things for you to learn too, Miss Catherine.'

'Could you please call me Kitty, like my sisters do,' she whispered.

Mrs Mortimer held out her arms to the little girl. 'Certainly, Kitty. Would you like to call me Aunt Stephanie?'

The girl shyly accepted the hug.

Suddenly she threw her arms around Mrs Mortimer's waist and hugged her back. 'I would rather call you Mama. I never had one before.'

'You can call me whatever feels right to you, Kitty,' replied Mrs Mortimer softly, as she looked up at Mr Bennet, who looked on with tears in his eyes. He caught her gaze and nodded, both in acceptance and resignation.

~~~oo0Ooo~~~
~~~

3 Changes

Since Mrs Hill had been forewarned, it did not take long for the girls' trunks to be packed and loaded onto Mrs Mortimer's carriage.

When Mrs Mortimer asked, 'Mr Bennet, would you and Jane like to come along to see the girls settled into their new home?' both immediately agreed.

It was a little crowded in the carriage which took them to Brook Hall.

Mr Bennet, who had not been to the estate before, was impressed by the house, which, although smaller than Netherfield Park, was larger than Longbourn. The gardens and everything else that he could see, were well maintained and prosperous looking.

They were greeted at the door by Mrs Kirby, the housekeeper.

Mrs Mortimer smiled and nodded at the woman, indicating that her offer had been accepted, whereupon Mrs Kirby broke into a big smile as she said, 'Welcome home.'

After introducing the housekeeper, the two women escorted the sisters and their father upstairs to the family floor.

Mrs Mortimer entered a room and explained, 'I had these rooms prepared for you in the hope that you would come to live with me.' She indicated doors on either side of the room. 'There are two more bedrooms to either side, which will allow you to visit each other without having to traipse around the hall.'

Elizabeth and her sisters were astonished. 'You mean this room is just for one of us? We each get a room like this?' she asked looking around the large room with the elegant appointments. The bed was easily large enough to hold all three sisters, and yet it seemed they would not have to share.

'Indeed. I believe everyone needs some privacy at times.'

Mary, reluctant to believe such splendour could be hers, went to one of the indicated doors and stepped into the adjoining room. It was just as large and well-appointed as the first.

She had to know that it was all true and rushed to the door opposite, which led into yet another similar chamber.

The other girls followed in her wake. Jane commented with a delighted smile, 'these are indeed splendid chambers,' when Mary collapsed onto a small sofa under the window and started to cry quietly.

Mrs Mortimer sat beside the girl and put a comforting arm around her shoulders. 'Is something amiss? If there is ought about the room which you do not like, you are welcome to change it, you know.'

Mary just shook her head, unable to speak.

Mr Bennet, who had followed them into the room, said in a shamefaced manner, 'Mrs Bennet assigned one room each to Jane and Lydia, but she had the others share a single room. The smallest.'

The other girls crowded around Mary. Jane took her sister's hands and exclaimed, 'your new room is so much nicer than mine. I am so very happy for you.' She beamed at Mary.

Mary, had expected to be berated for her unladylike tears, which were caused by her feeling overwhelmed at the sight of the paradise which would now be hers.

Instead, her new guardian was comforting her, and telling her that if she did not like the perfection before her, she could change it.

It was too much happiness to bear. She turned into Mrs Mortimer's arms and buried her face in the woman's neck. 'Thank you, Mama,' she whispered through her sobs.

Mrs Mortimer, touched by the declaration, returned the hug and said, 'you are very welcome.' The moisture in her eyes might have been caused by the dust of the recent cleaning.

The moment was disturbed by Mrs Kirby arriving with the footmen delivering the girls' trunks.

<p style="text-align:center">~~~ooo0Ooo~~~</p>

Mrs Mortimer smiled at the girls and suggested, 'I think I shall let you explore and decide which rooms you would like, without me hovering.'

After she and Mr Bennet left the room, the girls hugged each other with delighted squeals.

When they broke apart, the younger girls rushed off to explore their new home.

Elizabeth was a little pensive. 'What is wrong?' asked Jane. 'You do not seem as happy as the others. I would have expected you to be overjoyed. After all, did you not tell me what a wonderful lady Mrs Mortimer is?'

'It just seems too good to be true. This morning I was sharing a tiny room with Mary and Kitty, and being chided by Mama for being a hoyden, and now I am here… and all this…' she waved around the room. 'It is just too much…'

Now it was Lizzy's turn to lose her composure. Jane held her while she was weeping, partly in sadness at having to leave her home, partly in relief that she would no longer be subjected to Mrs Bennet's ire.

Elizabeth gasped when she realised that she had been thinking of the woman as Mrs Bennet, not as Mama or even Mother.

Her head came up and her tears stopped. A slow smile spread across her features. 'Yes, I think I shall be very happy to be here. I just wish you could join us.'

'You heard Mrs Mortimer, I shall be having lessons with you. We will see each other all the time.'

Elizabeth smiled even more in her relief. 'That is true. We shall have a wonderful time.' She took Jane's hand. 'I think we had better see what the others are doing.

They found Mary and Kitty bouncing on the bed in the farthest room. After some discussion the girls decided that Elizabeth should take the middle room to allow each of her younger sisters easy access to her, should they need it.

The footman who had waited patiently moved each girl's trunks into their selected rooms, and then sent a maid to help them unpack.

~~~ooo0ooo~~~
~~~

While Jane helped her sisters get settled into their rooms, Mrs Mortimer offered refreshments to Mr Bennet.

'Would you like tea or something stronger? Or possibly a brandy with your tea?'

Mr Bennet opted for brandy with his tea.

He was sipping his brandy thoughtfully while Mrs Mortimer watched him quietly.

'I have made many mistakes in my life and many bad decisions, but today I think I made the best decision I have ever made.' Mr Bennet looked at his hostess. 'While I am devastated that I could not provide a happy home for my daughters, I was glad to see them relaxed and joyous as they were earlier. Thank you, Mrs Mortimer. You have my eternal gratitude.' He raised his glass in salute.

'In that case, we are even, Mr Bennet. By entrusting your precious daughters to me, you have given me the family I have always wanted.'

Mr Bennet spoke about his daughters to his captive audience. He surprised Mrs Mortimer by how much he had noticed about the girls. That discussion forged a bond of friendship between them which lasted for years.

<div align="center">~~~oo0Ooo~~~</div>

Mr Bennet was nursing a glass of port in his book-room after his return from Brook Hall. While he was happy to see his neglected daughters so happily settled in their new home, he felt melancholy. It had been brought home to him that a complete stranger could make his daughters happier and feeling loved than their own parents.

Lizzy at least seemed ambiguous about the change in residence. When he said goodbye, she had asked him if he would be well without her in the house. He had been touched at her concern, but told her he would be better for knowing that she and her sisters were well loved and cared for.

He had become peripherally aware of some noise in the house, indicating that his wife had returned from her visits, when he heard a shriek, 'Lizzy.'

At the next moment his door burst open and his wife demanded, 'is that useless girl hiding with you again?'

'There is only one useless girl in this house as far as I know, and last I had heard she was in the nursery.'

'I was just in the nursery and Lizzy is not there,' huffed Mrs Bennet.

'I was not speaking of Elizabeth, I meant Lydia.'

'How dare you call my precious child useless,' screeched Mrs Bennet.

Mr Bennet ignored the question and asked, 'why are you looking for Lizzy?'

'I need her to run into Meryton to collect some ribbons and sweets for Lydia.'

'Lizzy is not Lydia's servant to be sent on errands for her,' Mr Bennet pointed out.

'It is the only thing she is good for. Why did I have to be saddled with three ugly daughters? I wish to god I did not have to acknowledge them,' lamented his wife.

'Do you truly wish to be rid of Elizabeth, Mary and Catherine?'

'Of course, I am. They are only using up funds which I need for my beautiful girls.'

'In that case, you will be pleased to know that I have granted your wish. The girls are gone.' Mr Bennet grated angrily. His melancholy was gone, replaced by anger at the callous woman who cared nothing for his treasured daughters.

Mrs Bennet looked at him dumbfounded for a moment before she became angry. 'Mr Bennet, you only say that to vex me. Who would take those useless, ugly girls?'

'They have gone to live at Brook Hall.'

'You have put them in service? How clever of you.' Suddenly Mrs Bennet was all smiles. 'I thought that was all they were good for, but I did not think you would allow me to arrange positions for them. How wonderful. How exceedingly delightful. You have made me inordinately happy today, Mr Bennet,' gushed the woman, oblivious to her husband's thunderous expression.

'Shall you want to collect your reward tonight?' she asked in a flirtatious manner and blushing slightly.

'No, Mrs Bennet, I have not the least interest in your dubious charms. The time is long gone that you could make me forget my responsibilities to my children,' he growled at his wife, who was flushing at the harsh rejection. 'And no, the girls are not at Brook Hall as servants. They are there as the beloved daughters of Mrs Mortimer.'

Mrs Bennet now openly gaped at her husband's vitriolic tone of voice, as well as the news he had imparted. 'Mrs Mortimer? But she is rich and well-connected. Why would she want those girls? If she wanted to give consequence and advantages to girls, she should have taken Jane and Lydia. Those beautiful girls deserve a better life than you can provide for them, not those three useless chits.'

Before Mr Bennet could answer, she mumbled, 'we will see about that,' and stormed out of the room.

~~~ooO0oo~~~

The following morning Mrs Bennet put on her newest day dress and had Jane and Lydia dressed in their best outfits as well. As soon as polite visiting hours allowed, she presented herself and her daughters at Brook Hall.

Mrs Mortimer, who had been showing the girls their new home, left them in the care of the housekeeper, and went to receive her guests. After polite greetings, Mrs Mortimer enquired as to the purpose of the visit, since Mrs Bennet had never called before.

'I have come to take away those useless chits my husband foisted off on you. Instead I am prepared to offer you my beautiful daughters,' declared Mrs Bennet.

Despite having an inkling of Mrs Bennet's character and attitudes, Mrs Mortimer was still shocked at the callous manner in which the woman acted. Treating her daughters as nothing more than chattel that could be traded.

'There are no useless chits in my home, and your husband did not foist anyone off on me,' replied Mrs Mortimer coldly.

'But Mr Bennet said that he had sent the girls to live with you.'
~~~

'Yesterday I adopted Elizabeth, Mary and Catherine… by my request. They are lovely girls and most certainly not useless, as you claim. They are now my beloved daughters and I would not trade them for anything in the world.'

'But Jane and Lydia are beautiful and deserve the advantages you can give them. Those other girls would do just as well as servants. I am sure I can find them positions. After all, no man will ever look at them. Why would you want ugly daughters?'

'They are beautiful, no matter what you may think. Blond hair alone does not make a girl beautiful.'

'But just think, you could have Jane, who is not only beautiful but very sweet tempered. And my lovely Lydia, who is so very lively…'

At that moment they heard a crash where the *lively* Lydia had just knocked a bonbon dish off a side-table because she could not quite reach into the dish.

Mrs Mortimer raised an eyebrow at the sight. 'I doubt that Lydia would be happy in my home, since I would curtail that kind of liveliness. She would be expected to learn manners and decorum, and she would not be the centre of attention. Although the girls are welcome to share lessons with my daughters, when they are ready.'

Mrs Mortimer turned to Jane with twinkling eyes. 'Miss Bennet, would you like to learn a lady's accomplishments?'

'I would be most grateful for the opportunity, Mrs Mortimer,' replied Jane just as courteously.

'Mrs Bennet, are you agreeable to your daughter Jane having lessons in how to be an accomplished lady? I am afraid that Lydia is still too young to benefit from that opportunity.'

Even Mrs Bennet could see that Lydia's actions had put paid to her chances at this time. She reluctantly agreed that Jane should learn whatever accomplishments she could, to help her catch a husband in a few years.

'Then it is agreed. I will send my carriage three times a week to collect Miss Bennet for her lessons,' Mrs Mortimer finished the conversation with satisfaction.

~~~ooO0Ooo~~~
~~~

4   New Beginnings

Mrs Kirby had nearly finished the tour of the house, when Mrs Mortimer joined the group again.

'I was going to take them to the library next,' Mrs Kirby informed her Mistress.

'Thank you, Mrs Kirby, I will take them.'

When Mrs Mortimer opened the doors to the indicated room, Elizabeth thought that she stood at the gates to paradise.

The room was in the centre of the house and extended up to the first floor. While it had no windows, the skylights provided excellent light. There were bookcases covering all the walls, with a mezzanine to reach the books at the upper level. The girls had never seen so many books in their short lives.

Lizzy was awestruck. 'Even the lending library does not have this many books,' she gasped. 'Are we allowed to read them?'

'Naturally. Choose anything you like. If you have trouble understanding anything, come and ask me and I will try to help. But there is another room you have not yet seen. Come along.'

When she entered another large room next to the library, she said, 'this is the ballroom, but I use it as a salle.'

'A salle is for fencing, is it not?' Elizabeth asked tentatively.

'Correct. Your father informed me that you would like to learn to fence. Is that true?'

'Yes, and shoot and ride, so that I can become a pirate.' The girl now grinned enthusiastically. 'Can you fence?'

'Yes, I can. I can also shoot and ride. Would you like to learn?' she asked all the girls.

Elizabeth agreed with shining eyes. Mary and Kitty were uncertain.

'Then you shall learn, Elizabeth.' She turned to the other girls. 'Mary, Kitty, you do not have to learn to shoot or fence unless you wish to do so, although I think you will enjoy riding. But I think it is time that we sit down and discuss the future.

~~~ooO0Ooo~~~

Elizabeth almost floated back to the parlour. Instead of being told she was a hoyden, their new guardian was offering to teach her some very unfeminine things. She had never dared to hope that she would have the opportunity.

She knew full well that being a pirate was not a possible career for her, but it had been a way to express her longing for more physical pursuits.

She was still wool-gathering when they settled on sofas in the parlour. Lizzy noticed with amusement and a little envy, that Kitty had sat down next to Mrs Mortimer and was snuggling into her side.

The lady automatically put an arm around the girl's shoulders.

'Now then. About your future. While I can teach you the accomplishments appropriate to a gently born lady, which each of you are, I think it would be wise to hire a governess for you.'

'Does that mean we have to move to the nursery?' Kitty whispered.

'No of course not. At least not unless you want to. Do you?'

Kitty shook her head, looking relieved. 'I like my room very much.

'I am glad that you do. And I must say, it was delightful to have cheerful company at breakfast. But to get back to the subject. While I can teach you many things, I cannot teach you everything. And since there are three of you and only one of me, I thought to engage a governess to share the load.'

'Also, I have other responsibilities, such as the running of this estate, which means that I will not always have time for you. While I am happy for you to learn about those duties as well, I think that is a lesson for the future.'

'Now, are there any particular subjects you would like to study? Any special skills you would like to learn?'
~~~

The girls listened with growing astonishment. After years of being ignored or berated, this lady was concerned about what was best for them and considered their interests.

'Papa allowed me to read about history and philosophy…' said Elizabeth hesitantly.

'As I said, my library is open to you. You may read whatever you like, as long as you are careful of the books and replace them when you are finished.'

Elizabeth fervently agreed.

'Now, Mary, you said you wanted to improve on the pianoforte. Do you have any other interests?'

'I would like to learn to play the harp…' Mary suggested timidly. Like her sisters, she found the change in her circumstances rather intimidating. Wonderful, yes, but somewhat scary. She had never been asked her opinion before.

'What about you, Kitty. What do you enjoy doing?' Mrs Mortimer asked the little girl gently.

'I like drawing but I am not very good at it. Mrs Bennet did not want me to waste paper on my horrible scribbles…'

'You shall have all the paper you like,' reassured Mrs Mortimer. 'I am convinced that since you love it, you will improve with practice.'

Kitty beamed. Not only would she be allowed to engage in her favourite activity, but also the faith Mrs Mortimer had in her abilities, gave her confidence.

'None of you have mentioned sewing or embroidery.'

Lizzy made a face. 'We can all sew after a fashion. Mrs Bennet insisted on it, but I always preferred to be outdoors.'

'It is a useful skill and I shall expect you to learn it to an adequate standard. I also expect you to learn how to do accounts and even the basics of cooking.'

Elizabeth looked sceptical when she heard the last. 'We were told by Mrs Bennet that ladies should not learn such menial skills.'

'If you do not know at least what is involved in cooking, how can you ensure that your cook is not cheating you? And even if you have a good and honest cook, when you plan a menu, it helps to ensure that you are not asking the impossible from your staff. Such as demanding five dishes which need to be baked, when you only have ovens sufficient for four items.' suggested Mrs Mortimer.

Elizabeth looked startled as realisation set in. 'I had not considered those issues.'

'I would not have expected you to have learned these things just yet,' Mrs Mortimer assured the embarrassed girl. 'I realise that there will be things which each of you will be reluctant to study. But if you apply yourself to the necessary subjects, I will ensure that you will have the opportunity to learn those which you enjoy.'

Mary smiled in delight and squeezed Elizabeth's hand. 'Thank you, Mama, I will do my best to become proficient in all things.' Suddenly her face fell. 'But what if I should fail in some things?'

'It is impossible to be proficient in all things. As long as you do your best, that is all I ask for.'

The girls started to chatter about the things they were hoping to learn while Mrs Mortimer listened with quiet pleasure.

<center>~~~ooo0Ooo~~~</center>

That afternoon Mrs Mortimer took the girls into Meryton to visit the dressmaker.

Mrs Brown was surprised to see the girls with Mrs Mortimer, whom she knew because the lady had commissioned several dresses from her, when she came out of full mourning.

The lady wasted no time on explanations, she simply said, 'Mrs Brown, I would like you to meet my daughters, Miss Elizabeth Mortimer, Miss Mary and Miss Catherine.'

'*Your* daughters?'

'*My* daughters, and as you can see, they have outgrown their old dresses and need new ones.'

'Of course, Mrs Mortimer. I will be delighted to make beautiful dresses for your beautiful daughters.' Mrs Brown smiled pleasantly.

She did not say that although she was pleased to have the business of making the dresses, she was even more delighted to see the girls in the care of a woman who seemed to appreciate them.

For the next hour the girls were measured and consulted about colours, fabrics and styles for several dresses each.

Mrs Mortimer also ordered a quantity of nightdresses, chemises and stockings.

While the younger girls giggled excitedly over the attention they received, Elizabeth felt overwhelmed and withdrew into a quiet corner to regain her composure.

Mrs Brown came across her when she was passing, and stopped to gently pat Elizabeth on the shoulder. 'Cheer up, Miss Mortimer. This is no more than you deserve,' she said kindly.

Lizzy looked startled and asked, 'do you truly think so?'

'Indeed I do. Everyone in town will be pleased with your good fortune as well.' Mrs Brown nodded decisively and moved on, leaving behind an even more bewildered girl.

Lizzy thought that if Mrs Brown was representative of people's opinions, Mrs Mortimer might have the right of it and Mrs Bennet was wrong. She was a worthwhile person after all.

Elizabeth re-joined her family with a big relieved smile, just in time to go to the next shop.

They spent the rest of the afternoon going from shop to shop, buying bonnets, gloves and ribbons, as well as ordering slippers and boots.

In each shop their reception was the same, initial surprise followed by delight at the girls' good fortune. The delight was only enhanced by the extra business the shopkeepers received.

The news spread like wildfire, and by the time they stopped at the teahouse for a treat, it seemed that all of Meryton had heard the story and heartily approved.

~~~ooo0Ooo~~~
~~~

Over the next two weeks, the new family settled into a routine.

In the morning, after they broke their fast together, Mrs Mortimer took care of her own duties, leaving the girls in the care of one of the maids who had several younger siblings and was good with children.

During that time the girls were free to find their own amusements. They played, read, went for walks, explored the estate, or the house when the weather was inclement.

They became acquainted with all the staff, from Mr Kirby the butler and Mrs Kirby, the housekeeper and their staff, to the cook and her staff. Elizabeth, who liked to be outdoors also made friends with the grooms and the gardeners.

In the afternoon, Mrs Mortimer spent time with each of the girls conducting lessons in reading and writing for Kitty, improving Mary's fingering on the pianoforte, and teaching Elizabeth the basics of fencing.

On the days that Jane joined them, she discussed the duties incumbent for the Mistress of the house and the estate.

One evening Elizabeth commented, 'you told us that we would have to learn to sew and cook and do accounts. But so far, all our lessons have focused on what we enjoy doing. Mind you, I am not complaining,' she finished with a cheeky smile.

'I decided to leave the unpleasant lessons to your governess,' explained Mrs Mortimer. 'Which reminds me. I have written to friends and asked for recommendations and I have had several replies. I will need to go to London next week to interview four ladies. Would you like to come along and visit your Uncle Gardiner?'

Kitty bounced in her seat with excitement. 'I have never been to London before. Can we truly come with you? I would like to see Aunt Gardiner. She is ever so nice.'

'Very well, it is decided. You shall come with me.'

~~~ooO0Ooo~~~

The following Sunday, Mrs Mortimer took the girls to attend services in Meryton. The sisters were wearing their new Sunday Best dresses which had been delivered the day before.
~~~

When they arrived, they were greeted by many of their neighbours, who commented on how well the girls looked.

Mrs Goulding was particularly effusive in her expressions of delight. Mrs Mortimer wondered about the reason for this, until she heard a dismissive sniff behind her, and Mrs Bennet's voice complaining, 'come along, Jane. You know how it vexes me when you dawdle.'

Mrs Bennet brushed past, ignoring Mrs Mortimer and her daughters, while Mr Bennet, who had followed slowly, stopped to greet the ladies.

After the obligatory pleasantries, he looked at his daughters and told them with a delighted smile, 'you all look very well and exceedingly pretty. Those colours suit you very well.'

Elizabeth asked quietly, 'how are you, Papa? I hope you do not miss us too much.'

Mr Bennet gave her a gentle pat on the cheek. 'Bless you my dear for thinking about me, but I am well enough. As a matter of fact, I am all the better for knowing you are so well loved and taken care of.'

He added with a mischievous smile at Mrs Mortimer, 'Jane reports to me after every visit, to reassure me that her sisters are not only well but thriving. She also tells me that she will not be coming to you for lessons this week since you are off to London. If you are going to see my brother-in-law, Mr Gardiner, would you take a letter to him, in which I explained the change in circumstances?'

'Certainly, Mr Bennet. I was hoping you had written to him since I am taking the girls and they hope to visit with his family.'

Mr Bennet passed over the letter before making his farewells to join his wife and daughter in the church.

Mrs Mortimer and the sisters found their own place and settled in to enjoy the soothing ritual.

<div align="center">~~~ooo0Ooo~~~</div>

5   Meetings

It was a cheerful and somewhat noisy trip to London. The girls spent much of their time looking out the windows of the carriage and exclaimed over each new vista.

As soon as they arrived in London, Mrs Mortimer sent the note she had prepared, together with Mr Bennet's letter to Mr Gardiner. She received a reply late in the afternoon, inviting the family to tea the following day.

Once she had heard from Mr Gardiner, Mrs Mortimer arranged to interview her prospective governesses two days hence.

Tilly, Mrs Mortimer's personal maid had come to town with her mistress, and was happy to share the information about the girl's background with the housekeeper. Mrs Carter was incensed to hear about the treatment the girls had suffered in their former home.

Meanwhile the girls spent the afternoon exploring the townhouse under the indulgent supervision of the staff. It had been many years since the house had rung with the laughter of children, and Mrs Carter was delighted for her Mistress to have been granted such lovely girls.

~~~oo0Ooo~~~

In the morning, Mrs Mortimer, together with Tilly and two footmen, took the girls for a walk in Hyde Park, which was near the townhouse.

Mrs Mortimer thought it wise to let the girls work off their excess energy before their visit. She was amused at Elizabeth's reaction.

'It is a very nice park, I suppose. But it is very tame and boring.'

'Considering it is very popular with fine ladies, they would not be best pleased having their expensive dresses torn by having to scramble through brambles,' suggested Mrs Mortimer.
~~~

She was startled by a quiet chuckle behind her. 'No indeed, they would be most vocal about such an unseemly occurrence. Although it would be amusing to watch.'

Mrs Mortimer turned towards the voice and was pleasantly surprised to see a familiar face. 'Lady Matlock, what a delightful surprise. I had not expected to encounter you on our outing.'

'I was never one to take my exercise during the fashionable hours, as you should know. Although you seem to have forgotten my name, I am still pleased to see you again.'

'I endeavour to be a good role model for my daughters, *Lady Matlock*.' Mrs Mortimer sported a mischievous smile as she emphasised the lady's name.

'Daughters? I had not heard that you had been blessed with three lovely girls, *Mrs Mortimer*. Will you not introduce us?'

Mrs Mortimer obliged, and all the girls managed creditable curtsies and polite responses, until it was Kitty's turn who finished her greeting by asking, 'what is a countess? Is she a lady who counts?'

Lady Matlock surprised them with a friendly chuckle and the reply, 'I certainly count my blessings every day.'

To prevent any more awkward questions, Mrs Mortimer suggested that the girls might like to feed the ducks at the nearby pond.

When the girls had moved away, Lady Matlock addressed her friend. 'They are delightful girls, Stephanie, but I know for a fact that you and Gerald never had children together. Where do they come from?'

'I adopted them, Susan,' replied Mrs Mortimer and proceeded to give her friend some of the background of the Bennet family and her reason for being in town while they strolled around the park.

'You always had a soft heart, Stephanie. You even managed to mother Gerald's boys, despite the fact that they were older than yourself.' Lady Matlock chuckled, remembering the bemused expression on James Mortimer's countenance as his younger stepmother fussed over him when he had broken his leg in a fall from his horse.

'I just hope Lizzy will be more careful than James. She reminds me of myself when I was her age.'

'Is she also climbing trees or riding the most unruly stallion in the stable or having her nose stuck in a book when she is not doing any of those things?'

'Luckily I do not have any unruly stallions... Mine are perfectly well behaved.'

Lady Matlock just shook her head. 'No wonder you could not resist.'

The ladies chatted a while longer, with Lady Matlock extolling the virtues of her own children, until they returned to the pond where the girls were ready to return home.

<p style="text-align:center">~~~ooO0Ooo~~~</p>

When Mrs Mortimer and the girls arrived at the residence of Mr Gardiner, the girls forgot about decorum the moment they spied their aunt and uncle.

Mrs Mortimer looked on with a pleased smile as the couple returned their enthusiastic hugs and greetings.

Mrs Gardiner recovered her aplomb a little before her husband did, to greet their visitor.

'Please forgive us this unseemly display, Mrs Mortimer. My husband and I have been concerned about the girls and are thrilled at the change you have wrought in their demeanour in such a short time.'

'There is nothing to forgive, Mrs Gardiner. I too am pleased to see my charges so very happy.'

Mrs Mortimer did not say how relieved she felt that Mr Gardiner was nothing like his sister and that Mrs Gardiner's genteel manners were a pleasant surprise as well. Their home, while on the fringe of Cheapside, was spacious and tastefully furnished. She could see the delicate touch of the lady of the house in many of the appointments.

Tea was served and it was obvious that Mrs Gardiner had catered to the preferences of her nieces.

Elizabeth and her sisters alternated between enjoying the treats and regaling their relatives with all the news of the last fortnight.

When Mrs Mortimer had finished her tea, and while the girls were still chattering away, Mr Gardiner asked for a private word in his study.

'Do you know what was in my brother's letter?' asked Mr Gardiner when they had settled at his desk.

'No, Mr Gardiner. Mr Bennet asked me to pass on his letter to you when he found out that we were planning a trip to London. He did not explain what it contained and I did not think it was my business to ask. I assumed it was an explanation to you about the fact that I adopted his daughters.'

'It was that and more. He informed me that every quarter he would transfer all the money he would have had to spend on the upkeep and pin money for the girls, to me, to invest in my business. That money and the profits would be his contribution to their dowry.'

'It is not necessary for Mr Bennet to do this, since I am in a position to ensure that my daughters will have everything which they need. But I understand his desire to contribute to their future.'

'I should probably not say this, since Mrs Bennet is my sister, but I suspect Thomas is doing this to vex her, since she would expect to spend that extra money on fripperies for herself, Jane and Lydia.'

Mrs Mortimer gave him a quizzical look. 'You and your sister appear to be very different people,' she said cautiously.

Gardiner sighed. 'You mean I am not obsessed with physical beauty and nothing else? That I care about my nieces even though they are not spitting images of their mother? I am afraid the fault lies with our mother. She was a beautiful woman but of mean understanding. My older sister Martha, now Mrs Phillips, takes after our father in looks. Our mother largely ignored Martha in favour of Fanny, who resembled her a great deal.'

He shrugged. 'When Fanny managed to attract a gentleman and Martha only a *lowly* solicitor, it confirmed to her that our mother was seemingly correct. What can I say… she but continues what her mother started. Of course, the entail does not help the situation. I am not certain if Fanny was worried that the middle girls would not find husbands because they do not live up to her standard of beauty, or if she was afraid that the girls would in some way detract from Jane's and Lydia's prospects.'

'I admit, I had wondered if there was a defect in Mrs Bennet's mind, which could have been inherited by one of the girls. But since it was only a faulty example, I imagine the girls will do quite well.'

'But you were still prepared to adopt them. You are indeed generosity itself.'

'No, Mr Gardiner. I was a lonely woman unable to have children. Now I have three lovely daughters to brighten my days. It was worth the risk. And just because a child is imperfect does not make it any less loveable.'

'That is where your opinion differs from my sister… I am exceedingly pleased to say under the circumstances.'

They spoke a little longer about the financial arrangements for the sisters before re-joining them and Mrs Gardiner.

Eventually, after each group promised to correspond and visit when the opportunity arose, Mrs Mortimer took the girls home.

~~~oo0Ooo~~~

The last interview for the governess position Mrs Mortimer had scheduled was with Mrs Taylor, a young widow of eight and twenty, who she hoped would be a more suitable option for her girls.

Of the first three, while all of them had the necessary accomplishments, two were exceedingly inflexible about what constituted proper accomplishments for a young lady. Both had been horrified at the idea of allowing girls to read books about history, philosophy and science. According to them, those books would turn their charges into bluestockings, and they claimed that no man wants a wife who might be better educated than he is. At least in their limited opinion, thought Mrs Mortimer.

On the other hand, Miss Carstairs, the first candidate, had no issues with bluestockings, after all, she was one herself, but she was only in favour of exercising the mind but not the body. While she admitted that a gentle stroll in the garden could potentially be beneficial, she was horrified at the idea of her charges mounting filthy beasts like horses.

Now Mrs Mortimer was down to one candidate.

Two minutes before the agreed time, Mrs Taylor was announced.
~~~

Mrs Mortimer was pleased that her potential employee was punctual. After their greetings, she immediately launched into the questions which had proven problematic for the first three candidates.

'Mrs Taylor, how do you feel about girls learning about subjects traditionally reserved for men?'

'If a young lady is interested in a subject, I believe she should be allowed to pursue it, although not to the detriment of the subjects which society requires ladies to know.'

'What about physical pursuits other than dancing?'

Mrs Taylor blushed but she steadfastly met Mrs Mortimer's eyes. 'As a child I was known to climb the occasional tree. I do not believe it has done me any harm, but if you disapprove of such activities, I will do my best to curb such behaviour.'

'What if I am in favour of such activities?'

'In that case I would be happy to teach them how to do it safely.'

'That will not be necessary,' replied Mrs Mortimer with a laugh. 'I have already demonstrated the proper technique to scale a tree.'

Turning serious again she said, 'I am planning to have my daughters instructed in ways how to defend themselves against physical attacks.'

Mrs Taylor's eyes lit up. 'In that case, might I be so bold to request to be included in those lessons? Provided of course that you would want to employ someone who has somewhat unconventional ideas.'

Mrs Mortimer enquired about her more conventional skills.

'While I am not expert, I can draw and I can play the pianoforte. In both cases I am quite familiar with the techniques, but I simply do not have outstanding talents in those areas. My embroidery on the other hand is exquisite, even if I do say so myself. I also speak and write French and German fluently. My Latin is better than my Italian, both of which are better than my knowledge of Greek. But I know enough to read Homer in the original.'

'What about mathematics?'

'I am competent with the basic mathematical operations, since all of them are necessary for managing the accounts for a household budget.'

'Do you think that there is anything a young lady should not learn?'

'Being too forward with gentlemen or using foul language...'

Mrs Mortimer laughed at the quip and started to relax. This young woman seemed to have the right attitude towards education. She rang the bell and requested tea.

'Since I have more questions, you will need the tea, unless you prefer coffee.'

Mrs Taylor said that she was partial to tea.

When tea had been served, Mrs Mortimer requested, 'please, tell me more about yourself and why do you apply for this position?'

'I was born and raised in Kent. My father was a minor gentleman. I have four younger sisters and a much younger brother. It was a great relief to my parents when he was born since the estate is entailed to the male line. Our estate is not large and with six children, five of them girls, our dowries were meagre. Although my parents had ensured that we had all learned the accomplishments expected of ladies. There were few gentlemen in our area which made finding a husband difficult.'

Mrs Taylor blushed, making such a personal admission. 'Three years ago, I thought I was on the shelf, and went to visit relatives in Southampton in the hope they could help me find employment. While there I met Mr Taylor, who was a Lieutenant in the navy. We formed an attachment and married. Unfortunately, six months ago he developed a fever and died. While we had some savings, it is not enough for me to live on. Therefore, I decided to look for employment.'

'Very concise. I think we will suit, provided the girls like you. When can you start?'

'Tomorrow, if that is soon enough.' Mrs Taylor smiled, relieved that her forthright manner had not put off her potential employer.

She was also grateful that there was only the Mistress of the house to deal with. Her first foray into employment had ended abruptly when she had slapped the Master for trying to take liberties. She had only escaped because her screams for help had brought the housekeeper and the butler to the room. As a reward, his Lordship had backhanded her across the face and dismissed her.

Now she felt, she would be not only safe, but in a household where she would be appreciated.

~~~oo0Ooo~~~

The meeting between Mrs Taylor and the girls went well. The lady had a relaxed and friendly demeanour, which put the sisters at ease.

She enquired into their interests and assured them that she would help them improve. When Mrs Taylor showed the girls an example of her embroidery, even Elizabeth reluctantly agreed that it might be worth her effort to learn that skill to subtly enhance her dresses.

As a result, on Saturday, the carriage returned to Brook Hall with an extra passenger.

~~~oo0Ooo~~~

6 Lessons

Mrs Taylor was astonished to be assigned a room on the family floor rather than the nursery. She was even more surprised to find that each of the girls had a room of her own across the hall from her.

Mrs Mortimer's explanation, 'why would I adopt the girls and then banish them to another part of the house, when I enjoy their company?' raised her employer in Mrs Taylor's estimation to even greater heights.

'I have had the end bedroom set up as a schoolroom since it has the best light,' Mrs Mortimer informed the governess.

The girls, who had accompanied the adults, immediately rushed off to inspect their new domain. They found the room set up with low tables and chairs as well as a small dining table and chairs suitable for adults.

Several bookcases had been moved into the room and contained paper, pencils, pens, ink, paints, slates, chalks, and sewing supplies, as well as some books. Stacked against a wall were easels and a chest, which on investigation revealed toys.

Mrs Mortimer who had caught up with the trio smiled indulgently. 'You cannot work all the time, you also need a chance to play.'

'If you need any other supplies, please let me know and I will arrange for them.'

Mrs Taylor looked around the bright room with a delighted smile. 'I believe that you have provided everything we will need for the moment. This is an excellent space for learning.'

'I can show you the music room, after you have refreshed yourself, Mrs Taylor,' offered Mary.

'You must come and see the library,' enthused Elizabeth.

'Is there anything you would like to show me, Kitty?' asked Mrs Taylor of the one girl who had remained silent.

'My pictures?' Kitty offered hesitatingly.

'I would be delighted to see everything.'

Within two weeks, Mrs Taylor was part of the family.

~~~ooO0oo~~~

After luncheon one Monday, Mrs Mortimer asked the sisters, including Jane, to come outside, where she led them to the stables.

When they arrived, they found a groom holding a lovely small mare and a pony. Jackson, the stablemaster grinned at the delighted expression on the girls' faces. 'Do you think you could give these girls a bit of a workout?' he asked.

'These are for us?' Lizzy breathed in wonder. She approached the mare and stroked her head. She giggled when the horse gently whiffled her hair.

'Yes, I bought them for you but you will have to share. The mare is for you and Jane, and the pony for Mary and Kitty. They will have to grow a little more before they are ready for a horse. By which time I expect you will have outgrown Honey.' Mrs Mortimer indicated the mare.

The youngest girls had already claimed the pony, who seemed to enjoy their pats.

Mrs Mortimer noticed that Jane eyed the saddle on the mare dubiously. 'Do not fret, Jane. Honey is also trained to side saddle. I presume you would prefer to ride like a lady?'

Jane looked relieved. 'Yes, please. I would not wish to do anything to raise the ire of Mrs Bennet.'

'I understand, child. You shall be a most accomplished ladylike young lady.' Mrs Mortimer turned to Elizabeth. 'Lizzy, if you go to your room, you will find a riding habit suitable for riding astride. Mary, Kitty, there are outfits in your rooms as well.'

By the time Mrs Mortimer stopped speaking, Elizabeth was already racing back to the house. The younger girls followed immediately after.
~~~

'Jane, there is an outfit for you in the room along the hall next to Mary's.' Mrs Mortimer told Jane, and added conspiratorially, 'and there is absolutely no lace on it.'

Jane's eyes were suspiciously moist when she curtsied and said, 'thank you, Aunt Stephanie.'

'You are welcome. Now go and change.'

While the girls were gone, servants brought a small table and some garden chairs, and placed them just outside the paddock, giving Mrs Mortimer a good view of the lesson.

Elizabeth was of course the first one to return, wearing what appeared to be a dress, but was in actuality a split skirt, like extremely wide pantaloons.

Jackson boosted her into the saddle and adjusted the stirrups before instructing her in the proper posture. When she was comfortable, he started to lead the mare in a circle at a gentle walk, keeping up his instructions.

Lizzy's expression was ecstatic.

Within the week, she was riding out daily with a groom. Within six months she graduated to a gelding, leaving the mare entirely for Jane's use.

On her twelfth birthday, she received the second greatest treasure of her life so far. A grey stallion whom she named Phoenix.

<center>~~~ooo0ooo~~~</center>

Mr Bennet became a weekly visitor at Brook Hall. Every Wednesday he accompanied Jane to her lessons.

Unbeknownst to his wife, Wednesday's lessons always featured history and literature… taught to his daughters by himself.

He had mixed success. Lizzy, as he knew, was a voracious reader and devoured any book he suggested. He was pleased that Mrs Mortimer's library exceeded his own, and that she was willing to let him borrow books he was not familiar with. Elizabeth was in heaven.

Mary discovered the philosophy section and over time proceeded to analyse and compare the contradictory texts. Discussing those discoveries gave her and her father great joy and even greater frustration until Mary burst out one day, 'people are not rational'.

Her father grinned at her and said, 'congratulations, Mary. You have discovered the greatest secret of mankind.'

Kitty was still too young to appreciate the history texts and much of the literature, but she did enjoy reading novels. Mr Bennet decided that at least since she was reading, it was a good start.

Jane turned out to be his biggest challenge until she had mastered the basics of French. Perusing the shelves with texts in French, she discovered Voltaire. She suddenly discovered an interest in politics and to his astonishment, a fascination with military strategy. Mrs Mortimer indulged her by acquiring a copy of the French translation of l'Art de la guerre by the French Jesuit Jean Joseph Marie Amiot.

It appealed to Mr Bennet's sense of humour to sit in a fashionable drawing room and discuss such unlikely subjects as Greek philosophy or Napoleon's military strategy with his daughters while they were busily stitching some intricate embroidery.

It also gave him a much-needed respite from the increasingly vociferous demands for more money from his wife.

<p style="text-align:center">~~~ooO0Ooo~~~</p>

It was not long before Mrs Mortimer introduced the sisters to estate management, by the simple expedient of taking one or more of the sisters along on her visits to tenants.

Often the younger girls would play with the tenant's children, while the adults discussed issues. After the visits, Mrs Mortimer would discuss what, if anything, needed to be done and why.

After one visit, Mary asked, 'when can I take a basket of food to Carol and Eddie?'

Since neither Mr or Mrs Grant had made any mention of money being tight, or that they were unable to feed the family, Mrs Mortimer asked, 'why?'

'Because they are hungry,' was Mary's obvious answer.

'Their parents did not mention any problem, Mary. Did Carol and Eddie tell you why they are hungry?'

'Carol said that her father had been sick and Mr Jones had to come to help him. Now they have no money for food.'

'I thought Mr Grant looked unwell. But I guess he is too proud or stubborn to ask for help.'

'That is what Carol said her mother said.'

'In that case, since you found out about the problem, would you like to arrange for a basket of food with Mrs Kirby and then take it out to your friends?'

'May I go there on Sophia?' Mary asked excitedly.

Mrs Mortimer laughed at the enthusiasm displayed by the young girl. 'Yes, you may take the pony, but a groom must accompany you.'

Mary threw her arms around Mrs Mortimer. 'Thank you, Mama. I told Carol that you would fix it.'

'I did not fix it. You did. And I am very proud of you.'

<div align="center">~~~ooo0Ooo~~~</div>

All the girls benefitted to a greater or lesser extent by everything Mrs Taylor had to teach. Playing the pianoforte, singing, drawing, sewing, comportment, languages, how to make polite conversation and more.

Once Mary and Kitty reached the limit of what Mrs Taylor could teach them about music and painting respectively, Mrs Mortimer took them to London for a month of intensive instruction with masters in their subject.

While Elizabeth had become proficient at playing the pianoforte and had a lovely singing voice, she had neither the interest nor the dedication needed for the intensive music lessons, and lessons in painting were totally wasted on her.

Instead, Elizabeth received lessons at Angelo's Fencing Academy. She was such an enthusiastic student, she even impressed Henry Angelo, who mourned the fact that she was female, otherwise he could have let her try her skill against his other students.

While Elizabeth was disappointed that her teacher was the only man with whom she could practice, she was thrilled by the fact that he treated her seriously and made no special allowance for her sex.

The family and Mrs Taylor repeated this trip three times every year.

~~~oo0Ooo~~~

'En garde,' cried Miss Julia Martin. She was sparring with her newest student, Miss Elizabeth Mortimer, in the ballroom of Brook Hall.

Miss Martin considered herself exceedingly fortunate to have obtained the position as arms-mistress from Mrs Mortimer. While having once been a very pretty child, a case of smallpox had removed her chances of marriage. No man seemed to be interested in a woman with a badly scarred face. At least not without a substantial dowry.

While the situation of her family had allowed her the opportunity to learn the accomplishments needed to become a governess or a lady's companion, her appearance had worked against her in this area as well. Children were frightened by her scarred face and ladies wanted a pleasant faced companion.

Fortunately for her, a cousin had introduced her to Angelo's School of Fencing. There she had learned all that she could about fencing with a variety of weapons. Her cousin, who served in the army, had also taught her about unarmed combat.

They both felt that while her looks made her ineligible for refined company, as the protector of a lady her scars would not be an issue, particularly once she changed to male clothing. Having an androgynous figure allowed her to successfully avoid notice.

For several years she had protected the daughters of the Duke of ---, who was thrilled that the girls would have a guard who would not endanger their virtue. But since the last remaining daughter married recently, Miss Martin's services were no longer required.

Now she was teaching the oldest of Mrs Mortimer's daughters to improve her fencing skills.

Twelve-year-old Elizabeth was a natural with a blade. In Julia's opinion Mrs Mortimer and Angelo had done an excellent job to bring
~~~

the girl to her current standard. Lizzy had excellent reflexes and was utterly fearless.

The lessons which they now focused on were designed to take the girl from a polite duelling style with a foil, to expand her ability with other weapons. Lizzy, who had blossomed in the three years under Mrs Mortimer's care and tutelage, took to those lessons like a duck to water.

But the lessons were not limited to bladework. Mrs Mortimer insisted that all her daughters should learn to defend themselves against unwanted advances. Mary and Kitty found that they quite enjoyed the rough and tumble of the exercise, but refused to touch the edged weapons.

While most gentlemen would behave with propriety, Mrs Mortimer knew that some men refused to take no for an answer. Unfortunately, in those situations society always put the blame on the women. Mrs Mortimer was determined that her daughters should be safe from those libertines. Mrs Taylor, who had first-hand experience with such a situation, was thrilled to join the lessons.

The girls had been shocked when they met Miss Martin. Not because of her scarred face, of which they had been informed beforehand, but because she wore breeches rather than dresses.

Elizabeth had immediately seen the advantage in the freedom of movement which breeches allowed and had requested permission to wear similar apparel.

Mrs Mortimer had countered the request. 'You may wear breeches for half of your lessons, but the rest of the time I expect you to wear dresses.' When Elizabeth had wanted to argue, she explained, 'if you ever need to use your skills in earnest, you will probably be wearing a dress. If you are not used to defend yourself while wearing a gown, you will lose.'

Elizabeth had seen the wisdom in the argument and now alternated between outfits

<p style="text-align:center">~~~oo0Ooo~~~</p>

7 Visits

Elizabeth, Mary and Kitty were visiting Lucas Lodge. This time without Jane, who was required to dance attendance on Mrs Bennet while she went visiting.

To everyone's surprise Elizabeth and Charlotte Lucas had become fast friends despite their difference in ages. Charlotte was quite intelligent and she found that Elizabeth's quick mind matched her own.

Mary, who had become much more confident due to her adopted mother's influence, had taken the younger Maria Lucas under her wing. Maria, who was of a similar age to Kitty, had been rather flighty, but was settling down a little because of the older girl's influence. Although on occasion all three could be found giggling or comparing the relative superiority of various ribbons.

Charlotte commented, 'I am so sorry for Jane. Mrs Bennet has the worst taste. Did you see the monstrosity she made Jane wear last Sunday? Frills and ruffles and lace everywhere. Does she truly think that is tasteful?'

'I am afraid some of that may be my fault since I despise over-decorated frocks. Mother agrees with me that simple styles are much more tasteful as well as more practical, both to wear and to clean. Mrs Bennet is trying to show us up by having Jane wear dresses with an abundance of lace because they are more expensive.'

'I understand that. She thinks that expensive equates to tasteful.'

'Precisely. But Jane is being made to suffer, since some of the boys snigger at her, because of the overdone dresses she wears. She would prefer something simpler, but she is not given a choice.'

'Lydia on the other hand is loving it. If she had her way, her dresses would be entirely made up of ribbons and lace.' Charlotte shook her head. 'I just wish Mrs Bennet would make the effort to give the girl at least a basic education. I heard that Lydia is learning to dance, but she can barely read or write.'

'I know. Her argument is that men do not like women who are better educated than they are. Since Lydia is but eight years of age, she still has a little time to improve, but I think Mrs Bennet is deliberately encouraging Lydia's laziness when it comes to study.' Elizabeth sighed. While she did not particularly like her youngest sister, she thought it unkind of Mrs Bennet not to give the girl more opportunities. Her musing was interrupted by her friend.

'Jane was telling me the other day that Mrs Bennet is planning to put her out into society as soon as she turns five and ten. *And* she expects Jane to be married within a year.'

'Poor Jane. She feels so very pressured. I am not certain now if it was a good idea to have had her sharing our lessons,' Elizabeth suggested with a frown. When Charlotte looked puzzled, she clarified. 'Jane is not only very beautiful, but now, thanks to Mother, she is also exceedingly accomplished. If she had a decent dowry, men would stand in line to marry her. Even so, I suspect she will have offers, making Mrs Bennet insufferable if Jane does not accept the first offer, because she does not love the man.'

'I shall certainly support Jane's decision,' declared Charlotte stoutly, despite the fact that her attitude towards marriage was much more practical, rather than romantic.

'At least in this situation, Father will support us, irrespective of what Mrs Bennet wants,' declared Elizabeth with conviction.

<div align="center">~~~ooo0Ooo~~~</div>

Elizabeth was having a great deal of trouble keeping a straight face. Mr Mortimer's grandsons by his first wife had arrived for a visit with their *grandmother*. She could not decide if they were deliberately teasing Mrs Mortimer by calling her Grandmama, or whether they were oblivious to the fact that it was incongruous to call a woman who was younger than their fathers by that title.

The lady in question must have been used to the address since she showed no discomposure. Indeed, she appeared to enjoy the irreverent attentions of Gerald, James and Charles Mortimer.

Although when Gerald, at the ripe old age of one and twenty tried to call Kitty, who was ten years old, "Aunt Catherine", the address was too preposterous. Elizabeth suggested, and everyone agreed, that they should all be honorary cousins.

They were on their way to Cambridge after the summer holidays. The two older cousins were to continue their studies, while Charles, brother to Gerald and the youngest of them was about to start his first year.

This was their first visit without their parents, and unlike previous occasions, they planned to spend several days enjoying Mrs Mortimer's hospitality.

'While I thoroughly enjoy your company, I wonder what occasioned this visit?' Mrs Mortimer wanted to know.

Charles looked extremely embarrassed and uncomfortable at the question, while his brother and his cousin sniggered.

Gerald answered for his brother. 'It seems that Charles has an ardent admirer. The lady saw his youth and innocence and thought to catch him while he remained thus. Father caught on to this and thought it best if we removed from Tamworth before she could place him in a position where he could not escape.'

'I would not have thought any lady would be quite so determined as to prevent an escape if a man is truly set against her.'

'She had many years of practice, unsuccessful, mind you, of setting traps and is getting desperate. Desperate people will do desperate things I am told.'

'If she had years of practice, she either started very young...'

'Or she is well and truly on the shelf.' Gerald completed the sentence.

'So, I have come to throw myself at your mercy to host us until the start of University. Yours is the only house where we feel safe, since our cousins, delightful as I am certain they are, are not of marriageable age,' Charles appealed to Mrs Mortimer with a pleading look.

At this point Elizabeth lost the battle with her countenance. A grin spread over her features. 'Mama, how does it feel to be in a position of rescuer, saviour even, to a group of gentlemen?' she chuckled.

'I find the notion quite charming and very appropriate,' the lady answered with perfect dignity.... and twinkling eyes.

Elizabeth looked mischievous as she added, 'although I miss her company, I must admit that I am rather pleased Jane is visiting the Gardiners in London at present. If Jane were at Longbourn, and Mrs Bennet found out that there are three unattached young gentlemen staying here, we would have to barricade all the doors and windows.'

'Heaven forefend. Please, Cousin Elizabeth, do not give us away,' cried James. 'I could not bear to have my liberty curtailed. Not even temporarily, never mind permanently... at least not until I am ready.'

'In that case, you may have the liberty of the estate, but you had better not go into the village,' suggested their hostess. 'Otherwise Mrs Bennet might recall Jane from London, and the girl does so enjoy her visits with her relatives.

'Very well, we will bow to your greater experience in such matters.'

~~~ooO0oo~~~

At breakfast Mrs Mortimer requested, 'Elizabeth since I will be busy this morning, would you be so kind and show your cousins around the estate?'

Elizabeth agreed, and finding that her cousin's horses needed some rest, arranged for mounts to be readied for all of them.

When she met her cousins at the stable, she wore her favourite riding habit with the split skirt. It was a compromise between the comfort and practicality of breeches, and the propriety of a dress which ladies were supposed to wear. When standing up or walking, the difference was not noticeable to the untrained eye.

Just as she arrived, the grooms were leading out four horses for them.

The cousins looked at the mounts, and Gerald noticed that there were three geldings and a spirited grey stallion. 'What a beautiful stallion. You have chosen an excellent mount for me, although the
~~~

stirrups need lengthening considerably,' he declared, holding out his hand for the reins.

The groom leading the stallion smirked at Gerald and walked past him, handing the reins to Elizabeth instead.

Lizzy grinned. 'Sorry, Cousin, but Phoenix is my horse, and the stirrups are just perfect.'

She offered an apple to the stallion who took it gently from her hand. After a brief pat on his neck, she swung up into the saddle before the cousins had a chance to react.

Gerald looked on in consternation. 'Ladies do not ride stallions,' he protested. 'You need to be able to grip with your legs to control them.'

'It is lucky that I am not yet a lady then, and can ride astride, is it not?'

Charles started to chuckle at his brother's discomfiture. 'Gerald, even though you are the oldest of us, you will not be able to claim the privilege of the best horse. You will have to settle for a gelding like the rest of us mere mortals.' He bowed to Elizabeth with a flourish. 'In this household the ladies are preeminent.'

Gerald collected his scattered wits. 'My apologies for my presumption, Cousin, I am unused to ladies whose accomplishments are not confined to embroidery and playing a musical instrument.'

'You are forgiven if you could stop wasting time.'

They took off at a gentle trot while Lizzy showed them the extent of the estate. When they came to the edge of the long field, which had just been harvested, she stopped. 'Here is the perfect spot if you would like to have a good run.'

James' eyes lit up. 'I hope you do not mind if we leave you behind, Cousin,' he said politely.

'I do not mind at all,' answered Elizabeth and gestured for them to take off.

The cousins were enjoying their gallop and had covered about a quarter of the distance when they heard hoofbeats behind them.

By the time they realised what was happening, a grey blur sped past them, with Elizabeth crouched low over Phoenix' shoulders.

Her cousins urged their mounts to greater speed but they could not catch her, until she stopped at the far-end of the field, where she waited for them.

Her face was flushed, her bonnet had slipped off her head and was dangling down her back, as was her hair. She was laughing with joy when her cousins arrived.

'Do not feel bad. Phoenix is the fastest horse in these parts and I am lighter than any of you,' she called out to them.

'Foiled yet again. I was hoping to show off my exquisite seat, but instead I was reduced to watching yours.' James shrugged good-naturedly.

Gerald shook his head. 'Elizabeth, is there anything you are not good at?'

'I am terrible at painting. Kitty, at the age of six and without any training could do better than I can after four years of instruction. Once I tried to paint Phoenix and Mother congratulated me on having painted a recognisable hippopotamus. I have since decided to stop wasting paper on those laughable efforts.' She shrugged. 'Shall we continue?'

She did not mention another failing. She felt guilty because she felt nothing for Mrs Bennet despite the fact that the woman had given her life. She did not even hate the lady for mistreating her. Elizabeth simply felt nothing. As far as her emotions were concerned, Mrs Bennet simply did not exist, and Lizzy felt troubled by that indifference. If it had not been for the fact that she dearly loved her sisters, her father and Mrs Mortimer, she would have thought herself incapable of feeling.

Their last destination was Oakham Mount. At the top they dismounted to let the horses rest for a few minutes while Elizabeth pointed out the various estates and landmarks.

'I love this place. I wish I could paint so that I could capture this view at sunrise. To me it always looks magical,' she said wistfully.

She cheered up. 'This is also the place where I met Mrs Mortimer, and my life changed for the better.'

'Then let us return and see if she can make things better for us too,' cried Gerald.

'Sorry brother, you are a lost cause...'

~~~ooOOoo~~~

Two weeks later the cousins were on their way to Cambridge.

That afternoon, Mrs Mortimer handed a flat parcel to Elizabeth. 'James has asked me to give this to you.'

'Why did he not give it to me himself,' Elizabeth wondered as she unwrapped it.

As soon as she could see the content properly, she understood why he had deputised Mrs Mortimer to do the honours.

Her eyes flooded when she saw a perfect sunrise viewed from Oakham Mount.

~~~ooOOoo~~~

8   Collins

In March 1805, when Jane had recently turned sixteen, Mr Bennet breathed his last. His wife's ceaseless demands for more money for yet more dresses for her daughters had worn him down. The final straw came when Mrs Bennet berated him for supporting Jane's refusal of a proposal from Mr Pogson, the owner of a largish estate in the next village. Mrs Bennet did not care that Mr Pogson was fifty years old, unpleasant to look at as well as odiferous, and had already worn out three wives through childbearing. She was determined that her most beautiful daughter must marry.

When Mr Bennet realised that he was slipping away, he was grateful for his release, secure in the knowledge that his daughters would be safe.

Everyone expected Mrs Bennet to be wailing enough to be heard all the way to Meryton when she discovered that her husband was gone.

Instead she took the news moderately calmly.

She had her plans in place. The heir to Longbourn was Mr William Collins, a man older than her husband had been. She herself was not yet five and thirty and according to her looking glass, she was still as beautiful as ever. Maturity and children had only added to her womanly curves. Therefore, once a minimal mourning period was over, she would happily change her name from Bennet to Collins, and ensure her continued position as Mistress of Longbourn.

And if perchance Mr Collins was not interested in a mature woman, there was always Jane, who at six and ten had grown into the beauty that was her birthright. Any man would have to be blind not to be interested in her older daughter.

Jane had come out the year before at the insistence of her mother, who wanted her daughters well married and settled, before Mr Bennet died. Even to a woman as oblivious as Mrs Bennet, it had become obvious that her husband was not much longer for the world.

Since her hopes for an early marriage for Jane had been dashed, due to her husband's refusal to approve the marriage with Mr Pogson, it left her beautiful daughter free to secure their home for their future.

She sent a carefully worded letter to Mr Collins, informing him that his inheritance awaited him.

~~~oo0Ooo~~~

Mrs Mortimer had taken her daughters to London for some shopping and to go to the theatre and the opera. While in town, they also visited with the Gardiners, who were still the girls' favourite aunt and uncle.

They had just returned from an outing in the afternoon, when an express arrived from Mr Phillips, informing the ladies of Mr Bennet's death.

They made plans to leave early the next morning, to be on hand to lend their support to Jane.

Overnight a storm blew up from the southwest, which, combined with a heavy downpour, made the roads between London and Meryton impassable.

They eventually left town as soon as the roads could be traversed, albeit with caution and at moderate speeds.

It was already four days after Mr Bennet's death.

~~~oo0Ooo~~~

Mr William Collins Senior and his son arrived at Longbourn two days after receiving the express from Mrs Bennet.

They arrived from Bedfordshire. While the early part of their journey had been relatively easy, the last ten miles had taken the better part of the day, since the coach-driver refused to risk the horses or the carriage on the muddy roads.

Mr Collins, whose temper was always problematical, was even more irascible than usual. When the door was not opened, the instant he exited the carriage, he pounded vigorously on the front door.

He was a tall and solid man, who would easily go to fat if he could afford to eat the way he would have liked. His formerly dark hair was mostly gone, and what was left was more salt than pepper.

Mrs Hill, had been busy looking after Mrs Bennet, who was having the vapours yet again, had barely cracked the door open, when Collins pushed it open fully, and she was rudely shoved aside.

'I will see the body of my cousin now,' demanded Mr Collins.

'May I ask if you are Mr Collins?' Mrs Hill asked politely, even though her hip hurt, where it had connected with the door.

'Who else would come calling?'

'The undertaker,' replied Mrs Hill, still polite, but she would not give that brute the satisfaction of seeing her cowed.

'Do I look like the undertaker?' blustered Collins. That incompetent woman had to go as soon as he was in charge.

'No, Sir,' answered Mrs Hill, thinking that the undertaker was a very pleasant man. She was also privately amused that for a man, who was in such a hurry, he was wasting time on silly questions and answers, when he could have simply confirmed that he was Mr William Collins.

'I am Mr Collins and I will see my cousin's body. Now,' he declared, pulling himself up to his full height. The frown he directed at Mrs Hill appeared to be a permanent fixture on his visage.

'Certainly, sir.'

Mrs Hill was trying to shut the door, when she heard a timid voice say, 'pardon me.'

She saw a physically smaller replica of Mr Collins trying to enter the house. The young man was maybe eight or nine and ten years of age. Even though he was moderately tall, he was stooping as if to hide himself away. His features, while similar to his father, were much softer and pleasant, but currently worried looking.

'Come along, boy. You know I hate it when you dawdle.'

'Yes, Sir. I was just telling the driver to unload our trunks, like you told me to do,' the young man said deferentially, as he slipped inside the door, which Mrs Hill promptly closed. A footman would see to the trunks.

She led the way into the morning room, which, since it faced east, was the coolest of the public rooms. Mr Bennet had been laid out in his coffin. It was disconcerting to many of the staff, as well as his family, that for the first time in years Mr Bennet's face had relaxed into a peaceful smile.

One of the footmen had commented, 'he is the first man I ever saw who looked happy to be dead.'

Mr Collins Senior looked down at Mr Bennet with a satisfied smile. 'You were five years younger than I, but I outlived you to claim what should have been mine in the first place,' he addressed the corpse.

It was surely a trick of the candlelight that Mr Bennet's smile seemed to deepen.

William Collins, who had followed his father into the room, looked at Mr Bennet, and with sorrow thought *I think I would have liked you.*

~~~oo0Ooo~~~

Meanwhile, the noise of his arrival had alerted Mrs Bennet to the presence of Mr Collins. She checked in her looking-glass to ensure that every hair was in place and she presented the perfect picture of a grieving, but composed, widow.

She descended the stairs and followed the voices to the door of the morning room. After seeing the smile on her husband's face the first time, she refused to enter the room. 'Welcome to Longbourn, Cousin Collins,' she addressed the older man.

Mr Collins turned at the sound of the greeting, and looked at Mrs Bennet from head to toe, as if she was a side of beef in a butcher's window.

'Cousin,' he acknowledged her greeting with a barely perceptible bow.

William Collins showed better manners. He bowed and said, 'I am sorry for your loss, Mrs Bennet.'

'Thank you, Cousin William.'
~~~

His father was not a man to worry about people's feelings, at least not in private. He might pay lip-service to propriety when in public, but only as long as it did not inconvenience him.

'You said in your letter that as Master of Longbourn, I should consider taking a wife.'

'Yes, Cousin Collins, that would be expected of you,' simpered Mrs Bennet. 'Naturally, I would have to observe at least a nominal mourning period...'

'I have no interest in used and used up goods,' interrupted Collins.

Mrs Bennet blushed, to be referred to in such a way. Very well, if she could not entice him into marriage, Jane would have to become Mrs Collins, to ensure that they would not lose their home and their station in the community.

But Jane had locked herself in her room, overcome with grief at the loss of her father apparently. She explained this to the towering man, when they heard giggles.

'Your daughter does not seem as discomposed as you made her out to be,' Collins accused Mrs Bennet.

'That is Lydia. She is full young yet to understand the tragedy which has befallen her. Losing her father at but nine years of age.' Mrs Bennet sighed. 'Jane on the other hand, was my husband's favourite, and she is devastated by his loss. She will need time to compose herself. Perhaps after the funeral...?'

'When is the funeral?'

'It can be tomorrow. We were just waiting for your arrival.'

'Very well. We will have the funeral in the morning and the reading of the will in the afternoon. Then you can introduce me to my potential bride. I hope she lives up to the picture you painted of her,' Collins ordered callously. 'Now I would like to refresh myself, then I want dinner and afterwards you may entertain me.'

~~~ooO0Ooo~~~
~~~

Jane was hiding in her room behind doors that were securely locked and barricaded. On Mrs Hill's advice, she had even locked the servants' door.

A short while ago, Mrs Hill had brought her a tray of food and tea, as well as information that she would have preferred not to know. It appeared that her mother was trying to barter her oldest daughter, to a man five years older than Mr Bennet, for the privilege of living at Longbourn.

Even in her room, Jane had heard the arrival of the man, and had been afraid of the rough and domineering tone of his voice. Now she was terrified.

Oh, why did her father have to die while Mrs Mortimer was so far away? She knew that on the death of her father, that lady would become her guardian. It had been a relief to her to know that this caring lady would be there to defend her against her mother's demands that she marry, no matter how unsuitable the man.

But now the torrential rain was preventing her saviour to return, and the potentially worst possible suitor had put in an appearance instead.

She could not even run away since such an action would potentially ruin her reputation. Even if she had somewhere to run to. All she could do now was to keep her doors locked and barricaded, and pray for deliverance.

~~~ooO0Ooo~~~

That evening, spurred on by Mr Collins' rude dismissal of herself as a potential wife, Mrs Bennet was prodded into one act of defiance.

When Collins demanded her favours as he deemed it his right as the Master of Longbourn, she told him that since the will had not yet been read, he was still the heir presumptive, not the Master, before flouncing off to her chambers.

Mr Collins, stung by the rejection, followed her... and refused to take no for an answer.

Meanwhile his son hid in his room, feeling pity for the widow.

~~~ooO0Ooo~~~

9   Upheaval

It was late in the afternoon, four days after Mr Bennet's death that the mud-covered carriage pulled up in front of Longbourn.

The journey had been fraught with delays and consequently Elizabeth had been fretful. Five years at Brook Hall had not erased the memory of her mother's mercenary nature. Her grief over the death of Mr Bennet was overshadowed by her concern for Jane.

Her constant fretting and restlessness had worn on Mrs Mortimer's nerves, particularly since her own suspicions of Mrs Bennet's likely actions was making her anxious as well. While both Elizabeth and Mrs Mortimer shared the same fears, neither had been prepared to voice them, afraid that to speak of them would make them come true.

Mrs Mortimer slowly descended from her carriage. She shook out her travelling dress, to make herself look a little more presentable.

In the meantime, Mr Phillips, whom she had alerted to her return on the way through Meryton, exited his own carriage and offered her his arm to approach Longbourn.

Mrs Mortimer's carriage, sans footmen, left to take the girls to Brook Hall. Mr Phillips would convey Mrs Mortimer to her home, after the reading of the will.

Mrs Hill, alerted by the servants' grapevine was ready to open the door as soon as they approached. She took them to the parlour and announced, 'Mr Phillips and Mrs Mortimer.'

Collins, who had been thwarted yet again by having the reading of the will delayed until all interested parties could be present, growled at Mr Phillips, 'are you here to make me wait even longer? When will *all the interested parties be assembled*? I think you are just dragging your feet, trying to annoy me.'

'Not at all, Mr Collins,' said Phillips deliberately pleasantly.

The quarrel which had divided the family had happened before his own marriage to Mrs Bennet's sister. He had therefore only met Mr Collins today. He had taken the measure of the man at the funeral and was not impressed.

'Now that Mrs Mortimer has arrived, all interested parties are present.'

'You mean you made me wait on the convenience of some woman?' snarled Collins.

'This lady has been on the road from London since the crack of dawn and has only just arrived. She did not even take the time to go home to change or refresh herself, so that she could be here as early as possible.'

'Then she should have left yesterday,' Collins was still argumentative.

'I tried to leave two days ago, but the rain made the roads impassable. You are lucky I made it here today,' Mrs Mortimer said coldly, dismissing the man. 'Now that I am here, I would prefer it if you did not keep me waiting.'

She turned to the solicitor. 'Mr Phillips, if you would be so kind...'

'If we could adjourn to the study...'

Once they reached the room, Mr Phillips settled himself behind the desk to the chagrin of Mr Collins. He pulled out his papers and looked at his audience, which now included William Collins senior and junior, Mrs Bennet as well as Mrs Mortimer. Jane could have been present, but on the advice of Mrs Hill had stayed in her room until everyone was assembled in the study.

Mr Phillips cleared his throat and started to read. 'This is the final will and testament of Thomas Henry Bennet.'

He went on to list a number of bequests, such as a sum of fifty pounds to Mrs Hill for her longsuffering service, as well as other items for each of the servants.

Then he came to the provisions for Mr Bennet's family.

'To my daughter Jane, I leave the personal jewellery of my mother, as per the attached inventory.

To my daughter Lydia, I leave Nellie, the horse of which she is so fond.

To my daughters Elizabeth, Mary and Catherine, I leave the books, sheet music and art which I have acquired in my lifetime, as per the attached inventory.

To Mrs Mortimer I leave the care and guardianship of all my daughters. I know they will be in the best of hands.

To my wife I leave nothing, as she has already taken everything I was able to give – and then some.

If my wife should be delivered of a son within ten months of my demise, the rest of estate, as per the entail, will go to my son and held in trust for him until he reaches his majority, by my brother-in-law, Mr Phillips, who will also be his guardian.

If no son is born in the specified period, the rest of the estate, as per the entail, can go to that unprincipled son of a deleted expletive, William Collins.

Thomas Henry Bennet

There was stunned silence for a full minute. Then Mrs Bennet started to screech, 'he left me nothing? After all these years of looking after him and giving him five daughters. And he leaves me nothing?'

'Did you say five daughters? Where are the others? Were you trying to fob off the worst of the lot on me, thinking that should satisfy me, while keeping the prime stock for some milksops? If I let you live under my roof, I want it to be worth my while.'

'Jane, my oldest, is only just turned six and ten. She is even younger than your son. Are you so perverted that you would want a true child as a wife? I am sorry to disappoint you, but I do not have a babe in arms to present to you as a bride.' Mrs Bennet now turned her vitriol onto the irate Collins.

Mr Phillips and Mrs Mortimer exchanged disgusted looks at the relentless selfishness of the two loud antagonists.

Mrs Mortimer spared a glance at William Collins and saw embarrassment, mingled with sarcastic amusement, on the countenance of the young man, as he watched his father being thwarted.

Mr Phillips let the two opponents rant for a while, until he judged the time to be right to end the argument.

'Enough,' he thundered.

The shout, delivered with such authority, stopped the other's shouts and screeches.

'Keep your arguments for another time. Mr Collins, for your information, none of Mr Bennet's daughters will be able to marry you, since I suspect that Mrs Mortimer will not give her permission.'

'I most certainly will not. If and when they do wed, the girls will marry men suitable to them in age and character. Considering Jane is only barely six and ten, that leaves Mr Collins out of contention.'

'Just so,' Phillips agreed. 'Mrs Bennet, your personal belongings and any items which you brought into the marriage are yours to keep. Your husband left an inventory of those items as well.'

'Mr Collins, you may act as the caretaker of Longbourn until Mrs Bennet is delivered of a son, if she is expecting, or until it is confirmed that she is not expecting. The established period for such confirmation is four months from the day of Mr Bennet's death.'

'Until you are confirmed as the heir and Master of Longbourn, Mrs Bennet is entitled to remain in her home and her usual pin money from the profits of the estate.'

At that point the door to the study opened quietly, and Mrs Hill poked her head in briefly and nodded at Mr Phillips, who was the only one facing the door. As soon as he had seen her, she withdrew.

Mr Phillips seemed to reconsider his last statement based on his observation. 'Fanny, if you are expecting, I suggest you come and stay with us and let your sister take care of you.'

Although Mrs Bennet was not a particularly intelligent woman, she was cunning enough to realise what her brother-in-law was suggesting, particularly after the actions of Mr Collins the previous evening. 'A sister's presence would be of great comfort at such a time. Thank you.'

'Very well. That is all I have to impart. I will leave you now to rest after this difficult day.'

Mr Phillips put away his papers, rose and offered his arm, 'Mrs Mortimer, I think you also need to get home and rest.'

'Thank you, Mr Phillips,' she replied as she took his arm and allowed him to lead her from the study.

In the foyer Mrs Hill was waiting to see them out. 'Everything you need is in the carriage or on its way to Brook Hall with the footmen,' she said cryptically.

'Thank you, Mrs Hill.' Mr Phillips smiled at the housekeeper.

Mrs Mortimer had her own ideas to add. 'Mrs Hill, there will always be a place for you and your friends at Brook Hall, should you require it,' she said softly as they headed out the door.

~~~ooO0Ooo~~~

As soon as Mr Phillips and Mrs Mortimer had settled onto the front bench of the carriage, the driver took off.

'My apologies for having to share such close quarters, Mrs Mortimer, but there were some critical items I have to convey.' Mr Phillips gestured towards a blanket covered bundle on the back seat.

'No matter, Mr Phillips. I know you to be a gentleman.'

Mr Phillips looked out the window and after a few minutes commented with a smile, 'since we have now left the grounds of Longbourn, I can now deliver your inheritance to you.'

At his words, the bundle on the other seat moved, and Jane extricated herself from the blankets and sat up. Her movement also exposed a sleeping Lydia lying on the seat.

'Aunt Stephanie, you have no idea how happy I am to see you. Mrs Bennet was going to marry me off to that horrid man,' Jane said tremulously. After the harrowing day she had spent, knowing Mrs Bennet's intentions, she could not bring herself to think of the woman as her mother.

'That was never going to happen, Jane. I am certain Mrs Hill and all the staff would have spirited you away had you been in any danger,'
~~~

said Mrs Mortimer as she manoeuvred herself onto the seat beside Jane, and gathered the trembling girl in a comforting embrace.

'I gather Mrs Hill did not expect Lydia to come along voluntarily,' Mr Phillips nodded at the sleeping child.

'As soon as you arrived, Mrs Hill sent her some hot chocolate laced with laudanum. She said Lydia should sleep through the night and give us all a chance to get at least one good sleep.'

Mrs Mortimer chuckled, 'that lady would have made an excellent general. I certainly hope she takes up my offer and comes to Brook Hall.'

Then she turned serious. 'Jane, I am dreadfully sorry you lost your father, but I hope you will be happy at Brook Hall.'

'It will be good to be with all my sisters again. I always enjoyed coming for lessons with them, but I hated having to leave. Now I can stay.' Jane looked wistful. 'To my shame I must admit that I envied my sisters having you as their mother.'

'Now that I am officially your guardian, I will be happy to be whatever you need me to be. Your friend, your adopted aunt or even your adopted mother. The choice is yours,' offered Mrs Mortimer while giving Jane's shoulder an extra squeeze.

Jane looked up at the smiling face, threw her arms around her and said, 'thank you. After all that has happened, I know who my true mother is.'

<p style="text-align:center">~~~oo0Ooo~~~</p>

Mrs Bennet knocked on the door to Jane's room. When there was no answer, she tried the handle and the door opened to reveal an empty room. Not just empty of the occupant, but emptied of Jane's possessions as well.

She rushed to Lydia's room and found the same emptiness.

When she returned to her own room, she rang for Mrs Hill.

'Where are my daughters?' she demanded of the housekeeper, when she entered.

'Miss Bennet and Miss Lydia left with their guardian.'

Mrs Bennet sat down heavily. 'All alone,' she murmured, staring blindly at a piece of paper she was still clutching.

She felt drained. Her earlier outburst had been fuelled by relief that Jane would not be forced to marry that brute.

While she had thought Collins to be an older version of her husband, polite and weak, she had thought him a good match, since she believed that she and Jane could easily manage the man.

But after the man's actions the previous night, Mrs Bennet's stunted maternal instincts had awoken enough to be concerned for her oldest daughter. Now that Jane and Lydia were out of danger, there was only herself to endure Collins' attentions. Was the position of Mistress of Longbourn worth the price?

After sitting and thinking for several minutes, she looked up and saw Mrs Hill waiting for her to come out of her funk.

Mrs Bennet realised she was still holding the paper. Glancing at it again she came to a decision. She handed the list to the housekeeper.

'Hill, please have everything on this list and all my personal belongings packed up, and delivered to Mr Phillips. I think I shall go for a walk to clear my head.'

Mrs Hill nodded in understanding. 'I will send Bob to escort you, Madam. Your things will be delivered later this evening.' She curtsied and left the room.

Mrs Bennet, with the help of her maid Sally, quickly changed into a costume suitable to wear outdoors.

When they came down the servants' stair, Mrs Hill was waiting at the bottom with Sally's stout boots and coat. 'You had better go with the Mistress. It is not safe for you to stay either,' she said gruffly to the maid, and handed her a small valise.

'Mrs Hill is right, you had better come along,' agreed Mrs Bennet, and a minute later the two women, accompanied by Bob the footman, slipped out the side door.

It was a cold walk, but they made it safely to the Phillips residence, where Mrs Phillips was already expecting them.

<p style="text-align:center">~~~ooo0Ooo~~~</p>

10 Consequences

When Mrs Mortimer arrived at Brook Hall, Elizabeth and her sisters were anxiously waiting for them.

When Jane walked through the front door with Mrs Mortimer, she felt herself engulfed in a hug from Elizabeth. A moment later the other sisters joined them.

'We have been so worried about you. Wondering if Mr Collins had arrived. We heard some absolutely horrible stories about him.'

'He arrived yesterday, but Mrs Hill had me lock myself in my room until Mother arrived,' she said, nodding in Mrs Mortimer's direction, to the delight of her sisters.

'But I must admit, despite the locked door, I have never before been so terrified in my entire life.

Just then, Mr Phillips entered, carrying Lydia. 'Where would you like me to put her?' he asked.

Elizabeth answered, 'I had Mrs Kirby prepare the rooms down the hall from us.' She looked questioningly at Mrs Mortimer.

'Excellent thinking, Elizabeth. Please show your uncle and sister the way.'

<p style="text-align:center">~~~ooO0Ooo~~~</p>

They all retired early that night, exhausted from the day's events. Jane volunteered to sleep with Lydia, in case the girl woke up and needed reassuring.

But Mrs Hill had judged the dosage perfectly. Jane had just finished her morning's ablutions, when Lydia stirred.

She looked around in confusion and asked, 'where are we?'

Jane sat next to her on the bed and took her hands. 'We are at Brook Hall and Mrs Mortimer is now our guardian. That is what Papa wanted and arranged.'

'Brook Hall? Truly?'

'Yes, indeed.'

Lydia suddenly beamed. 'La, what a joke. Mama was always moaning about us being thrown into the hedgerows when Papa died, and now we get to live in a much nicer place than Longbourn.'

Jane was horrified at Lydia's cavalier attitude. 'Are you not upset that Papa is gone?' she asked.

'No. Why should I be. You know, I hardly ever saw him.' Lydia looked around. 'Where is Mama?'

'She stayed at Longbourn, but may have gone to Aunt Phillips' house by now.'

'Why would she go to Aunt Phillips? Their house is very small. She should be here. We could have so much fun.'

'Mama would not be happy here. You know she does not like Elizabeth, Mary and Kitty.'

'Oh, I forgot. The ugly girls.'

'Our sisters are not ugly,' objected Jane, angrily.

'But Mama always said they were.'

'Mrs Bennet is wrong,' declared Jane firmly.

'You had better not let Mama hear you say that, or you will not get any new dresses for months,' cautioned Lydia.

'Mrs Bennet cannot tell me what to say anymore. Mrs Mortimer is our guardian now.

'In that case, I can get even prettier dresses. Mama always said that Papa's slut was ever so rich.'

'Lydia,' cried Jane, horrified at Lydia's words. 'Do not ever use such words again. Mrs Mortimer is a true lady, and your language is offensive.'

'Jane, do not carry on so. It is just words.'

'Very bad words. You are never to use them again. Do you hear?'

'Whatever you say, Jane,' Lydia answered casually. 'But I am hungry. I want some breakfast.'

~~~ooO0oo~~~

After breakfast, which all the sisters shared with Mrs Mortimer, the lady decided it was time to discuss the future with Lydia.

'Lydia, did Jane explain that your father appointed me your guardian to ensure that you are taken care of, when he passed on?'

'Yes, she did.'

'How do you feel about this arrangement?

'Your house is much nicer than Longbourn. I expect I will like it here.'

While Mrs Mortimer was not impressed by the mercenary and callous attitude, she was relieved that at least she would not have to deal with the major tantrums of a traumatised child.

Lydia had a question of her own. 'What should I call you?'

'That depends. Your sisters call me mother since I formally adopted them and have been their mother for years. If you are not comfortable with that, you may call me Aunt Stephanie. If that is too familiar for you, then you may call me Mrs Mortimer. Do you have a preference?'

'Can I call you what my mother called you?'

'What is that?'

'Slut.'

'No, you may not call me rude names.'

'But Mama said you were Papa's slut,' Lydia exclaimed defiantly.

Instead of arguing, Mrs Mortimer rang the bell.

While they waited for the maid, Mrs Mortimer explained. 'Lydia, in this house you will behave with decorum, you will attend lessons, you will not throw tantrums and you will not use foul language. Is that clear?'
~~~

'Why should I do anything you say? Mama likes how I behave. She says that I am lively. She says men like that.'

'Your mother is wrong on all counts. Your father was a gentleman and always behaved as such. On the other hand, *your* manners are atrocious, and apart from the fact that you are much too young to even consider what men might like, no decent man wants a woman who behaves and speaks like a harlot. Which is how your *lively ways* will be perceived.'

'La, you cannot make me do anything I do not want to, or stop me doing what I do want to.' Lydia remained defiant.

Just then a maid entered, and the lady said, 'Miss Lydia has a filthy mouth. It needs washing.'

Lydia's reputation had preceded her. Therefore, the maid asked, 'the lye soap, Madam?'

'Definitely the lye soap. We need to make sure it stays clean from now on.'

The maid returned shortly, carrying a bucket and soap. She was accompanied by two footmen, one of whom carried a jug of water and a cup. Mrs Mortimer supressed a smile when the maid handed her the soap. She could tell by the smell that it was definitely not lye soap, but the gentler soap everyone used in their bath. But Lydia would not know that.

'Lydia, you will now learn the consequences of unacceptable language or behaviour.'

Mrs Mortimer washed Lydia's mouth with the soap, while the footmen held the squirming girl who was trying to scream imprecations at her guardian while also trying to bite her hand.

Mrs Mortimer appeared unmoved. 'The longer you keep that up, the longer it will be until you can rinse your mouth. What is it to be?'

While Lydia was spoiled and headstrong, she was not stupid. She shut up. Mrs Mortimer handed her a cup of water and allowed her to rinse her mouth. When Lydia looked like she would spit the water onto the carpet rather than into the bucket, Mrs Mortimer raised the soap in warning. Lydia understood the message.

~~~oo0Ooo~~~

When the younger girls went to their lessons, and Mrs Taylor had taken Lydia away for basic lessons in manners, Mrs Mortimer asked Jane to sit with her and chat.

'Something you said last night made me think. You said you were terrified even with your door locked.'

Jane nodded. 'I felt so helpless. Like a rabbit with a wolf sniffing around.'

'Just so. You should know that for the last five years your sisters learned not only ladylike accomplishments, but also how to take care of themselves.'

'What do you mean, take care of themselves?' Jane was puzzled.

'I hired an arms-mistress for them, to teach them shooting, fencing and unarmed combat. Although only Lizzy wanted to learn shooting and fencing, they all learned how to defend themselves. Whilst most men are bigger and stronger than women, there are a number of dirty techniques that can bring down even the strongest man. Those techniques are not ladylike or even gentlemanly, but they are effective.'

'But why...'

'There are some nasty people in this world, and I would not have my daughters be victims. Knowing how to defend yourself will give you confidence. Confidence is a very attractive quality in anyone.'

Mrs Mortimer grinned. 'The delightful consequence is, that if you act in a confident manner, those nasty people are much less likely to pick on you. They are usually bullies, and will back down when confronted. After all, they are looking for victims, not a fight which they might lose.'

Jane was thoughtful for a minute, remembering the terror she felt when Mr Collins had stomped about the house, and worse, when she heard her mother's cries. 'I do not want to be, or even feel like a victim again. Thank you. I would like to meet your arms-mistress.'

Mrs Mortimer rang the bell, and a moment later a smiling woman in an outlandish costume entered the room. If it had not been for Mrs Mortimer calling her the arms-mistress, Jane would have taken her for a young man, in her short jacket, breeches and hessians.
~~~

'Julia, I have another victim for you…'

'Good. With her looks, she will need all that I can teach her.'

~~~ooO0oo~~~

Life settled down in the Mortimer and Phillips households. Miss Martin, who had had a gentlewoman's education, started to assist Mrs Taylor with lessons for the older girls, while the governess focused on Lydia.

Jane wanted to show respect for her father's death, but she did not wish to importune Mrs Mortimer for new dresses as soon as she joined the household. As a compromise, she gratefully removed all lace from her dresses and trimmed several of them with black ribbons instead.

Mrs Mortimer, who had been considering mourning clothes for the sisters, thought Jane's solution to be an excellent compromise, and suggested similar alterations to some of the sisters' outfits as well.

Lydia did not like the new regime. She was used to being the centre of attention in her mother's life. Now she had to deal with a guardian and four sisters who were unmoved by her demands. When she threw a tantrum, she was taken to her room until she calmed down.

As a precaution, all breakable items were removed from Lydia's room.

About a fortnight into her residence at Brook Hall, she demanded new dresses. When Mrs Mortimer explained that she had quite enough dresses, Lydia threw yet another tantrum.

Mrs Taylor took her to her room and left her to stew, while she helped Mary learn a new piece of music.

When she returned to look in on Lydia, she found that the girl had pulled all her dresses out of the wardrobe, and was in the process of tearing them to shreds.

'Now I have nothing to wear. I will need new gowns,' Lydia declared triumphantly.

'Not at all, Lydia. I suspect you will get very tired of wearing the same dress every day. But you have only yourself to blame,' replied Mrs Taylor pleasantly.

Lydia stared at the governess in open mouthed horror.
~~~

When she looked like she was about to start screaming imprecations, Mrs Taylor walked out of the room, closing the door behind her.

At dinner that night, having been forewarned about Lydia's exploits, no one commented on the fact that Lydia was still wearing her day dress and an expression which was both sulky and furious.

Conversation amongst the other ladies was pleasant and lively until Lydia spoke up with a complaint. 'Mrs Mortimer, I was ringing the bell for an hour for the maid to come and tidy up my room, yet no one came. You have very lazy staff. At Longbourn this would not be tolerated.'

'At Longbourn your bad behaviour was tolerated. In my house it is not. You made the mess in your room, therefore you shall clean it up. If you are careful, you may even be able to salvage some dresses and repair them,' Mrs Mortimer calmly explained.

'You want me to do a servants job...' Lydia was flabbergasted.

Mrs Mortimer shrugged. 'You need to learn that in this house bad behaviour has consequences. If you destroy something, you shall fix it. If you make a deliberate mess, you shall clean it up. My servants have better things to do than to indulge a spoiled child.'

Lydia started shouting imprecations. After the administration of soap to her mouth, she was taken to her room. A footman was stationed at her door to ensure she stayed there, while the rest of the family enjoyed a quiet dinner.

Lydia had three more encounters with the soap, but she was gradually improving her manners. Since she was deprived of many of her usual amusements, she eventually started paying attention to some of her lessons out of sheer boredom.

Meanwhile, Julia Martin was impressed by the dedication Jane displayed in her practice. 'It is amazing what a good scare will do to focus someone's attention,' she mused.

Mrs Bennet did not send word that she wanted to see any of her daughters.

~~~oo0Ooo~~~

Two months later, the rumour started that Mrs Bennet was expecting.
~~~

Mr Phillips confirmed the rumour to Mrs Mortimer at one of his visits to check on his nieces. While he had no concern for their safety, it was a pleasant break for him to be out of the house and away from Mrs Bennet's voice.

When Mrs Mortimer displayed incredulity at the news, he related what his sister-in-law had confided in him regarding the events of Mr Collins' arrival.

Mrs Mortimer could not help a sardonic chuckle. 'I certainly hope it is a boy. It would serve Collins right if the consequences of him acting as Lord of the Manor, loses him the manor.'

Mr Phillips heartily agreed. Under the circumstances, he also decided it was safer for Mrs Bennet to remain in the house, to ensure that no *accidents* could befall her.

Especially since Collins had received the news of Mrs Bennet's pregnancy... badly.

~~~oo0Ooo~~~

Nine months to the day, after Mr Bennet's death, in the early hours of Christmas Eve, Mrs Bennet was delivered of a healthy baby boy.

Mr Phillips grinned wolfishly when he was presented with his nephew by the proud and exceedingly pleased mother.

Lady Lucas had attended the birth, and her husband, in his role as the magistrate, had kept company with Mr Phillips to provide an independent witness that the baby was undoubtedly that of Mrs Bennet, should it prove to be a boy.

He added his congratulation as he confirmed the sex of the child. He too would be pleased to see Longbourn return to the Bennet family.

Collins had tried to run roughshod over the tenants, but had been prevented of the worst excesses by threats of legal consequences. He had been smart enough to know that as a newcomer to the area, the word of even a tenant farmer carried more weight than the heir presumptive of Longbourn.

As soon as it got light, a contingent of footmen, borrowed from several neighbours, accompanied Mr Phillips and Sir William to Longbourn.
~~~

Collins was blearily breaking his fast when the delegation entered the dining room.

'Mr Collins, at three thirty-three this morning Mrs Frances Bennet, widow of the late Mr Thomas Henry Bennet, was delivered of a healthy son, Joshua Thomas Bennet. According to Mr Bennet's will, that son is now the heir of Longbourn. Also, according to the will, Mr Phillips will be the trustee of Joshua and Longbourn. Therefore, your services as caretaker for Longbourn are no longer required.' Sir William finished his rehearsed speech.

By the time he finished, Mr Collins was wide awake and furious. 'I bet that boy is no son of Thomas Bennet. I am sure that slut opened her legs to anyone who tipped his hat at her,' he exclaimed.

'You, Sir, are slandering a respectable widow. You should know that since the day she left Longbourn to live at my house, Mrs Bennet has not been in unchaperoned company with any man. Apart from the fact that she was in mourning, what you suggest is vile,' accused Mr Phillips.

'But be that as it may, the law states that a child born to a widow within ten months of her husband's death, is legally her husband's child.'

Mr Phillips was pleased to see the chagrin spread over Collins' face as he realised, he had only himself to blame for the current state of affairs. But he would not give up without a fight.

'I like it here well enough; I think I shall stay. After all, possession is nine tenth of the law; Collins crossed his arms and leaned back in his chair.

Mr Phillips and Sir William exchanged a look. Phillips handed Collins a document, which the man reflexively accepted.

'This is an order of eviction. The bailiffs are currently packing up your belongings, which they will be taking to the post stop. You had better get your coat. It is a cold day outside.'

'You cannot make me leave,' Collins blustered.

At that moment, four burley footmen entered, one of whom was carrying his coat and said, 'you better put that on or you'll be leavin' without it.'

Collins put on the coat with ill grace, and then without warning lashed out a fist at the nearest footman.

The footman, Smith, whose father had been a smith, and the son worked for him until he found an easier position, swayed lightly on his feet. Collins' punch missed, but Smith's return punch connected solidly.

'I guess we'd better pile him onto the cart too,' he said phlegmatically.

As the cart with the unconscious Collins and his possessions was leaving, the cook handed a packet of food to William Collins, who dejectedly followed the cart on foot.

~~~ooo0Ooo~~~
~~~

11 Contrasts

Lydia received the news of the birth of her brother with glee. She had heard about the entail all her life and knew that her brother was now the heir of Longbourn, rather than that horrible Mr Collins.

Since her brother was the heir, Collins would have to leave and her mother would return to Longbourn with her son.

If her mother could return to Longbourn, then so could she.

Although Lydia had learned to mind her manners over the last nine months at Brook Hall, since she did not like the consequences her former behaviour garnered her, she would have preferred to live with her indulgent mother. But not if it meant living in the small house of Mr and Mrs Phillips.

When she found out about her mother's condition, she daydreamed about the wonderful time they would have at home with her mother and baby brother. There would no longer be anyone to deny her anything. Since Papa was dead, Mama would now be in charge of the estate, and holding the purse-strings.

They would no longer have to scrimp and save to afford the latest fashions. They could have as much lace as they wished.

It was going to be wonderful. She would have her mother back, who catered to her every whim. Lydia rejected all overtures by Mrs Mortimer and her sisters to make her part of the family. She was not yet prepared to be part of a family where she was not the centre of attention. But her loneliness would not last much longer. She could mind her manners for a few months.

Now that Longbourn had an heir, she just had to convince Mrs Mortimer to let her visit her mother, and everything would be perfect.

~~~ooO0Ooo~~~
~~~

On Christmas Day, the Mortimer ladies attended services in Meryton. When they arrived, the whole congregation was abuzz with the news of the heir to Longbourn.

Mrs Bennet would have been delighted to attend and accept the congratulations of her neighbours, but she would not be parted from her son and saviour. No matter how much she would have enjoyed the attention, she would do nothing to jeopardise her future.

In her stead, Mrs Phillips spoke to all the neighbours, promising to relate their good wishes to her sister.

Meanwhile Mr Phillips greeted Mrs Mortimer and his nieces. Lydia saw her chance and politely suggested, 'I would love to meet my new brother.'

Mr Phillips was surprised since Lydia had not expressed any desire to visit her mother in all the months that she had been at Brook Hall. Admittedly, neither had Mrs Bennet suggested that her favourite daughters should visit her.

'I would be delighted to collect you tomorrow for a visit. Your mother should be recovered enough to enjoy the company by then,' he suggested.

Lydia beamed at him. 'Thank you, Uncle Phillips. That would be wonderful.'

Jane sent a questioning glance at Mrs Mortimer, who smiled and nodded encouragement.

'I believe I too should welcome our brother,' she offered diffidently.

'Of course, you must come too,' Mr Phillips offered. The time was arranged and he joined his wife to attend the service.

<center>~~~ooO0Ooo~~~</center>

On Boxing Day, Mr Phillips collected Jane and Lydia to visit their mother and new brother.

Jane and Lydia entered the room where Mrs Bennet reclined in her bed with her son in her arms. 'Ah, girls, I would like you to meet Joshua Thomas Bennet, the new Master of Longbourn.'

The sisters were appropriately complimentary. Mrs Bennet looked pleased at the attention until Lydia asked, 'Mama, now that Mr Collins is gone, how soon can we all move back to Longbourn?'

Mrs Bennet frowned. 'I am sorry, Lyddie, but Joshua needs me to look after him. I do not have time to waste on you. Your Uncle Phillips has been telling me that Mrs Mortimer is taking good care of you. You had better make the most of what she can give you.'

What Mrs Bennet did not say, as she did not even admit it to herself, was that she did not want anyone at Longbourn, who was present the night that Joshua was conceived.

She had been desperate enough to maintain a roof over her head that she had considered marrying the man, and even, heaven help her, for Jane to marry him. But after his actions that night, she had done her best to forget the circumstances of her son's conception and had almost convinced herself that Joshua was Mr Bennet's farewell gift to her.

Seeing Jane today reawakened her feeling of guilt. Although the fact that Jane and Lydia were now in the care of a lady who could provide them access to a greater number of eligible men, salved her conscience somewhat.

'But, Mama, you always said I was your very special girl.'

'Of course, you are a special girl, Lyddie. But you are only a girl. Now I have a son who will be the Master of Longbourn.' Mrs Bennet gazed adoringly at the infant sleeping in her arms, while hoping that Lydia would stop pushing. She did not wish to hurt her favourite daughter, but she had to break the connection.

'But...'

'Do not vex me, Lydia. My nerves cannot stand one of your outbursts and Joshua needs me,' Mrs Bennet said dismissively.

Lydia was dumbstruck. Her mother, who had always doted on her every whim, had just callously discarded her. Lydia's world crumbled around her.

She flung herself from the room, tears streaming unheeded down her face, as she stumbled blindly down the stairs.

Strong arms caught her as she tripped on the last step. 'What is wrong, Lydia?' asked Mr Phillips.

'Mama does not want me anymore, now that she has Joshua,' sobbed Lydia.

Mr Phillips briefly closed his eyes in sympathetic pain for his niece. He had known how self-centred his sister-in-law was, but he had not expected her to be so cruel as to reject her favourite daughter.

When he opened his eyes again, he saw Jane coming down the stairs looking concerned. 'Uncle, would you do us the kindness to take us home? Home to Brook Hall.'

Jane, who had not been as surprised as her younger sister about their mother's attitude, held and tried to comfort the weeping girl as they were conveyed to their true home.

Over the next several days a very subdued Lydia tried to come to terms with having been displaced in her mother's affections.

<p style="text-align:center">~~~ooO0oo~~~</p>

In the afternoon of New Year's Eve, a very bedraggled looking young man knocked on the door of Mr Phillips' home. He was gaunt and shivering and seemed to be on his last legs.

Mrs Hill, who had come to look after Mrs Bennet, happened to be in the hall and opened the door.

She was surprised to recognise young William Collins, and shocked at his appearance.

'I am sorry…, I did not… know… where else to go… My father… was killed… in a… drunken brawl… two days ago…' he said with chattering teeth.

'You had better come in then,' offered Mrs Hill. Taking another look at the state he was in, she took his arm and guided him to the kitchen. Settling him in a chair at the table near the fire, she dished up a bowl of the soup, which was keeping hot on the stove.

'Get that into you, boy, while I get Mr Phillips.'

William Collins gratefully started to eat the soup which emitted a wonderful aroma and heat. He had nearly finished when Mr Phillips entered the kitchen and sat down across the table from him.

'When you feel up to it, tell me what happened.'

William finished the last few mouthfuls and replied, 'I can tell you now, Mr Phillips.' He sighed and after briefly closing his eyes, he explained. 'When you threw us out of Longbourn, not that I blame you for that, I know what my father was like. But as I started to say, father recovered consciousness when we arrived at the post station. We were just in time to take the chaise to St Albans. Father said he knew someone there who could help.

When we got there the friend was away. Father sold most of our belongings to get some money and we took a room at an inn.' Collins gave a tired laugh. 'Calling it an in is an overstatement. Be that as it may, we had a room and we waited for father's friend to return. He started drinking and became angrier by the day. Because of what had happened at Longbourn and because his friend did not return. Then, by noon, two days ago, he started arguing with another customer.'

Collins shrugged helplessly, 'to make a long story short, it was a drunken brawl and he was killed when he fell against a table and broke his neck. Unfortunately, he had spent the last of our money on drink. I had but the clothes I stood up in. There was nothing I could do, so I just walked out.'

He sighed, 'to be honest I did not know what to do or where to turn. I have no family anymore other than the Bennet's. I know my father behaved badly but I was hoping you could help me get a job or... something.'

Mr Phillips had listened thoughtfully. 'You know that Mrs Bennet is a guest in my house?' William nodded. 'I am convinced that you understand that my sister-in-law thinks poorly of your father and by extension of you.'

William nodded again, sadly. 'You are saying that you cannot help me.'

'I am saying that you cannot stay in this house.' When Collins started to rise, looking defeated, Mr Phillips held up his hand to stop him. 'But...

I know someone who *might* help you. Stay here and warm up while I have the carriage brought around.'

~~~ooO0Ooo~~~

Mr Kirby opened the door when they arrived at Brook Hall. Knowing that Mr Phillips was always welcome, he escorted the visitors to the parlour where Mrs Mortimer and the sisters were having tea.

The ladies were all startled when they saw William Collins trailing behind Mr Phillips, who after a brief greeting, requested of Mrs Mortimer, 'I have come to you in the hope you can assist Cousin William, who is now an orphan. I would do so myself, but Mrs Bennet would not be happy encountering him in my house.'

'You appear injured. Were you beset by highwaymen?' Elizabeth had noticed that William Collins moved with difficulty.

Collins shook his head, looking embarrassed. 'No, my father took his anger out on me after we left Meryton.'

'By the look of you, more than once, I wager,' surmised Mrs Mortimer.

William nodded while looking at his hands which he had clasped in front of him; refusing to meet anyone's eyes.

Mrs Mortimer rang the bell. When Mr Kirby answered the call, she requested, 'please have a guest room prepared and arrange for a bath for our guest, as well as a tray in his room. Could you also find him some clean clothes? I believe one of my grandsons left some behind, which he grew out of while he was visiting.'

Meanwhile, Lydia, who for the first time since Boxing Day, had joined the family for tea, was horrified at seeing her cousin. Her initial horror was about the fact that he looked unkempt and dirty, until she realised that what she perceived as dirt on his face were bruises. And then she found out that his own father had inflicted them.

Seeing him like this struck a chord with Lydia. While her mother had only rejected her verbally, Mr Collins had done so much worse to his son.
~~~

Without even thinking, she rose from her seat next to Jane and went to William, where she took his hand and reassured him, 'it will get better. You are safe here. Mrs Mortimer is kindness herself.'

Seven pairs of astonished eyes looked at Lydia at this statement.

The one that mattered did not have to raise his eyes very much to look at the young girl. Seeing the concerned and sympathetic look on her face, he was overcome with gratitude.

'Thank you,' he murmured. 'I am sorry we displaced you from your home.'

'La, do not concern yourself. When Papa died, I was destined to leave home and live with Aunt Stephanie. I am better for being here. It just took me a long time to realise it.' She smiled encouragingly at the young man. 'You will be better for it too.'

Mrs Mortimer watched the interaction with a pleased little smile. At last something had touched Lydia's heart, and broken through the shell of learned selfishness.

'Mr Collins,' she said only to be interrupted by him.

'Please call me William. Mr Collins was my father...'

'William, tomorrow we can discuss your future. For now, go to your room, have a bath, dinner and rest. Things will look brighter in the morning.'

Mr Kirby, who had returned, escorted their guest out of the room.

'That was well done, Lydia.' Mrs Mortimer smiled at the girl in gentle approval.

Lydia blushed in pleasure at the compliment but refusing to be daunted, shrugged and declared. 'I know what it feels like to be unwanted. At least Mama only beat me with words.'

Mrs Mortimer went to the girl and enfolded her in an embrace, 'well, you are welcome here.'

Lydia returned the hug and said quietly, 'I know. I am only sorry it took me so long to realise it.'

~~~oo0Ooo~~~
~~~

12 Further Education

The following morning William joined the family for breakfast. Now that he was clean and not blue with cold, the bruises on his face stood out even more.

The footman, who had helped William with his bath, had reported to Mrs Mortimer, that the young man's body was similarly adorned. The lady thought it a miracle, or possibly proof of his desperation, that he had managed to walk all the way from St Albans in the depth of winter.

She smiled pleasantly at the young man. 'You look much improved this morning.'

'Thanks to you, I *feel* much improved today. You are all generosity and charity. I am forever in your debt, since I do not know what I would have done if you had not been so exceedingly kind to me.' William blushed, being the recipient of compassion.

'I would like you to know that you are welcome here,' confirmed Mrs Mortimer, and all the sisters added their welcome.

Mrs Mortimer would have welcomed anyone, even the devil himself, who was able to break through the shell of Lydia. That girl had been resistant to all overtures, to become a member of the family. Her self-absorption had seemed limitless. While her manners had improved, she was still the same selfish, uncaring creature she had always been. Until the previous day. Something about William Collins had touched the girl. For that reason alone, Mrs Mortimer was prepared to take in yet another stray, and support him as long as needed.

William, who had never known kindness from his father, was overcome that a stranger and his cousins would welcome him in this fashion. Lydia, who was sitting next to him, quietly passed him a handkerchief when she noticed the moisture in his eyes.

'It seems you have caught a cold in this miserable weather,' she commented mendaciously.

William was grateful that the ladies all appeared to accept that statement as truth.

After the meal, Mrs Mortimer invited him to her study.

When they were comfortably settled, she informed him, 'William, last night Mr Phillips told me that once Mrs Bennet moved back to Longbourn, you would be welcome in his house, and that he would sponsor you to whatever education you are interested in.'

'After what my father did to his sister...' Suddenly realising what he was saying, he stopped and blushed. 'Ah...'

'Never mind. You are not responsible for your father's actions. On the contrary, you were one of his victims.'

William looked relieved even while still blushing.

'But that is irrelevant to our discussion. I suggested a different solution. Last night was the first time Lydia cared about someone other than herself. I am hoping that if you stay here, she will come out of her shell even more. Therefore, I suggested to Mr Phillips, that I would host you for the foreseeable future, while he can arrange for your education.'

'You wish me to live under the same roof as my cousins? Are you not afraid that I might... ah...'

'Considering your reaction just now, no, I am not concerned. Now about your future... William, if you had the choice to do whatever you wanted, do you have any idea what you would like to do with your life?'

William looked startled at the question. 'I do not know. You see, all my life all I ever wanted was to have a chance to be free of my father. I never truly thought beyond that...'

His composure broke and he wrapped his arms about himself and started to sob. 'I am sorry... men... should not... cry... but... since... my mother died... no one ever... showed me... any kindness...'

Mrs Mortimer moved to sit next to him on the sofa and put a comforting arm about his shoulders. 'Men do cry when they are badly hurt, and you have obviously been badly hurt. And I do not just mean physically.'

She passed him another handkerchief and waited patiently for the emotional storm to subside. When he started to get himself under control, she rang for sweet tea to be brought.

The hot sweet beverage helped soothe his raw emotions. 'Thank you. I have no better words to express what I feel...'

'You are most welcome and you can stop thanking me in every other sentence. While it is good to see that, unlike your father, you can feel gratitude, I truly do not need you to express it with such frequency.'

'I am sorry...'

'You also can stop apologising,' she grinned at him when he opened his mouth to apologise yet again, and then closed it without saying anything.

'Now I would like you to think about the question I asked you. Is there anything you like to do? Take your time.'

William considered the question while sipping more sweet tea. The taste brought back memories.

'I just remembered the last time I had sweet tea. Our vicar, Mr Renshaw, used to teach me to read and write using the bible, and he would discuss scripture with me. I used to envy him his peaceful life. He was a kind gentleman, and very good with his parishioners. I always wanted to be like him.'

'Would you like to be a clergyman?'

'I am not certain I have the faith to enter the church, but I would dearly love to do some good with my life.'

'In my opinion, having concern for your parishioners and wanting to help them to live good and decent lives is more important than blind faith. Although I suspect it would be best not to mention that to a devout clergyman.'

For the first time, William smiled. 'Your secret is safe with me, Mrs Mortimer.'

'Thank you, William, I appreciate that.' Mrs Mortimer smiled mischievously. 'I would like you to consider my question for a few days and then give me a final answer. In the meantime, Mrs Taylor, the girls' governess, can help you brush up on your academic subjects. It will also help you if you learn at least the basics of fighting, so that you do not have to be a victim again. Miss Martin will see to that.'

'I am to learn fighting... from a lady?' William was stunned. Both at the subject and the teacher.

'Indeed. You will find that in this household ladies can and will do more than just embroider and look pretty.'

William tried to get his head around that idea. 'If you say so...'

~~~oo0Ooo~~~

Over the next few days William Collins learned several valuable lessons.

The obvious lesson was how to stay alive in a fight. Miss Martin showed him every dirty trick in the book and drilled him until he was ready to collapse. It was unpleasant, painful even, and certainly humiliating to be thrown around by a woman smaller than himself, but he learnt to defend himself.

The less obvious lesson came from the humiliation he felt, being bested in a physical activity by a woman.

His father had taught him that men were superior to women, particularly when it came to physical ability. William slowly came to realise that his father had been wrong in many ways.

Listening to his cousins' discussions in the evening, where topics were wide-ranging and often esoteric, opened his eyes to their mental capacity. All girls, except ten-year-old Lydia, were better educated than he was. Even eleven-year-old Kitty was more knowledgeable.

Previously he had felt sorry for women, thinking them the weaker sex, both physically and mentally. But now, since he was being bested physically by Miss Martin, and mentally by his young cousins, he developed a new respect for ladies.

As a consequence, he came to a decision. He approached Mrs Mortimer.

'The other day you asked what I wanted to do with my life. I have had time to observe the ladies in this household, and learnt that what my father taught me about women is wrong. But I have also realised that his attitude is quite common. While I cannot change the attitude of
~~~

all men, I believe that as a clergyman I could at least influence a community. I may not succeed in all cases, or possibly even most of them, but I would like to try.'

'That is certainly a worthwhile endeavour, William. Women have very few rights under the law, and anything that improves their situation will be welcomed.' She smiled at the young man, who blushed at the praise.

'My dear boy, even if Mr Phillips had not offered to pay for your education, I would have been delighted to cover your expenses to help you achieve your dreams. If even one woman benefits from your efforts, I would be well rewarded.'

~~~oo0Ooo~~~

Having decided on a course of action, William, with the assistance of Mr Phillips and Mr Stewart, the rector of the church in Meryton, threw himself into his studies. He had much to learn before he could attend university.

Mr Stewart was pleased to encourage such devotion, and sponsored him to a place at Cambridge. By the start of Michaelmas term William was ready to take up his studies in earnest.

'You may not be the most advanced student to enter university, but if you apply yourself with the same enthusiasm you have shown the last six months, you will do well enough,' Mr Stewart told his student, as he made ready to leave.

William was affectionately farewelled by Mrs Mortimer and his cousins, and promised to correspond and to visit at Christmas.

~~~oo0Ooo~~~

During this year new lessons were added to the sister's curriculum.

Mrs Mortimer hired a dancing master to instruct her daughters in all the popular dances. Lydia was ecstatic, at last these were lessons she could excel in.

As it turned out, all the sisters were very light on their feet.

It was a source of amusement to the girls when their teacher exclaimed, 'I have never before been blessed with such coordinated students.'

Nobody pointed out to him that the ladies had learned their coordination in very unfeminine pursuits.

~~~oo0Ooo~~~

After she had recovered from her confinement, Mrs Bennet, with the assistance of her sister and Mr Phillips, busied herself with the refurbishment of Longbourn. She was determined to remove every trace of *that man* from her home. She even used every penny of her pin money to pay for it.

The final step was hiring new staff for every position.

Mrs Hill, although concerned that she had to find a new position, understood Mrs Bennet's desire to remove any reminder of her ordeal. When it became known that Mrs Hill would not return to Longbourn, Mrs Nicholls, the aging housekeeper at Netherfield, encouraged Mrs Hill to take over her position.

Mr Phillips hired a highly recommended steward to manage the estate. He also sat down with Mrs Bennet and educated her about the realities of her finances.

She had thought that with Mr Bennet gone, she would be in charge of all estate matters. Her brother-in-law disabused her of that notion.

'Fanny, according to your husband's will, the estate now belongs to Joshua, and I am the trustee for your son. Currently you do not have any money to spare, there is barely enough to maintain the estate. Between your husband's indolence and Collins' recklessness, it will take years for Longbourn to recover and be profitable.'

He went over the figures in detail, and while Mrs Bennet had been frivolous and reckless in her spending, she could learn when someone took the trouble to explain. Although she did not like the reality of the financial situation, she realised that she had no choice but to abide by the budget Mr Phillips set for her. At least in the near future.
~~~

Finally, after weeks of intense activity, during which the house had been remodelled and redecorated, Mrs Bennet and Joshua moved into the new Master suite of the estate.

Mrs Bennet, who at last knew that she was secure in her home, relaxed and no longer suffered from nerves. Although she hired a nurse to assist with the care of Joshua, Mrs Bennet spent much time with her beloved son.

As the weeks went by, she found that she missed the company of adults, but did not wish to leave her son alone at home with only his nurse to look after him.

Eventually she discussed the situation with her sister and Mr Phillips, and made an offer.

'Brother, since you are Joshua's guardian, do you think it would be beneficent for him if you lived in the same house? Longbourn was designed for a large family and currently there are only two of us. There is more than enough space for all of us, and I would feel better to have a man living in the house.'

Since Longbourn was only a mile from Meryton and his office, Mr Phillips readily agreed. Mrs Phillips, although she liked being in the centre of the village, and the centre of gossip, concurred with his decision. After all, there were benefits to living on an estate. Apart from that, Joshua had stolen her heart.

<p style="text-align:center">~~~ooO0oo~~~</p>

Christmas that year saw the return of William Collins for his promised visit to Brook Hall.

The change which the last year had wrought in him was amazing. Gone was the boy, battered in spirit and body. Instead he was a healthy, cheerful and confident young man who had found himself, and for whom life was good.

'Mrs Mortimer, it is wonderful to see you again.' Collins took her hands and bowed, as he beamed at her and gushed. 'I hope you are as well as you look. You have been in my prayers of thanksgiving to the Lord every day for the opportunity you have given me...'

'Slow down, William. It is good to see you as well and in such high spirits. I gather your studies are going well?'

'They do indeed. I have acquired a mentor, Mr Pickering, who has been most helpful and encouraging. He thinks that I will be able to be ordained within three years.'

'That is excellent news. But will you not greet your cousins? They have been impatiently awaiting your return.'

'Please forgive me, Cousins. I did not mean to slight you in my excitement. I am overjoyed to see you all again.'

'Cousin, you look ready to burst,' laughed Lydia.

'I used to pray for deliverance every night, and dreaded to wake up the next morning. Now I greet every new day with joy. It gives me quite a heady feeling. And I have all of you to thank for my elation.'

William managed to calm down enough to sit down and partake of tea, while regaling the ladies with tales of his life at University.

~~~oo0Ooo~~~

At Longbourn Mrs Bennet, together with Mr and Mrs Phillips quietly, but joyfully celebrated the first birthday of Joshua Bennet, followed by an equally relaxed Christmas.

The most exciting event on Christmas Day was when Joshua took his first unassisted steps, before tumbling at the feet of Mrs Phillips, whereupon he yelled in startlement and frustration.

When Mrs Bennet tried to rush to him and smother him with her concern, she was held back by Mr Phillips. 'Leave him be. He is not hurt.'

Mrs Bennet reluctantly subsided back into her seat, but was rewarded for her restraint, when a few minutes later, her son managed to toddle to her.

As far as she was concerned, Christmas was perfect.

~~~oo0Ooo~~~

13 Coming out

Jane and Elizabeth were nervous. They had come to London for their first season. Mrs Mortimer had offered to launch Jane into society the previous year, but Jane had demurred.

Although Elizabeth had made a few friends over the years, when Mrs Mortimer had brought her into town for lessons, shopping trips and visits to the theatre, Jane had only been with them during the last year. When she had come to London previously, it had been to visit the Gardiners, and while they were an elegant and sophisticated couple, they did not move in the same circles as Mrs Mortimer.

Jane wanted at least one guaranteed friendly face amongst the crowds. Therefore, she had opted to wait another year until Elizabeth, who was about to turn seven and ten, was just old enough to join her.

The previous year had flown past for the sisters in intensive lessons on comportment in society, dancing practice and practice to make their curtsy at their presentation. While the younger girls were not yet ready to be launched into society, they participated in all the lessons, although they remained in Meryton with Mrs Taylor for the time being.

Now Jane and Elizabeth were both in London, where they had been presented at court. Mrs Mortimer sponsored Elizabeth of course, while her sister-in-law, Lady Middlebrook, had offered to do the honours for Jane, who was in equal parts excited and humbled at the privilege.

Having survived the presentation, they were about to attend their first major ball. The invitation had come from Lady Matlock.

They had new ballgowns, which, although fashionable, had been adjusted by the knowledgeable modiste to flatter each girl. While the gowns featured a minimum of lace, they were subtly enhanced by embroidery. The gowns were complemented by jewellery, gifted to them by Mrs Mortimer. The hairpins, earrings, necklaces and bracelets, while obviously of the finest quality to the discerning eye, were elegant rather than ostentatious.

They had spent much of the day being primped and pampered until the experienced maids had declared them perfect. While Jane had endured the preparation without complaint, it had taken a bribe in the form of a long walk in the early morning for Elizabeth to submit to the experience.

'I feel like a chicken, being plucked and garnished, to be displayed in a butchers' window,' she complained.

'The things we suffer in the name of fashion...' sighed Mrs Mortimer sarcastically, although she sympathised with Elizabeth. The preparation had been a reminder why she usually chose to reside in the country, rather than in town.

~~~oo0Ooo~~~

By a stroke of luck, three of Mr Mortimer's grandson were in town for the season. They ranged in age from one and twenty to nine and twenty, and were in the market for brides. They had hoped to attend the Matlock ball, but had been unable to get an invitation.

When Mrs Mortimer offered them the opportunity to attend as escorts to herself and her ward and her adopted daughter, they were happy to oblige. Particularly, when Patrick, the oldest of them, waxed lyrical about the charm of the ladies, whom he had met briefly the previous year.

James and Charles were delighted when they joined Mrs Mortimer and the girls for dinner, a few days before the ball that Patrick had not deceived them. Their memory from several years earlier was of a very gangly and rather hoydenish Elizabeth. Neither of them had met Jane before she came to live with their grandmother.

Before Patrick had a chance, the younger cousins claimed the first set from Jane and Elizabeth.

Patrick not to be outdone addressed his hostess, 'I am obliged to James and Charles for giving me the opportunity to ask the loveliest lady for a dance. Would you do me the honour and reserve the first set for me?'
~~~

Mrs Mortimer laughed. 'I would be delighted to dance the first with you, dear boy. But you should be careful. If you indulge in such outrageous flattery with young ladies, you shall quite turn their heads.'

'Never fear, Grandmama. I am significantly more circumspect with single ladies unrelated to me.'

'I am pleased to hear that.'

~~~oo00oo~~~

When they arrived at Matlock House, Mrs Mortimer introduced Jane and her grandsons to their hosts, finishing with 'you may remember my daughter Miss Elizabeth Mortimer.' Although not technically true, Mrs Mortimer, with the agreement of Jane and Elizabeth, had decided to introduce both of them as her daughters to avoid confusion and explanations.

'You are lucky to have such escorts. My grandson is still in the nursery,' chuckled Lady Matlock. 'I would introduce you to my nephew, Darcy, but I expect he is hiding in the shadows again.'

'I gather he still does not like dancing.'

'He likes dancing well enough, but he hates being prey.' Lady Matlock smiled at her friend, who nodded in understanding. 'I doubt that you will need help introducing your daughters. You will find many familiar faces here tonight. They may be a little greyer than you remember them, but they still speak of you fondly.'

So it turned out. It did not take long for the girls' dance-card to acquire an impressive list of names. Although Elizabeth had the foresight to add the name R.M. Feet to the set after the Cotillion, to have a chance to rest and catch her breath. While she was fit from her constant exercise, she was not used to stuffy and overheated ballrooms.

The girls enjoyed the first set with their cousins. All of them were good looking and superb dancers. Since they were family, both Elizabeth and Jane felt relaxed in their company.

If Charles was paying particular attention to Jane, it went unnoticed by the young lady, who thought he was simply considerate to a young cousin.

~~~oo00oo~~~

The Cotillion finished and Elizabeth slipped into the shadows at the edge of the ballroom with a glass of lemonade, to ease her parched throat.

She found an unobtrusive chair on which to rest in the shadow of a pillar, where she could still observe the dancing.

The music for the next set had just started when Elizabeth noticed a young man on the other side of the pillar, looking pained. He appeared to be very tall and would have been exceedingly handsome if not for his expression. She noticed that his dark hair had a tendency to curl despite his valet's obvious attempts to control it.

In the break between the two dances of the set, he suddenly looked panic-stricken and dodged behind the pillar. He had been so focused on watching the room that he had been oblivious to Elizabeth's presence, and consequently collided with her legs.

He let out a startled oath, but had the decency to blush when he realised that the young lady heard him.

Elizabeth grinned impishly at him. 'I gather you are hiding too?' she suggested.

The young man's blush deepened at being found out, but the mischievous smile and the sparkling eyes of the lady, as well as her words put him at ease.

'Just so,' he admitted with a chagrined smile.

Elizabeth scanned the room and noticed a red-haired woman looking searchingly around. She remembered hearing the young lady's name when she heard her speak with a nearby group earlier in the evening.

Miss Bingley had given the impression of being a mercenary social-climber, therefore, when Lizzy glanced back at the young man and saw the worried look on his countenance, she could not blame him for hiding.

She lifted the glass to her lips and behind its cover murmured, 'if you stay perfectly still, she will not be able to see you.'

The young man looked startled at her perceptiveness and bowed his head in gratitude. 'My thanks for the advice,' he murmured with a relieved smile.

While the dimples which the smile produced were very appealing to Elizabeth, she thought herself much too young to consider any man in a matrimonial light for some time to come.

Instead of paying any more attention to him, she watched the room again. After a while she advised, 'move a little to your right.'

He raised his eyebrows but complied.

A few minutes later she announced, 'the hounds have moved on,' as she rose, and with a final quirk of an eyebrow at the fellow she returned to Mrs Mortimer.

She left behind a very amused, intrigued and grateful Mr Fitzwilliam Darcy.

~~~ooO0Ooo~~~

Lord Neville Banning was dancing the supper set with Jane. He was charming and witty and very attentive to his partner. He was also light on his feet and pleasant to look at.

Jane was thrilled to have such a gentleman paying attention to her. While she had gained in confidence in the three years she had spent with her guardian, she was still basically quite shy and modest.

She did not consider her beauty to be exceptional and none of her accomplishments were outstanding. Yet this son, albeit the third son, of a duke, had singled her out for the supper set.

'Are you enjoying your stay in London?'

'It is very different from the society I am accustomed to in sleepy little Meryton.'

'Where is this lucky Meryton that has you as a resident?'

'In Hertfordshire. Only about fifteen miles past St Albans.'

'It is my misfortune then that I hail from Buckinghamshire. It has robbed me of the opportunity to meet you earlier. Now I have to stand in line with all your other admirers.'

'I did not notice a line.'

'Perhaps, in that respect, my perception is superior to yours.'
~~~

He continued to flirt with Jane throughout supper. While it was flattering that he paid such attention to her, she also felt embarrassed. Jane also thought that the whole conversation was rather superficial.

Before they parted after their meal, Lord Neville asked if he might call on her. Since she had no good reason to refuse and thought that a ballroom was possibly not the best place to get to know someone in more depth, Jane agreed.

~~~ooO0Ooo~~~

That night, while they were getting ready for bed, Jane and Elizabeth compared their experiences.

Lizzy was impressed that a Duke's son was interested in her sister. 'I can only say that he has excellent taste,' she declared. Privately she thought, *it is lucky that Mrs Bennet is not here. She would never rest until Jane had secured him, even if she was unsure if they would suit.*

Since Jane seemed pensive about her potential suitor, Lizzy related the episode about the young man by the pillar. The story cheered up her sister, especially when Elizabeth imitated the *hound*.

'I believe the young man may have been Lady Matlock's nephew, Mr Darcy. I heard someone mention that Miss Bingley has her cap set on him and clings to him like a limpet whenever she gets a chance.'

'In that case, I can understand his reluctance.' Elizabeth found herself oddly disturbed at the thought that Miss Bingley might get her talons into the handsome young man.

~~~ooO0Ooo~~~

Over the next few weeks, Lord Neville became a frequent caller at Mrs Mortimer's home, where he paid a great deal of attention to Miss Jane Mortimer.

His conversation was practiced and gracious but completely meaningless. When she tried to steer it to anything other than inanities, he would claim that the subject was much too serious for such a pleasant occasion and went back to flattering her.

Jane tried to subtly discourage him, but he did not appear to notice her disinterest, and she was too polite and kind-hearted to tell him to go away and not come back.

He did not restrict himself to press his suit only during polite calls. He invited Jane to walks in the park as well as a visit to the museum, the latter which she declined on the grounds that she was not interested.

Every time they met at a function, he made a point of paying obvious attention to Jane, and in the process discouraging gentlemen she might have found more interesting.

She was starting to get desperate to rid herself of this most persistent and boring suitor.

~~~ooO0Ooo~~~

Meanwhile Elizabeth was having a lovely time. Since she was not interested yet in finding a husband, she enjoyed the dancing and the conversation, but whenever a gentleman showed an interest, she politely and kindly informed him that she was too young to consider marriage.

She noticed Lord Neville hovering around Jane. Since she knew about Jane's discomfort in the man's presence, she tried to stay close to her sister whenever she could.

Once or twice Elizabeth noticed the "young man by the pillar" at functions. She was amused that he still appeared to be in hiding.

She thought he was trying to approach her once, but, as she was being claimed by her promised dance-partner, she could not be certain.

Unbeknownst to either of them, they almost met several times in the park when one left just before the other arrived.

It seemed that fate had decided that they should just be ships passing in the night.

~~~ooO0Ooo~~~

14 Going Home

Mr Patrick Mortimer needed advice about a young lady. He rather liked her and thought that she reciprocated his feelings. But there was a slight niggling doubt, and he decided to consult an expert on ladies.

'Grandmama. is she interested in me or my money? I simply cannot tell,' he asked.

Mrs Mortimer looked uncomfortable. 'I hope you do not like her too much, because I am afraid that she is only interested in making a profitable match.'

He looked disappointed. 'Ah well, that is life in the Ton. Marriage is a business. Many people are perfectly happy tying themselves to someone they do not even like, as long as it improves their position or their finances. Or preferably both.'

'You are full young to be so very cynical.'

'What can I say. Some people will go to any length to get what they want. Just today I heard some chaps betting on whether Lord Neville will be successful in compromising a young woman so that he can get his hands on her dowry. It is disgusting, the men of the nobility are supposed to be gentlemen, but many of them are just titled cads.'

Mrs Mortimer had become distracted during Patrick's diatribe, but the name he mentioned caught her attention. 'Did you say Lord Neville Banning?'

'Yes, I did. He is another one of those...'

'Never mind that. Do you know the young lady's name?'

'No, the chap was only saying that Banning was a lucky devil because she is not only rich but also a stunning blond.'

'Damn. He has been calling on Jane. According to my enquiries there is nothing wrong with Banning, although Jane has been rather lukewarm about him. She feels flattered that a Dukes son is calling on her, but I believe she finds him rather boring and irritating. I was letting her deal with it, since she has not asked for help to get rid of him.'

'Cousin Jane finds him boring? Drat. Then chances are that he has his eye on her. She has enough beauty to make most men envy him, and her sweet and innocent nature means he sees her as too pliable to oppose him in any way. If her dowry is as respectable as rumour has it, he would think her perfect. We must warn Jane not to see him again.'

Mrs Mortimer shook her head in frustration. 'I wish I had known that two hours ago. Jane is currently in his company.'

~~~oo0Ooo~~~

'Lord Neville, what is wrong? Are you unwell?' cried Miss Mortimer in alarm, as the gentleman suddenly collapsed against her and gasped, while he held onto her to prevent himself from falling. They had been on their way out of Gunther's after having enjoyed their ices.

She turned to the other patrons, 'could someone please assist Lord Neville? I believe he has taken ill.'

Two gentlemen at a nearby table took one look at the white and suddenly sweating face, and immediately stood to assist Lord Neville to a chair.

'You are quite right, Miss. I think someone had better send for a doctor.'

'You broke my ankle,' grated Lord Neville.

'How dare you suggest such a thing,' retorted Miss Mortimer in a huff. 'If you have hurt your ankle, it must have been when you lost your footing and fell against me. Instead of accusing me of injuring you, you should be grateful that I supported you and did not let you fall.'

She gave him another withering look. 'I believe that under the circumstances I would prefer it if you did not call on me again.'

'Come, Tilly,' she ordered Mrs Mortimer's maid who had acted as her chaperone, 'we are leaving.'

She stalked towards the door with her head held high, while she was wondering how best to get home since they had come in his carriage.
~~~

Jane was almost at the door, when it opened and a very familiar and welcome gentleman entered.

'Cousin,' she smiled at Patrick Mortimer. 'What a delight to run into you.'

'I am equally delighted to see you, and looking so well, Cousin. I hope that I am not come at an inconvenient time, but your mother has asked me to come and fetch you. She has received some interesting news which she wished to share with you.'

'Your timing is exquisite. I was just leaving.'

'In that case, your carriage awaits you.' Patrick bowed with a flourish, indicating the carriage in front of the door.

When he straightened up, Patrick offered Jane his arm, which she gratefully took. Moments later, he handed her into the carriage and assisted Tilly as well, before settling himself on the opposite seat.

As soon as the carriage started to move, he asked, 'what happened? Your mother said you were going to Gunther's with Lord Neville.

'I did go with him to Gunther's, but just as we were leaving, he tried to compromise me. He grabbed hold of me right in the middle of the room.' Now that the excitement was wearing off, Jane started to shake.

'If he grabbed hold of you, why was no one even looking as if anything untoward had happened to you?'

Jane took a deep breath to steady herself. 'I made people think that he had taken ill and I was preventing him from collapsing.'

'If he was determined to compromise you, he would not have played along with such a ruse. I would rather have expected him to declare that you are his fiancée.'

'I did not give him a choice. He truly became ill.'

'How does a healthy man suddenly become ill?'

Jane looked rather shamefaced as she answered, 'I broke his ankle.' She demonstrated a very small but very sharp kick, which had gone unnoticed by everyone at Gunther's.

Patrick stared at her in disbelief for a minute. 'That will do it every time, I suppose,' he said before he started to chuckle.

He had rushed to Gunther's to save his cousin from being compromised, but apparently, she did not need rescuing after all. She had handled the situation with aplomb and in such a manner that Banning was not likely to try such a compromise again in a hurry. At least not with any lady named Mortimer.

~~~oo00oo~~~

Thankfully, the ride back to Mrs Mortimer's house was a short one. The Lady was anxiously waiting, hoping for the best, but fearing for the worst.

What if Banning succeeded. She would hate to see Jane forced into a loveless marriage by a fortune-hunter. But maybe he was not yet ready to act. He might be hoping that his position and charm would win her hand. Unless he had debts, which needed attention immediately.

She was pacing in the drawing room, the tea which had just been served, sitting forgotten on the table, and every time she approached the window, she checked to see if her carriage had arrived. She was approaching the window yet again for another look, when she heard the front door opening. A moment later, Elizabeth walked in, having returned from a visit to the Gardiners.

Before Mrs Mortimer could show her disappointment at seeing the wrong daughter enter, a chuckling Patrick, with the blushing Jane on his arm, entered the drawing room.

Their relaxed attitude made Mrs Mortimer heave a sigh of relief.

'Jane, are you well? Is everything all right? Did Patrick tell you why I sent him for you?'

'Yes, yes and yes, Mother.' Jane went to Mrs Mortimer and gave her a hug. 'I am perfectly fine.'

'So Patrick reached you before Lord Neville could try anything. I am exceedingly relieved.'

Jane looked partly embarrassed and partly relieved, when Patrick answered in her stead. 'As a matter of fact, I arrived just in time to provide transport to our conquering heroine.'

'Do you mean to tell me that Banning tried to compromise you and failed?'
~~~

'Compromise?' squeaked Elizabeth, completely unaware of the potential drama that had threatened Jane.

'Please remind me to thank Miss Martin for her excellent instruction.' Jane hugged Mrs Mortimer again. 'And I want to thank you for bringing Miss Martin to us. She saved my life. Or at least she saved me from a life where I would have been miserable.'

The shock of the situation was wearing off. Jane knew intellectually that she had hurt that man, and it was not in her nature to hurt anyone. But Patrick's information had confirmed that Lord Neville had meant to harm her, by forcing her into lifelong servitude as his wife. That knowledge somewhat mitigated the guilt she felt.

Elizabeth was asking, 'what happened?', while Mrs Mortimer was getting irritated by the snippets with which the pair was teasing her. 'Enough of this prevarication. I need you to sit down and tell me exactly what happened.'

She noticed the tea service again, and finding that the tea was still hot, she poured a cup for everyone, while Jane told the story of her narrow escape.

By the time she finished telling her tale, reaction to the events of the afternoon truly set in for Jane.

She became despondent. 'I always wanted to believe in the goodness of people, but Lord Neville's action makes me think that Lizzy has the right of it after all. I was so naïve to think that Lord Neville's motive were driven by affection. Instead he was driven by greed.'

She huffed mournfully. 'I must have appeared to be the perfect victim. A naïve country girl who could be manipulated.'

'But he miscalculated.' Mrs Mortimer pulled Jane into an embrace. 'You may have been too trusting, but when it counted, you were quick thinking and decisive. You did not become a victim to his schemes. I am so very proud of you, Jane.'

Elizabeth concurred. 'I wish you had no need to change your opinion of people. But you did the only thing you could. It is better for this despicable rake to hurt for a few days, than you hurting for a lifetime. And he only brought it on himself. Had he behaved like a gentleman you would have treated him as such.'

While Jane was comforted by the support of her family, her time in London had lost its spark. 'I would like to go home,' she pleaded, looking apologetically at her sister. 'I am sorry, Lizzy. I know you have been enjoying yourself…'

'Think nothing of it, Jane. You know full well that I only came to support you. I am perfectly content to return to the country,' Elizabeth reassured her sister.

Mrs Mortimer cautioned them. 'We must stay at least a few more days and be seen in company to ensure nobody connects our departure with the events of this afternoon. Otherwise there will be gossip.'

Jane reluctantly agreed, but was cheered by the prospect of escaping the now unpleasant company in London.

The following afternoon, Patrick reported that Lord Neville did indeed have a broken ankle, but he had not tried to blame Jane for the injury after that first thoughtless comment.

Patrick surmised that Banning had realised that it would make him a laughing stock if he persisted in his claims.

People would either not believe that sweet and gentle Miss Mortimer would do such a thing, and Banning would be seen as a sore loser who spread malicious lies because he had been rejected. On the other hand, if someone did believe him, his fellows would laugh at him for being so soundly defeated. In either case, he would lose.

Although, Patrick did not mention that one or two of the honourable gentlemen seemed to be carefully schooling their expressions to repress a smirk at Banning's misfortune.

<div align="center">~~~oo0Ooo~~~</div>

They remained in town for another fortnight during which they attended teas, dinners and balls as well as the theatre.

A few people commented on the absence of Lord Neville from the Mortimer drawing room, to which Jane blandly replied, 'I understand he has been taken ill, which is just as well since I am come to the conclusion that we would not suit. Lord Neville is inordinately enamoured of the weather, while I prefer a less airy conversation.'

An Unconventional Education

As soon as speculation regarding Lord Neville died down, Mrs Mortimer and her daughters returned to Brook Hall.

~~~oo0Ooo~~~
~~~

Part 2

15 Interlude

The last three years had brought about a number of changes in sleepy Meryton.

~~~oo0Ooo~~~

Longbourn had recovered, thanks to Mr Phillips' oversight and the hard work of the steward.

It had taken two years of careful management, but by then all repairs were completed, fields were drained, crop rotation was implemented, and Longbourn was solvent.

The income of the estate gradually increased from the previous two thousand pounds per annum to three thousand. But when Mrs Bennet argued that the additional one thousand pounds should be made available to her, Mr Phillips refused.

He increased the lady's pin money to the level it had been before her husband's death, and he ensured that Joshua and Longbourn was well provided in every respect. But he insisted that some of the excess funds should be used to create a buffer in case of bad years, while the rest should be invested with Mr Gardiner to improve the dowries of Jane and Lydia.

Mrs Bennet objected. 'Why should Joshua and I be made to suffer only to provide for those ungrateful girls who deserted me.'

'Fanny, have you forgotten that it was you who rejected them? They wanted to return to Longbourn with you after Joshua was born, but you treated them most cruelly and sent them away.'

'I remember no such thing. But I do remember that they have not once visited.'

'Sister, I was there on Boxing Day when the girls came to see you and Joshua. Lydia asked when she could come home to Longbourn with you
~~~

and you told her that you had no time to spare for her and did not want her.'

'This cannot be true. I would not do such a thing…'

'I also was there when Lydia burst crying out of your chambers, because you had sent her away,' Mr Phillips confirmed his wife's words.

'I do not remember…' cried Mrs Bennet, tears now streaming down her face.

Mrs Phillips took pity on her sister. 'You were under a great deal of strain at the time. Having to flee Longbourn so that you and your babe should be safe, and you had given birth to Joshua but two days prior.'

'Am I a bad mother?' whispered Mrs Bennet.

'You are a wonderful mother to Joshua.'

'But not to my girls. Is that not what you are saying?'

'You lived with the fear of eviction from your home for many years. It made you anxious…'

'I suppose it must be true. Jane and Lydia are better off with Mrs Mortimer. You say she cares for them well?'

'Very well indeed. But she should not have to shoulder the burden of a dowry for the girls. That is not fair on the other girls.'

Mrs Bennet looked sadly at Mr Phillips. 'I suppose you are correct. Make any arrangements that you believe are right. But I think I need to rest a little for the moment.'

Mrs Bennet went to her room in a very thoughtful state. After much deliberation she gradually accepted her part in the estrangement, and at last managed to let go of the anger she felt against her daughters and against Mrs Mortimer. She felt unequal to the task of rebuilding the bridges she had burned, but was pleased that the girls were happy.

<div align="center">~~~oo0Ooo~~~</div>

When Mr Phillips had approached Mrs Mortimer to inform the lady of the arrangement, she suggested a slight change.

Since Mrs Mortimer had adopted Elizabeth, Mary and Kitty, she would provide the dowry for her own daughters, while the Longbourn funds should be allocated to her wards.

The money which Mr Bennet had invested for the middle girls, should be split between Jane and Lydia and added to the funds already set aside for them, which gave each girl an amount of about five thousand pounds. That amount would keep growing due to Mr Gardiner's excellent business acumen, and increased by Mr Phillips' contribution.

~~~oo0Ooo~~~

When it was Mary's turn to come out into society at the age of seven and ten, she opted for the more relaxed atmosphere of Meryton, since the story of Lord Neville had made the sensitive girl uncomfortable with London society. Although she did visit London briefly with Mrs Mortimer to make her curtsy to the Queen.

Instead of a London season, Mrs Mortimer arranged a ball at Brook Hall and invited all the leading families in the area to attend.

The timing was perfect, since it was the beginning of summer and her grandsons were able to visit, as well as William Collins, who was a newly ordained member of the clergy.

There were heated arguments between the various cousins, Mortimer and Collins, about who would have the honour of opening the ball with Mary.

In the end, Mary asked Mr Phillips to stand up with her as her nearest male relative. The gentleman was touched by the request and did his best to be a credit to his niece.

Neither Mary nor her sisters lacked for dance partners that evening.

~~~oo0Ooo~~~

The years at university had been good for William Collins. By the time he returned after his ordination, he had grown tall and had filled out, and was a well-built young man of three and twenty.

Although he was not noticeably handsome, he was pleasant to look at, particularly when he displayed, what Lydia, to his embarrassment called, a sweet smile.

He remained in Meryton for several months, serving as a deacon to Mr Stewart, until he turned four and twenty years of age and could be fully ordained. An occasion that happened shortly before Easter the next year.

During that time, he enquired to see if a permanent position would open to him.

Due to a friend's intervention and advice, he was offered the living at Hunsford in Kent, the advowson of Lady Catherine de Bourgh.

~~~oo0Ooo~~~

During the summer, Mrs Mortimer encouraged Kitty to join in family gatherings with their neighbours.

While Kitty was a competent and confident young woman amongst her family, strangers made her exceedingly nervous.

Since Kitty's seventeenth birthday was approaching, Mrs Mortimer thought it wise to accustom her youngest daughter to company.

~~~oo0Ooo~~~

At the end of the summer of 1811 the news spread throughout Meryton that Netherfield Park had been let.

The new lessee was a Mr Charles Bingley, the son of a successful business man, who had bequeathed his money to his only son, with the hope he would purchase an estate and raise the family's standing to landed gentry.

Mr Bingley was to take possession of the estate at Michaelmas.

He visited briefly to sign the lease and arrange for staff, to ensure the house would be ready to occupy in a week's time when he planned to return.

His single, younger sister would act as his hostess, and he would be accompanied by a friend to help him learn about estate management.

~~~oo0Ooo~~~
~~~

16 Tempted

The assembly was in full swing when the party from Netherfield made their entrance. Sir William Lucas immediately rushed over and welcomed them, offering to make introductions. Mr Bingley declared he was delighted to meet the leading families of the area.

After introducing them to his own family, Sir William Lucas performed the introduction of the Netherfield party to Mrs Mortimer.

'A lady estate owner, how quaint,' murmured Miss Bingley in her most supercilious manner.

'Indeed, Miss Bingley? It is really much more common than you might think,' replied Mrs Mortimer with a pleasant smile. 'Even in our small community there are two others. I would be most pleased to introduce you.'

Miss Bingley looked as if she had just smelled something bad, but she recovered her composure enough to reply in her haughtiest demeanour, 'you are all graciousness. In the first circles one usually does not associate with members of the minor gentry.'

'Of course, Miss Bingley, I quite understand. I suppose with your background you are not overly familiar with country gentry, but in a small community such as this, we are always happy to assist new neighbours in the furtherance of their education.'

Mr Darcy who had observed this encounter, was hard pressed to maintain his stoic demeanour. He had expected to be displeased with the society in this small backwater. Instead, one of the first ladies he encountered had taken the measure of Miss Bingley, and politely and cleverly scored a hit. It was even funnier because Miss Bingley had missed the point.

He was so absorbed in his musings, he almost missed Sir William introducing him. 'It is indeed a great pleasure to make your acquaintance, Mrs Mortimer.'

'The pleasure is all mine, Mr Darcy,' replied Mrs Mortimer and added, 'I hope you will not mind my saying that I was sorry to hear about your father's passing, five years ago. He was a good man.'

'You knew my father?' Darcy was surprised to encounter someone who had known his family in this community.

'We were acquainted. My late husband's estate is near Tamworth in Warwickshire. It is not so far from Pemberley.'

'I went to Cambridge with a Gerald Mortimer who was from that area...' Darcy left the question hanging.

'Gerald is the grandson of my husband from his first marriage,' the lady explained before addressing the group. 'But let me introduce you to my daughters. Miss Jane Mortimer and Miss Mary.'

Bingley immediately asked Jane to dance, and she accepted with pleasure.

'I would introduce you to my daughter Elizabeth as well, but she is currently chatting with friends.'

The music was starting for the second set, and Bingley led Jane to the dancefloor. Miss Bingley clutched Darcy's arm and coquettishly demanded, 'this is our dance I believe, Mr Darcy.'

He grudgingly agreed and followed her brother.

~~~ooO0Ooo~~~

Once he had done his duty by Bingley's sisters, Darcy went back to his old familiar ways. He stalked the edges of the room, avoiding contact with everyone.

In the process he overheard several snippets of conversation.

When he heard a particularly shrill voice exclaim, 'I do not understand why that woman is making the girls wear such plain dresses. Hardly any lace at all,' he wondered if the woman had any daughters herself. He shuddered to think what they would be like with such a loud and crass woman as their mother. He had a glimpse of her and was not surprised to see the overdone lace ruffles all over her dress.

Another woman commented, 'Jane seems very pleased with Mr Bingley. I do not remember her ever being this animated.'
~~~

'The girls are lucky that Mrs Mortimer adopted them. There is no finer lady in all of Hertfordshire,' another voice chimed in.

Darcy thought about that comment. He had not noticed any familial similarity between the lady and Miss Mortimer or Miss Mary.

She must be an exceedingly generous woman to have taken in three girls. Based on his brief meeting with the lady, he agreed with the nameless voice. The girls were very lucky indeed.

~~~ooO0oo~~~

Another one of those lucky girls was having a wonderful time. She had danced four sets already with her friends.

When John Lucas asked for the fifth set, she suggested he should give another lady a chance to dance, while she rested her feet.

Since Jane, Mary and Charlotte Lucas were currently dancing, she collected a glass of lemonade from the refreshment table and found herself a chair where she could sit and discretely rub each foot against the other to relieve the strain.

As it happened, Mr Darcy had drawn near to Elizabeth on his perambulation around the ballroom.

She had noticed the entrance of the Netherfield party, particularly the tall, handsome gentleman. There was something familiar about him but she could not place the occasion when she might have seen him. She was simply amused to note Miss Bingley clinging to his arm.

As he drew nearer and then stopped, she took the opportunity to observe him discretely.

At the end of the first dance of the set, she saw Mr Bingley approach his friend and urge him to dance.

'You know how I hate the activity unless I am particularly well acquainted with my partner,' protested Darcy.

'I would not be as fastidious as you for all the world. There are many uncommonly pretty and amiable young ladies at this assembly.'

'You are already dancing with the prettiest one of the lot.'
~~~

'Yes, I know, she is an angel. But her sister is sitting just behind you. She too is exceedingly pretty and very amiable. Come, let me introduce you,' Bingley encouraged while gesturing towards Elizabeth.

Darcy sighed in exasperation. 'Bingley, please, just go back to your partner...' He did not get further. When his friend had gestured, he had automatically started to turn to look at the young lady, whom he had no wish to meet.

The cutting remark he was about to utter died on his lips, when he saw Elizabeth, as she was again rubbing one foot against the other, while raising her glass to her lips with an impish smirk.

The sight reminded him of that Matlock Ball three years earlier, where a young lady had guarded him from Caroline Bingley.

Despite his low spirits at the time, her attitude had cheered him up, and he had wondered who she might be. But he had never encountered her again. Until tonight.

There she was, watching him with amused eyes. He had the impression that she stopped herself from winking at him only by a major force of will.

'You,' he exclaimed.

He turned back to Bingley, who had taken him at his word and was heading back to Jane Mortimer.

'Bingley, wait,' called Darcy. When Bingley turned back, Darcy requested, 'would you be so kind as to introduce me to the lady.'

Bingley was startled, but eagerly complied with the request. 'Miss Elizabeth, please allow me to introduce my good friend Mr Darcy, of Derbyshire. Darcy, I have the honour of introducing Miss Elizabeth Mortimer, of Brook Hall.'

Elizabeth, who had risen to her feet at the start of the introduction, curtsied politely. 'A pleasure to meet you, Mr Darcy,' she acknowledged with twinkling eyes.

'It is indeed a great pleasure to see you again and at last make your acquaintance. I had despaired of ever finding you,' Darcy said while bowing extravagantly. When Elizabeth looked puzzled, he added, 'the Matlock Ball. Three years ago...'

Recognition at last set in for Elizabeth. 'The gentleman by the pillar...' she exclaimed in delight. 'I am sorry I did not recognise you immediately; but at that time, I was busy scanning the room for hounds...'

'I was most grateful for your assistance. Now I would be equally as grateful if you would honour me with a dance, if you have any available,' Darcy asked with a smile.

Bingley, realising he was now superfluous, returned to the dancefloor, pleased that his friend had decided to be sociable.

'I would be delighted to dance the next set with you, Mr Darcy. But for the moment I would like an opportunity to rest my feet a little longer. I am afraid my last dance-partner was not as light on his feet as I would have hoped,' she added in explanation.

'In that case, would you allow me to sit with you?' Noticing that she had finished her drink, he offered, 'after fetching some more refreshments for you perhaps?'

Elizabeth handed him her glass. 'I would enjoy the company and I most gratefully accept your kind offer. The lemonade is very refreshing.'

She watched his retreating back and admired the strong, muscular form. Now that he had reminded her of their previous encounter, she remembered that at the time he had been hiding from Miss Bingley. Considering how proprietarily the lady had clutched Mr Darcy's arm, did that mean that the hound had caught its prey? Elizabeth felt a pang of something she could not define.

In short order Darcy returned with two glasses of lemonade. He handed her one as he sat down. 'I am grateful for your recommendation. The lemonade is indeed refreshing and delicious.'

Elizabeth thanked him and then asked, 'What brings you to Hertfordshire, Mr Darcy. It is quite a long way from Derbyshire.'

'As I presume you know, my friend Bingley has just taken the lease of Netherfield to see if being a landed gentleman suits him. Since he is new to it, he asked me to help him learn to manage an estate.'

'Pardon me for saying so, but I would have thought you rather young to have such expertise to impart.'

'I wish I was not in a position to be an expert, but my father died about five years ago, and I have run Pemberley ever since.'

'That must be a daunting responsibility, Mr Darcy. I have heard of your estate and am aware that it is rather large. You must have many tenants and staff relying on you.'

Darcy was surprised. This young lady mentioned responsibility and tenants when referring to Pemberley, rather than wealth and status.

His impression at the Matlock Ball had been correct. This was a young lady he wanted to get to know better. For once a lady was treating him as a person rather than prey.

It was ironic. He had come to Meryton only to help his friend, but expected to dislike the company. Instead he had met the lady whom he had been searching for in London.

He determined this was going to be an enjoyable visit, Miss Bingley notwithstanding.

~~~ooO0oo~~~

The next set started and Darcy rose and offered his hand to Elizabeth which she accepted with pleasure.

She found that she was enjoying his company and conversation. The mention of Pemberley had led them to discuss estate management of all things. It was a subject dear to his heart and he was delighted to find a young lady knowledgeable on the subject. Elizabeth was gratified that the gentleman was not only willing to discuss something weightier than the weather, but took her opinions seriously.

Her lessons with Mrs Mortimer on the subject appeared to be even more useful than that lady had intended.

The dancing started and Darcy was entranced by the ease and grace of her movements. He became so lost in his admiration of his dance partner, that after several minutes he was startled out of his reverie when Elizabeth commented with a mischievous smile, 'come, Mr Darcy. We must have some conversation. It would appear quite strange if we stood up together for half an hour without speaking.'

'My apologies, Miss Elizabeth. I was lost in admiration and forgot my manners,' he replied without thinking.
~~~

Elizabeth blushed at the honest compliment, but managed to answer with a smile. 'Very well said, Sir. Since you managed to flatter my vanity, I will accept your apology.'

'I am grateful to have your forgiveness, but I must correct you. I did not flatter you. I simply spoke the truth.' He grinned when he saw her blush even more.

'Enough, Mr Darcy. You will quite turn my head.' Elizabeth managed to find her equilibrium again and teased, 'and if my head is turned, I will not be able to see where I am going and might step on your feet.'

'My feet are at your disposal, Miss Elizabeth.'

Elizabeth was astonished. No man in her, albeit limited, experience had ever been able to match her in a verbal sparring match. Yet Mr Darcy seemed to do so with ease.

Darcy meanwhile was astounded at himself. Normally he was tongue-tied in the company of women unless they were family. Yet here he was flirting with Miss Elizabeth and seemed to find the right words without difficulty.

Unbeknownst to each other, they each determined they would like to get to know the other better, if given even half a chance.

They thoroughly enjoyed their dance, even more so when they discovered a shared love of books.

When the set finished, Darcy escorted Elizabeth to Mrs Mortimer and requested her permission to call on them the following day.

Mrs Mortimer, after noticing the pleading look in Elizabeth's eyes, happily granted permission to Mr Darcy, and any friends he cared to bring. She was rewarded by beaming smiles from two people.

~~~oo0Ooo~~~
~~~

17 Getting Acquainted

The following day, Darcy and Bingley called at Brook Hall on their own. Miss Bingley was unfortunately indisposed, possibly due to too much punch at the assembly, and her sister stayed with her to offer comfort.

Miss Bingley might have made a quick recovery had she known that her brother and Mr Darcy planned to call on their neighbours, but Bingley had prevaricated and said they were going for a ride.

Darcy was pleasantly surprised when they arrived at Brook Hall. Although the house was smaller, the understated elegance of the décor was very similar to Pemberley. A circumstance which made him relax.

Darcy and Bingley were shown into the small parlour, where Mrs Mortimer and her three oldest daughters greeted them graciously. The staff was obviously efficient as tea was served immediately upon their arrival.

Since Bingley immediately monopolised Miss Mortimer's attention, it fell to Darcy to engage the other ladies in conversation.

'Mrs Mortimer, you mentioned that you knew my father…'

'Yes, I briefly made your parents' acquaintance. It must be about twenty years ago, when my husband and I visited at Matlock at the end of summer.' Mrs Mortimer smiled mischievously. 'As a matter of fact, I also met Master Richard Fitzwilliam and yourself, but I thought it best not to mention that fact last night.'

Darcy was puzzled. 'I do not see why you would not wish to acknowledge an acquaintance of such long standing. Although I must admit that I have no recollection of the meeting. Twenty years ago, I was but eight years of age and usually not allowed to mingle with the adults when the family had guests…'

'I thought you would not wish the circumstances of our meeting to be bruited about. I was afraid you might find it embarrassing.'

When Darcy still looked puzzled, she added, 'you were stuck in a tree at the time... and you promised not to tell anyone of our meeting.'

Comprehension struck Darcy. 'Oh Lord. The lady in the tree. You climbed up to release me because the back of my jacket had gotten caught and I could not get loose, and Richard was not strong enough to lift me.'

He favoured his hostess and her daughters with a bright smile. 'I was wearing a new coat and was terrified to rip it. Since I was not even supposed to be climbing trees in the first place, I could not send Richard for help. Then suddenly you were there and lifted me off that branch. At the time I wondered who you were, but I could not ask without giving away our secret.'

Mrs Mortimer laughed. 'I was trying to portray the perfect lady. It simply would not do if the story was spread about that I was climbing trees...'

Despite being seated, Darcy managed a polite bow. 'I am very pleased to renew our acquaintance.'

Reverting back to polite conversation, Darcy commented, 'you have a beautiful home, Mrs Mortimer.'

'Thank you, Mr Darcy. I know it is not a grand estate like Pemberley, but we find it quite comfortable. Would you care to see it?'

Darcy agreed with alacrity. While he found his hostess delightful, and her second daughter even more so, he struggled to find topics of conversation. Mrs Mortimer deputised Elizabeth and Mary to show the gentleman the house, while she remained behind to chaperone the oblivious Bingley and Jane.

Darcy offered his arms to Elizabeth and Mary, and Elizabeth guided them to the next room adjoining the parlour.

'On this floor, virtually all the rooms are interconnected,' she explained, as she led them through the various rooms. At the back of the house they crossed a hallway and entered the ballroom.

As always, when visitors were expected, the weapons and other equipment had been tidied away into cupboards lining the wall opposite the windows, leaving the floor completely clear and giving an even greater feeling of space.

Darcy was amazed at how light the room was, until he looked up... and up, to the skylights two stories above the floor.

'Yes, we are very proud of our ballroom. Due to the height of the ceiling, we can have fifty couples dancing in here without the atmosphere becoming too stifling,' Mary informed Darcy.

'It is also a useful space for exercise when the weather is inclement,' Elizabeth supplied with a pleasant smile, which hid the amusement she felt. Very few people were privy to the fact that the ballroom did double duty as a salle. The dichotomy of its function appealed to Lizzy's sense of humour.

'Indeed, it seems large enough to practice almost any sport in here. I admit, I did not expect such a grand room in any of the houses hereabouts. I am informed that Netherfield is the largest house in the area, but even its ballroom is smaller than this.'

They continued through the other rooms and finished the circuit in the large drawing room.

Darcy commented. 'This house is indeed exceedingly elegant and yet comfortable. Although I am surprised that there is no library. Considering your love of reading, I felt convinced you would have a room devoted to books.'

Elizabeth gave him a mischievous smile. 'You have judged correctly, Mr Darcy. But I have kept the best for last...'

She led them into the foyer, past the stairs to glass double doors.

Mary and Elizabeth each pushed open one side of the door and Elizabeth exclaimed theatrically, 'ta da...' as she gestured around the room.

The sisters released Darcy's arms to allow him to wander around the room and explore the various book cases.

Elizabeth and Mary smirked at each other. Darcy's reaction was typical of any bibliophile. The room was massive and two stories in height and had the same sky lights as the ballroom. There were doors on three sides, but all the other wall-space was hidden behind bookcases.

Mary quietly suggested, 'this could take a while,' before stepping outside the door and requesting that tea should be brought to the library.

Darcy was stunned at the sheer number of books in the room. When he had a closer look, he saw that the books were organised by topic, language and author. He became engrossed in examining the titles of the volumes on the ground level. He was about to climb to the mezzanine when he realised that he was a guest in Mrs Mortimer's home and had shamefully neglected his escorts.

He turned around and saw Miss Elizabeth and Miss Mary comfortably ensconced in a group of chairs, each with a book and a cup of tea.

Elizabeth looked up and said with a smile, 'welcome back, Mr Darcy. Would you like another cup of tea? It is still hot.'

'My most profound apologies, Miss Elizabeth. I am a most negligent guest...'

'There is no need to apologise, Mr Darcy. After our conversation yesterday, when you mentioned your love of books, I expected you to become distracted in this room. It has that effect on every bibliophile.'

'That is no excuse for my behaviour.'

'On the contrary, Mr Darcy. That is a perfect excuse. At least in this household. Here you are in likeminded company. But you did not answer my question. Tea?' She lifted the pot in invitation, and gestured towards the other chairs.

'Yes, thank you,' replied Darcy and took one of the indicated seats closest to Miss Elizabeth.

Before he had a chance to ask for sugar and lemon, Elizabeth fixed his cup to his liking.

'You are very observant, Miss Elizabeth. Thank you.'

'It is a lady's duty and pleasure to look after the comfort of her guests,' she replied primly, but the twinkling eyes belied her serious demeanour.

'Even guests who get lost in contemplation...'

'Especially those,' teased Elizabeth.

'Do you have particular favourites?' he asked both sisters, indicating the shelves in the room, which started a lively discussion of favoured books, authors and topics between the three of them. Mary, after a few remarks about the books which she loved the most, was content to sit back and enjoy watching the animated discussion between Darcy and her favourite sister.

Mary was pleased to note that for once Elizabeth was opening up to a gentleman. While Lizzy was teasing and pleasant with all the men whom they knew, she had always retained a certain reserve. That reserve was now in abeyance and judging by his response, Mr Darcy seemed to be equally relaxed.

While Mary thought he was intelligent and she appreciated his sly sense of humour, she found him just a little intimidating. But the more she listened the more convinced she became that Lizzy and Mr Darcy were well matched.

Meanwhile Elizabeth forgot the presence of her sister. She was engrossed in the discussion with Mr Darcy and revelled in the intellectual challenge. He had decided opinions, but was prepared to discuss and defend them, in the process he treated her as an intellectual equal, like no other man before.

Darcy was equally enchanted. Miss Elizabeth did not simper and fawningly agree with every statement he made. While they had similar taste in books, at times their interpretation differed. When she disagreed with him, she was prepared to stand up to him and defend her point of view.

They had just agreed to disagree on their latest argument, when he remembered something that he had been curious about.

Darcy took a sip of his tea. 'Pardon me if I digress, but I would like to ask a question if I may. It may be presumptuous, and I have no wish to pry, but last night, I heard someone mention that Mrs Mortimer adopted you and your sisters...'

'Indeed, she did. I was most grateful to my father to allow her to do so.'

'Your father is still alive?'

'No, unfortunately he passed away about six years ago. At which point Jane and Lydia came to live with us also.'

Darcy was confused. 'Pardon me if I misremember, but I thought your sister's name was Miss Mary?' he indicated the young lady who had listened with amusement.

Elizabeth looked a little uncomfortable, but she answered nonetheless. 'I think I need to explain. I am the second of five sisters. Mrs Bennet had difficulty dealing with so many daughters. Which was why, eleven years ago, my father allowed Mrs Mortimer to adopt three of us. Myself, Mary and Kitty, whom you have not met since she is still too shy to be comfortable in society.'

'I presume Miss Kitty is the youngest of you?'

'She is the youngest of us whom Mrs Mortimer adopted eleven years ago. Mrs Bennet was happy to keep Jane, our oldest sister, and Lydia, the youngest of us, at home.'

'It seems to be an unusual division of sisters.'

'Jane and Lydia are both blond and blue eyed.' Elizabeth shrugged. 'I should not speak ill of her, but I am afraid that Mrs Bennet is a rather shallow woman. She liked the looks of Jane and Lydia, who are most like her in appearance. The rest of us did not meet her standards.'

Darcy was shocked at the callousness of Mrs Bennet. 'That seems... cruel.'

'Although I believe that Mrs Bennet was not deliberately so, Mrs Mortimer agreed with you. She approached our father and offered to adopt us. He agreed because he was in poor health and could not contain his wife. Then, six years later, our father died. In his will he named Mrs Mortimer as the guardian for Jane and Lydia, and they came to live with us.'

'But if she is not adopted, how is it that Miss Jane is now known as Miss Mortimer?'

'Because Jane did not approve of Mrs Bennet's attitude and actions after our father's death, she prefers to be called Miss Mortimer. We all have great respect for our adopted mother. She is the dearest and most generous lady imaginable. Even Lydia has come to view her as such, and she was Mrs Bennet's favourite.'

Darcy shook his head in disbelief and wonder. 'You have been most fortunate. I am aware that in the first circles many parents treat their children with indifference, but in my opinion, it perpetuates the problem. People who were not loved as children, will not know how to love their own children. Emotions are stifled...'

'They do not know how to love, which is why they are perfectly content to marry for wealth and position rather than affection,' Elizabeth agreed.

'You sound as if that thought does not appeal to you.'

'My sisters and I have decided to only marry for love and respect. Living with Mrs Mortimer has taught us how important love is.'

'Indeed, it is,' said Mrs Mortimer from the doorway. 'Being loved as a child, generally makes for more pleasant adults.'

Darcy rose politely to his feet. He suddenly felt embarrassed to have spent most of his visit in the library, rather than in the parlour with his hostess. 'I beg your pardon, Mrs Mortimer. We should have returned...'

'Nonsense. Since Lizzy mentioned you liked books, I expected you would end up in the library.'

'You have an enviable collection. Although I hope you will not take it amiss when I admit that the library at Pemberley exceeds even your collection.' Darcy looked longingly at the books.

'Of course, I will not take it amiss. I have heard that the library at Pemberley is the work of generations.'

Darcy smiled in relief. 'Indeed it is, and I admit that I am proud to be the custodian of such a collection. I only wish that my friend had even a small fraction of those books...'

'You feel deprived because you do not have enough old friends to keep you company.' Mrs Mortimer gestured towards the shelves. 'Do you wish to borrow any particular volumes?'

'Might I impose on you?'

'It is no imposition since I just offered.'

'I did spot two or three books which I have not been able to find. I would cherish the opportunity to read them.' Darcy beamed.

'Go ahead Mr Darcy, borrow what you wish. I will even leave word with my staff that you may come and exchange books whenever you need more reading material.' Mrs Mortimer looked indulgently on as Darcy collected two books from different shelves.

She then informed Darcy that Mr Bingley was ready to leave.

When Darcy exited the library, he found Mr Kirby waiting for him, holding a set of saddlebags. 'For the books, Sir.'

Bingley who had come into the foyer, laughed, 'trust you to find someone willing to lend you books.'

On their way back to Netherfield, Bingley suggested slyly, 'at least when Caroline asks where we have been, we can truthfully tell her that we have been out to get you some reading material.'

~~~oo0Ooo~~~

After the gentlemen departed, Elizabeth and Mary returned to the parlour with Mrs Mortimer and Jane, where they were joined by Kitty and Lydia whose lessons had just finished.

When they had settled, Elizabeth asked, 'Mama, you were introduced to the party from Netherfield last night. What can you tell me about Miss Bingley?'

Mrs Mortimer was taken aback, since she had expected a question about a certain gentleman. 'Miss Bingley? I do not know much, other than that she thinks herself above the company in Meryton. Why do you ask?'

'Lizzy likes Mr Darcy and is worried that Miss Bingley has a prior claim,' Mary explained to the assembled ladies.

'Mary,' cried Elizabeth in consternation. She blushed at having been found out by her perceptive sister.

'I did notice them enter the assembly hall, and Miss Bingley was acting in a very proprietary manner...'

'Think nothing of it, Lizzy. Since I was beneath her notice during the introductions, I had the opportunity to watch them quite closely.' Mary paused for dramatic effect.

'Mary, stop teasing. What did you observe?'
~~~

Mary smirked. 'Miss Bingley would like to be attached to Mr Darcy, but he has not the slightest interest in her. Unless I completely mistook his expression, he kept wishing her into the next county. Especially when she kept clutching at his arm.'

Elizabeth beamed at the intelligence provided by her sister.

Mrs Mortimer smiled and asked, 'would you like my opinion of the gentleman?'

When Elizabeth nodded, she said, 'I have heard of his reputation in town. He is honest and honourable and everything a gentleman ought to be. He appears to be intelligent and well-mannered. I suspect he is a little shy in unfamiliar company, which he covers up by a haughty mien. But that is the worst I can say about him. Feel free to like him.'

'We only just met last night, Mama. It is too early to speculate. But I do like him and would like to get to know him better.'

'From what I saw, I suspect he will wish to exchange books quite frequently,' commented Mrs Mortimer and delighted in seeing Elizabeth blush even hotter.

'What about you, Jane. How do you find Mr Bingley?' Elizabeth asked to divert attention from herself.

It was Jane's turn to blush at being put on the spot. 'I quite like him. He is pleasant and amiable and he asked about my opinion regarding tenants visits.'

After that disaster in London during her season, Jane had become even more guarded. She was determined to only marry a man who took her seriously, rather than one only interested in her for her ornamental value.

'Nice to look at too,' remarked Kitty wistfully. She had been looking out the window when the gentlemen arrived, and had been taken by the smiling countenance of Mr Bingley. There was something very gentle and attractive about him.

'If Mr Darcy visits, I suspect Mr Bingley will not be far behind.'

<p style="text-align:center">~~~ooO0Ooo~~~</p>

18 Painful Lessons

Darcy and Bingley could not hide the fact that they were invited to tea at Brook Hall from Miss Bingley, since the invitation was for all of them.

Miss Bingley much preferred the society in town, and had only agreed to come to Netherfield Park as hostess for her brother's foray into being a landed gentleman, because Mr Darcy had agreed to come along to advise his friend on estate management.

The opportunity to be in company with the gentleman for several weeks, without the competition of the other ladies of the Ton, was too good to pass up.

To her disgust, as soon as they arrived in this savage backwater, her brother dragged her and Mr Darcy to that pathetic little assembly.

As expected, her brother had danced every dance, but he had the nerve to single out one young woman for a second set. Yes, the woman was beautiful and exactly the type her brother always fell in love with, but she had no sense for fashion. Miss Mortimer had worn the plainest dress Miss Bingley had ever seen.

Caroline had not bothered to look further, otherwise she would have noticed that the quality of the lightest pale blue silk was exquisite and the contrasting dark blue ribbon, which set off the apparently plain material, was shot through with gold thread. After years of enduring Mrs Bennet's obsession with lace, Jane rebelled by avoiding lace whenever possible.

Miss Bingley had no intention of allowing her brother to connect them to someone so obviously inferior. And to think that the woman's mother managed an estate. Who had ever heard of such unfeminine behaviour...

And then there was the second daughter. Miss Bingley wondered how the chit had managed to convince Darcy to do her the signal honour of dancing with her. He *never* danced unless acquainted with his partner.

Mrs Mortimer must be extraordinarily mercenary, since she quickly seized the opportunity to invite the gentlemen for tea. Miss Bingley chose to ignore the fact that the invitation had been for the whole party from Netherfield.

She was determined to foil the woman's designs. She would accompany the gentlemen on the visit to expose the complete unsuitability of the family to her brother and to Mr Darcy.

Miss Bingley's intentions did not go *quite* according to plan.

When the party from Netherfield arrived, Mrs Mortimer introduced Elizabeth, who had not formally met Miss Bingley, as well as her youngest daughters, who were joining them for tea.

Lydia had been allowed to join the gathering on the proviso that she remained quietly in the background. She was present mainly to ensure that Kitty was not left on her own. Since Lydia was as bold and outgoing as Kitty was shy, the younger girl, once she had accepted her place in the family, had appointed herself Kitty's champion and defender.

The gentlemen welcomed the addition of the girls, whereas Miss Bingley was less enthusiastic about anything related to Brook Hall.

The understated elegance of Brook Hall was entirely lost on Miss Bingley, who thought the decoration to be plain in the extreme.

Mrs Mortimer took one look at Miss Bingley's dress and thought that she had met Mrs Bennet's soulmate. Fortunately, Mrs Mortimer and her daughters were too polite to display any of the disdain or amusement they felt upon seeing Miss Bingley's elaborate gown.

Once Mrs Mortimer had served tea to all her visitors and her daughters, they made the initial polite conversation.

Mr Bingley immediately became quite distracted by Miss Mortimer, while Mr Darcy attempted to converse with Miss Elizabeth. Mary remained at her mother's side.

Miss Bingley decided that she could work on her brother later, but Mr Darcy must immediately be shown the superiority of herself in comparison with these country nobodies.

'Do you spend much time in town, Mrs Mortimer?' Miss Bingley asked.

'We visit from time to time, to go to the theatre and to spend time with family and friends.'

'Have you had the honour to meet Viscount Middlebrook?' asked Miss Bingley, planning to discuss the ball she had recently been allowed to attend, and expecting to score on her hostess.

'Yes, he is a charming man, do you not agree?'

Caroline was annoyed that this woman claimed to know a Viscount. This was obviously a ploy to make herself look well connected. 'Yes, Mrs Mortimer, a most charming man. Although I have to say that his wife is sadly not a fashionable lady.'

'I understand that she prefers to wear colours which favour her complexion, rather than what is in fashion. I always thought that she looks exceedingly well in blues.'

Since Lady Middlebrook had indeed worn a blue dress, Miss Bingley realised that Mrs Mortimer might actually have made the Viscount's acquaintance. 'Have you known them long?'

'I have known the Viscount all my life, although we have not been much in company in recent years.'

'You must miss the opportunity for such elevated company.'

'Not at all, although we visit London regularly, I enjoy living in the country. Providentially the Viscount is a very able correspondent.' Mrs Mortimer smiled in her most engaging manner. 'In his last letter he related a most amusing story about the ball he gave for his daughter's coming out. Apparently, one of his guests brought along a friend and his sister, and while the friend is perfectly charming, the sister made a complete fool of herself.'

Miss Bingley, who loved vicious gossip, hoped to gain more grist for her mill. 'Do tell, Mrs Mortimer. I was present at the ball...'

'Then I am certain you must have noticed her. It seems that the woman was dressed most unbecomingly in the latest fashion. I am certain you have seen that type... past the first bloom of youth, and to make up for it, they slavishly follow the fashions even if the style and the colours do not suit them at all.'

'Yes, I know the type. Absolutely ghastly, is it not?'

'Quite. But to continue with my story. It seems the lady, if I can call her that, was acting in the haughtiest manner to almost everyone present, other than her brother's friend upon whom she fawned in the most ridiculous fashion. Now, the company could have forgiven her atrocious sense of fashion, would you believe she wore a bright orange gown festooned with feathers, but for the daughter of a tradesman to act superior towards people of higher station, while fawning over the gentleman in such a way... What can I say... according to my brother, his friends thought she was most entertaining. Especially since she did not seem to notice that the gentleman whom she was fawning over detests her, and spent the evening trying to scrape her off his arm. Luckily the poor dear did not realise she was making herself the laughing stock of the evening, otherwise she must have felt utterly humiliated.'

Bingley's attention was caught when Mrs Mortimer mentioned the orange dress. 'Caroline, did you not wear an orange dress at that ball also?'

'Not at all, Charles. My gown was apricot. A much more becoming colour, do you not agree, Mrs Mortimer?'

'Of course, Miss Bingley, apricot is much more flattering than bright orange,' Mrs Mortimer replied with a bland smile.

Darcy was grateful for the years of practice he had in maintaining a stoic demeanour, no matter the provocation. He remembered that evening, and he was certain that Miss Bingley's dress had been bright orange. He saw enough of it, while he tried to escape the wearer of this dress.

He looked searchingly at their hostess. While her manner was all that was polite and proper, he suspected that she knew full well the identity of the lady in orange...

Caroline on the other hand, looked like she had bitten into a lemon. She had paid close attention to the fashions which the other ladies wore that evening, and knew for certain that only one lady had worn the fashionable orange gown.

Herself.

To find out that what she had considered a successful evening, was instead a complete fiasco, which she had been too oblivious to realise, was a bitter pill to swallow.

She seized on one apparently unconnected snippet to try and change the topic. 'You said your brother was at the ball? How did he manage to get an invitation? I understood that it was a very exclusive affair.'

'My brother did not have a choice but to attend the ball. He was the host.' Mrs Mortimer smiled beatifically.

'The Viscount is your brother?' gasped Miss Bingley.

'Indeed, he is. I am exceedingly blessed to have such a charming brother.'

Miss Bingley was remarkably subdued for the rest of the visit.

~~~oo0Ooo~~~

As soon as they returned to Netherfield Park, Miss Bingley excused herself, claiming a splitting headache.

Bingley and Darcy retired to the library for a drink and a discussion.

'Darcy, I do not remember another woman in an orange dress at that ball. I know I do not pay attention to those kinds of things, but that colour is so vile, I think I would have noticed it...'

Darcy sighed sympathetically. 'There was no other woman in an orange dress.'

'Oh dear. I hope Mrs Mortimer does not find out that it was Caroline at that ball.'

'Are you afraid that your sister would be embarrassed if the lady found out? Or are you concerned that Miss Mortimer might not wish to be associated with the brother of Miss Bingley.'

Bingley looked rather shamefaced. 'The latter is my main concern. I have just about given up on Caroline. For years I tried to tell her that her behaviour is unsuitable when associating with quality. But she refuses to listen to me.'
~~~

Bingley downed the rest of his drink and poured another one. 'I rather like Miss Mortimer and I am concerned that her mother might object to me based on my relationship with Caroline.'

'How do you think Mrs Mortimer acted towards you today?'

'She was all charm and graciousness. She is a wonderful lady.'

'I quite agree with you.' Darcy could not repress a smirk. 'But I believe she is also a veteran of the Ton... I suspect that she knew precisely who she was talking about. I admit that I am not certain if Mrs Mortimer was trying to point out the error of her ways to your sister, in the hopes that Miss Bingley improves, or if she decided to cut your sister down to size.'

Bingley looked stricken at the declaration. 'What am I to do about Caroline? If that is how society perceives her, what chance does she have for marriage in that circle.'

'Somewhere between zero and none, unless the man is desperate for money, and even then...'

Bingley sighed. 'I was afraid you would say that.'

~~~ooO0Ooo~~~

Miss Bingley was also the subject of discussion at Brook Hall.

Kitty, who had sat with Lydia during the visit, and observed the Netherfield party with interest, asked, 'Mama, are Miss Bingley's manners those of a fashionable lady of the Ton?'

'They are, for a certain element of society. These manners are usually practiced by young ladies who are trying to gain access to the first circles, but rarely by ladies who *are* members of that group.'

'Please do not misunderstand, there is no shame in having family in trade, no matter what members of the nobility might try to claim. Take Mr and Mrs Gardiner for instance. They are elegant, sophisticated and genteel, and an asset in any company. But I am afraid that Miss Bingley has not had the advantage to grow up in a genteel household.'

'You mean she is a stuck-up, supercilious, social-climbing strumpet.'

'Lydia, shame on you. I have taught you better than that. One must not use such language... however true it might be.'
~~~

Lydia, who half expected a set-down for her comment, was surprised and then thoughtful at Mrs Mortimer's admission.

'I am sorry, Aunt Stephanie, Miss Bingley irritated me the way she was trying to lord it over you and trying to treat you with disdain, when she has no reason to be proud.'

'Instead you can tell her the truth by pretending not to know that you are relating gossip about her,' chimed in Elizabeth, who remembered the letter from Uncle George, the Viscount.

'You knew this story was about Miss Bingley?' exclaimed Kitty in horror.

'Naturally. After all, I would never spread malicious gossip.'

~~~oo0Ooo~~~

Meanwhile, Miss Bingley reconsidered her position.

She realised that she had completely misjudged the company. Although she could not understand why anyone would prefer to live in this backwater, Mrs Mortimer obviously preferred it, even though she could well afford to live in town.

After finding out about the lady's connections, Miss Bingley at last paid attention to the gowns the ladies were wearing.

Since Lady Middlebrook preferred to wear styles that suited her, rather than whatever was the latest fad in fashion, perhaps Mrs Mortimer was similarly inclined.

When Miss Bingley examined the gowns the ladies wore, she realised that the colours of each were chosen to complement the wearer's colouring of hair, eyes and complexion. As she inspected the gowns more closely, she at last noticed the excellent quality of the fabrics and trims, and the subtle elegance of the cut.

In retrospect, she was chagrined that in that company, she looked like a peacock amongst a flock of swans.

She also knew from experience that this kind of elegance did not come cheap. To dress six ladies in this fashion required considerable wealth.
~~~

Maybe she had been wrong, wanting to separate her brother from Miss Mortimer. The young lady had a Viscount as an uncle, and her mother could afford the best of everything. Miss Bingley did not realise that in her ruminations, Miss Mortimer had changed from *that country chit* to the *young lady*.

The problem was only that if she encouraged her brother in the pursuit of Miss Mortimer, then there was a chance that Mr Darcy might spend more time in the company of Miss Elizabeth. Now that Mr Darcy was aware of the family's wealth and connections, Miss Elizabeth could be a strong rival for his attention, which was something Miss Bingley could not allow.

She completely missed one point of the tale. Mr Darcy detested her.

<p style="text-align:center">~~~oo0Ooo~~~</p>

19 Friends

Sir William Lucas was a sociable man and liked to entertain. To that end he had invited a number of neighbours to join his family for a party.

Since it was only family and friends, the younger girls were invited as well. When Mrs Mortimer and her daughters arrived, Mary, Kitty and Lydia immediately sought out Maria Lucas, while Jane and Elizabeth joined Charlotte.

After their greetings, Charlotte said, 'I hear that Mr Darcy is a frequent visitor at Brook Hall...'

'Mr Darcy comes to borrow books from our library,' Lizzy replied primly, while Jane hid a smile.

'He must be a voracious reader. I understand he never takes more than two days to read a book,' teased Charlotte.

'As you say. He is a prodigious reader,' answered Lizzy firmly, but could not help the blush spreading across her cheeks.

'Ah, speak of the devil. Pardon me, I meant the gentleman.' Charlotte nodded towards the door, where the party from Netherfield had just made their entrance.

At the first opportunity, Darcy and Bingley detached themselves from the rest of their party and Sir William. They scanned the room to find the ladies whom they were eager to meet again.

Darcy, with his advantage in height spotted Elizabeth, and made his way to her side with Bingley in his wake.

Miss Bingley was temporarily left with her sister and brother-in-law, although Sir William promptly escorted Mr Hurst to the refreshment table, leaving the sisters on their own.

While Miss Bingley and Mrs Hurst approached a group of matrons in search of gossip, Darcy and Bingley chatted pleasantly with their ladies.

Once Mr Darcy and Mr Bingley became engrossed in their conversations, Charlotte excused herself to greet the latest arrivals.

~~~oo0Ooo~~~

'You have had enough fun for the moment, Elizabeth.' Charlotte returned and linked arms with her friend. 'Now I must insist that you sing for your supper. Would you excuse us, Mr Darcy? Our guests demand a performance by our dear Eliza.'

Elizabeth laughed, 'since you insist, I suppose I must comply, although you know perfectly well that I never practice enough to give a polished performance.' She looked apologetically at Darcy. 'I am sorry, Mr Darcy, I must do my duty to our hosts.'

Elizabeth took her seat at the pianoforte and started to play her favourite song. After a few introductory bars, she raised her head and sang "Voi che sapete" to her spellbound audience. As she had claimed, her playing was not perfect, but she invested the song with such feeling that nobody cared, even if they noticed.

Miss Bingley took the opportunity to sidle up to Mr Darcy. 'I know what you must think. It is intolerable to have to listen to such a poor performance.'

'On the contrary, I have rarely heard this song performed better,' answered Darcy dismissively, without taking his eyes of the performer.

If looks could kill, Mr Darcy and Miss Elizabeth would have perished in an instant.

'There is no accounting for taste,' huffed Miss Bingley and flounced back to her sister.

When she finished, Elizabeth was urged to perform another song. At the end of that performance she cried off. 'It is someone else's turn now.'

Sir William requested, 'Miss Mary, would you play us some dance tunes. I feel certain that our young people have a wish to dance.'

Mary took her seat at the instrument and waited while the carpets were rolled up.

Darcy took the opportunity to request a dance from Elizabeth.
~~~

'Are you certain it will not damage your reputation to dance a reel in a parlour, Mr Darcy? I remember your aunt stating that you avoid dancing whenever possible.'

'If my aunt mentioned my dislike of dancing to you, then I am certain she also mentioned that my fondness of dancing, or lack thereof, is in direct relation to my feelings for my partner... It would give me the greatest pleasure to dance with you.'

'I would by no means suspend any pleasure of yours, Mr Darcy,' replied Elizabeth as she gave her hand to Darcy to lead her to the floor.

Other couples joined them, including, predictably, Mr Bingley with Miss Mortimer.

When the first dance finished, Bingley led Jane to where her other sisters were sitting. He planned to stay and converse with Miss Mortimer some more, but then noticed the wistful expression on Miss Catherine's countenance. In one of those lightning changes of purpose with which all his friends were familiar, he instead asked, 'would you honour me with the next dance, Miss Catherine?'

Kitty was stunned to be asked by this amiable gentleman, and could only shyly nod her agreement.

After the first dance, Darcy did not get another chance to dance with Elizabeth again for the remainder of the evening. Instead he danced with all her sisters, even Lydia, after asking permission of Mrs Mortimer. He even managed to coax Mary away from the pianoforte for a dance with him.

Bingley was astounded. That was the first time he had seen his friend dance so often, and what was even more astonishing, Darcy seemed to be enjoying himself.

~~~oo0Ooo~~~

The morning was still quite foggy when Darcy returned from his ride.

His friend Bingley was starting to get used to country hours, and while he did sleep later than Darcy, he now usually rose by the time Darcy returned from his morning ride.

Darcy joined Bingley in the dining room to break his fast.
~~~

'You look troubled, Darce,' commented Bingley. 'Is something on your mind?'

'I just wondered if there is something in the air around here that is making me start seeing things.'

Bingley looked baffled, 'what did you see that you think you should not…'

'I am wondering if this area is haunted and I saw a ghost.

'What kind of a ghost? A spectre?' cried Bingley in alarm.

'No, a grey rider on a grey horse moving at an impossible speed.'

'And where did you see that apparition?'

'Between Oakham Mount and Brook Hall. I had but a glimpse of it'

'It is not like you to be fanciful. I could almost suppose your mind has started to wander due to a particular lady in this neighbourhood…'

~~~oo0Ooo~~~

Providentially, for Darcy's peace of mind, it was but two days later that he uncovered the mystery of the grey ghost.

On his morning ride he decided to explore Oakham Mount. He had been told that the view from that spot was quite remarkable. Since the morning promised to be fair, he rode to the top of the hill.

When he arrived, he discovered that the location was already occupied… by Miss Elizabeth.

She was clad all in grey. She wore a long jacket over what looked like a slim wool skirt. The ensemble was topped, not by a bonnet, but a scarf, wrapped tightly about her head, confining her abundant hair.

She looked around when she heard Hermes' hoofbeats.

'Good morning, Mr Darcy,' she smiled in welcome. 'Have you too come to admire the sunrise?'

'I have indeed, Miss Elizabeth,' he replied as he dismounted.

'Did you walk up here alone?' he asked in concern when he could not see anyone else.
~~~

'Yes and no.' Elizabeth smiled mischievously. 'Since I did not walk, technically I did not come alone. Phoenix is enjoying his breakfast over there.'

Darcy looked in the direction she pointed and saw a magnificent grey stallion grazing a little way off.

A suspicion dawned on him. 'Do you often ride alone in the morning, Miss Elizabeth?'

'I do, but why do you ask?'

'Because for the last few days I thought I was losing my mind, since I had seen what appeared to be a ghost.' He gestured between the horse and Elizabeth.

'I am sorry you were troubled, Mr Darcy. Had you but asked any of the locals, they would have put you to rights.'

'I suppose I could have. But it was rather intriguing to imagine seeing a real live ghost.'

'A live ghost? Is that not a contradiction in terms?'

'Not at all. You and Phoenix looked like a ghost, but you both are very much alive.'

'Touché.'

They fell into an easy conversation while they watched the sunrise paint the countryside in a golden light.

Darcy divided his attention between the lovely view in the distance and the one beside him.

The more he spoke to Elizabeth the more he liked her. She was bright, intelligent and had an open friendliness which was refreshing. In their conversations she always spoke to Fitzwilliam Darcy, not the Master of Pemberley.

He admired the breadth of her education. Due to her knowledge of estate management and the needs of tenants, she would make an excellent Mistress of Pemberley. That thought felt so very right.

He could imagine her at Pemberley, presiding over meals, visiting tenants, walking in the garden, riding in the woods, curled up in the library with a book, in his ...

He stopped himself before his imagination carried him away. Those visions were much too tempting.

He wanted a chance to get to know her better, and to give her a chance to know himself. While she had been on his mind for three years and more, Elizabeth had only just met him. Darcy was determined to give her time to deepen their acquaintance.

He hoped that she would find him worthy of her.

She had so much in her favour that he was certain she had no lack of offers. The fact that after three years in society she was still unmarried indicated to him that she would be true to her stated desire to only marry for love and respect.

Elizabeth too enjoyed the view and the conversation. She relished the attention and Mr Darcy's acceptance of her ideas. This man was not intimidated by her intelligence, or put off by the fact she expressed her opinions so decidedly… on a great number of subjects.

And then there was this sensation when he touched her as they danced, or when she held his arm. Even when he smiled at her. It made her feel… something. She had no words to describe the delightful sensation.

~~~ooO0Ooo~~~

Darcy remembered something he had been curious about. 'Miss Elizabeth, I would like to ask… I mean, I wondered… I do not mean to pry…'

Elizabeth laughed softly at the suddenly awkward gentleman. 'Please, Mr Darcy, just ask your question.'

Darcy smiled in relief. 'I had wondered about your parents. You said that your father passed away, but I gather your mother is still alive…'

'You are wondering who my natural parents are.'

When Darcy nodded, Elizabeth said, 'my parents were Mr and Mrs Bennet of Longbourn. You can see the estate over there.' She pointed out her birthplace. 'It is the third largest estate in the area.'

She tilted her head and tried to repress a smirk. 'I am a gentleman's daughter, if that is what you wondered about.'
~~~

Darcy had indeed speculated about her ancestry. While being the adopted daughter of Mrs Mortimer gave her an excellent standing in society, there had been a small but niggling concern about her parentage. While it made no difference to him, he wanted to be prepared if necessary. Although hearing that she was a gentleman's daughter did relieve his mind.

She added fondly, 'he was a good man. He taught me to love books and started me on the path to an unconventional education. In retrospect I think that was part of the problem Mrs Bennet had with me. She was raised to value physical beauty. She had no understanding about the beauty of the mind.'

'Do you still speak to her?'

'In recent years we have exchanged polite greetings if we happen to encounter each other. Before that she ignored me. I admit, at the time I was pleased that I did not have to interact with her. But I have had many years of Mrs Mortimer's care, and she taught me to accept people as they are. Everyone is flawed to some degree. You know what it says in the bible, about casting the first stone…'

'You are very forgiving…'

'Not at all, Mr Darcy. But I realised that Mrs Mortimer has given me opportunities I would never have had otherwise. And protracted hate only hurts oneself. I prefer to be happy. My philosophy is, *think only of the past as its remembrance gives you pleasure*. But on that note, I must take my leave.'

'If you must.' Darcy rose and offered his hand to Elizabeth, who took it but rose without putting any pressure on it.

He walked with her to her horse and looked about for any feature she could use as a mounting block. Before he could find one, Elizabeth had swung into the saddle, at which point he realised that she was sitting astride, and what he had assumed was a skirt, was a pair of what appeared to be loose pantaloons.

Elizabeth raised an eyebrow at Darcy in challenge. Darcy smiled and bowed. 'I applaud your sense in ignoring customs. My sister too prefers to ride astride. Although her costume is not as subtle as yours. May I escort you to your home?'

'Do you wish to borrow another book?'

'Perhaps. But mainly I wish to prolong the pleasure of your company.'

'In that case, I would enjoy the company. I might even get Kitty to prepare a sketch of my outfit for your sister.'

~~~oo0Ooo~~~
~~~

20 and Enemies

'Charles you cannot mean to call on Miss Mortimer again,' protested Miss Bingley.

'Whyever should I not? Miss Mortimer is beautiful and charming and intelligent and genteel. I find her company exceedingly pleasing.'

'What do you know about her? Did she tell you that Mrs Mortimer is not her mother but her guardian? Do you even know who her true family is? I cannot think but that she is ashamed of her origins, which is why she uses her guardian's name rather than her own.'

'Caroline, it is irrelevant who her family is. Miss Mortimer is all that is good and gracious. Apart from that, she makes no secret of the fact that Mrs Mortimer is her guardian and that of her youngest sister Lydia. The other three sisters are the adopted daughters of Mrs Mortimer.'

'But that still begs the question, what kind of unsavoury characters are her true parents. For all you know, they could be servants or even peasants.'

'You are being ridiculous, Caroline. Mr Bennet was the gentleman who owned Longbourn, the third largest estate hereabouts.'

'Bennet? Did you say Bennet?'

'Yes, I did. What does it matter?'

'Mrs Bennet is still alive. Did you know that?'

'Yes, I did. But again, what does it matter?'

'Have you seen Mrs Bennet? Have you seen that ridiculous woman with too many lace ruffles on her dress? You know what they say, look at the mother to find out what to expect from the daughter.'

'You object to the lady because of lace ruffles?'

'Yes, because that woman has no sense of fashion.'

Bingley raised a single eyebrow, then pointed at Miss Bingley's skirt. 'That is the pot calling the kettle black,' he stated with a smirk.

Caroline realised that she had made a tactical error wearing her favourite dress with the swags of lace adorning the lower part of her skirt.

'Well. have it your own way. But do not come to me for sympathy if you make a fool of yourself,' she huffed.

'No one would ever be foolish enough to come to you for sympathy, since you do not know the meaning of the word,' said Bingley in disgust.

~~~ooO0oo~~~

The ladies from Brook Hall had been invited to a party at the Long estate. Several other families had also been invited, as well as some of the militia officers.

When Mrs Mortimer and her daughters arrived the were greeted affably by Mr Long, who also introduced them to the officers whom they had not yet met.

The officers were delighted at the addition of four lovely young ladies to the party.

Colonel Forster appeared particularly taken by Miss Catherine. 'You must come and visit my wife sometime. I feel certain that you and she could become dear friends, since you seem to be of an age, and she loves company.'

Kitty, who felt rather intimidated by the large man, who must have been at least twenty years her senior, suggested with a glance at Mrs Mortimer, 'my mother and I would be delighted to call on your wife, Sir.'

'Indeed, we would, Colonel,' agreed Mrs Mortimer. 'But I am surprised that your wife did not join you here today if she loves company.'

'I am afraid she is feeling indisposed, otherwise she would have been delighted to join this party,' answered the Colonel defensively. 'But there is no need for you to incommode yourself, Mrs Mortimer. Do you not find the chatter of young ladies tiresome?'
~~~

'Not at all, Colonel. I find their enthusiasm rather refreshing, and I never allow my daughters to go out without a chaperone.'

'In that case, of course you must come too,' Forster grudgingly agreed, before he excused himself to join another group.

Kitty surreptitiously squeezed Mrs Mortimer's hand. 'Thank you, Mama.' She and Mary went to join Mrs Long's nieces, while Mrs Mortimer wondered about the Colonel's determination for Kitty to visit without a chaperone.

Mrs Mortimer, Jane and Elizabeth drifted around the room chatting to friends until they joined in the various card games.

Elizabeth, had become bored with playing cards and was taking a break from the card-table. She was sitting by herself on a sofa at the side of the room when Lieutenant Wickham asked to join her.

Since he appeared charming and well spoken, Elizabeth was happy to have his company.

'Do you not like playing cards, Miss Elizabeth?'

'I like it well enough, although not for the entire evening. But I notice that you too are not playing either, Lieutenant.'

'Alas, while I like playing, I have not been blessed with a bottomless purse.'

'That is truly a misfortune if you enjoy that diversion.'

'I quite agree. In fact, it should not be so if it were not for the circumstance that I was denied my inheritance.'

'How shocking,' declared Elizabeth, although there was something about his statement, or possibly the way he said it that did not sit right with her.

'Indeed, it is shocking, since the man who denied me was my boyhood friend. Alas he became jealous of the fact that his father, who was my godfather, favoured me over him.'

Wickham sighed sorrowfully, while he carefully watched for Elizabeth's reaction.

Although she had reservations about his statement, Elizabeth was curious enough to ask, 'pray tell, how could such a thing happen?'

That was enough encouragement for Lieutenant Wickham. 'As it happened, my father was the steward at a large estate. The Master of the estate thought highly of my father, and to honour him, he became my godfather. As such he provided me with the same education as his son. The Master's son and I were of an age and we grew up together, almost like brothers.'

Wickham smiled charmingly as if in remembrance. 'As boys, we did everything together, but when we started school, he became very proud and haughty. He preferred to spend time with others of his rank and looked down on mere mortals. His father disliked the man he was becoming and preferred my amiable nature, which made the son jealous.'

He sighed. 'What can I say, my godfather wanted to ensure that I had the kind of living that my education made me fit for, and recommended me to the living which was in his advowson, when the incumbent died. Regrettably, my godfather predeceased the vicar, and when the living became available but two years later, the son denied it to me.'

'If your godfather recommended you in his will, there must have been legal recourse for you to claim the living.'

'Alas, the wording was informal enough that the son did not feel obliged to honour his father's wish.'

'That is indeed a great misfortune. But could you not have obtained a living somewhere else if you were already ordained?' Elizabeth asked reasonably. After all, her cousin did not have any connections, yet he had managed to secure a living.

Wickham was getting worried. While the young woman was sympathetic, she was also much too perceptive for his liking.

'I am afraid I was prevented from becoming ordained by being without funds, and could not afford the fees for the examination.'

Elizabeth looked puzzled, as she knew differently. 'That is most strange, Lieutenant. I happen to have a cousin who was ordained only this year, and he did not mention any fee attached to his ordination...'

'Different rules apply in different counties, Miss Elizabeth. In Derbyshire I could not afford the fee.' Lieutenant Wickham was becoming concerned, having to find justifications for his story.

'In Derbyshire, you say? Could you not have requested the assistance of another gentleman to help with the fees? I happen to know that Mr Darcy has a reputation of being a most generous gentleman.'

'Darcy would be the last man to help me,' spat Wickham.

'Oh...'

'I did not wish to name the culprit who forced me into penury, because I consider his father to have been the best of men, but Mr Darcy was the ruthless man who denied me the living.'

Elizabeth had been dubious during this recounting of his tale of misery, but when he suggested that Mr Darcy had acted dishonourably, she was certain that there was more to the story than the Lieutenant had told. She decided to see if she could get more information.

'If he denied you the living without grounds, you may confront him here in Meryton to demand justice.'

'What can you mean, Miss Elizabeth?'

'Simply that Mr Darcy is currently residing in Meryton.

'Darcy is here?' asked Wickham turning white.

Elizabeth noticed her companion's reaction but gave no indication of her true feelings. 'Indeed, he is, Mr Wickham. You see, fate has brought you together to improve your fortune.'

'You are kindness itself to suggest such a course of action. But you must have experienced it yourself, how arrogant and haughty Mr Darcy is. Once he has made up his mind, he will not budge from his position.'

Now she knew the man was lying. While Mr Darcy was a little reticent in company of strangers, he was always polite, and amongst friends he was delightful company.

'Possibly he had good reason for denying you the living.'

'Has he been blackening my name again? Every time I try to make a new start, he spreads vile slander about me.' Wickham protested.

'Careful Mr Wickham. It does not do to slander a gentleman. You should know that I have never before heard your name, but you have shown yourself to be careless with the truth.'

With that parting shot, Elizabeth rose and took the one free chair at one of the card tables.

~~~oo0Ooo~~~

Wickham stared at her retreating back, feeling baffled and furious. His story had always before garnered him the sympathies of his listeners. Yet today he had failed miserably.

Who was this young woman who refused to be drawn in?

Although Miss Elizabeth was a little old for his taste, she was a remarkably handsome and vivacious woman. That vivacity had drawn him to her side. He had felt certain that he could charm her and gain her favours.

Instead she had defended Darcy. Since she had not seemed like a fortune-hunter, it was incomprehensible to Wickham that she could speak favourably of his old enemy. After all, the poor sap was so uncomfortable in company, that he invariably came across as haughty and arrogant.

He had to find out more. Despite what Wickham had claimed, he knew Darcy never refuted him when Wickham blackened Darcy's name. Therefore, it was safe to make enquiries.

He strolled over to Mrs Long, who was pouring tea or coffee for her guests, and engaged her in conversation, being as charming as he knew how to be.

After complimenting the lady on the success of the party, he casually asked, 'I heard mention that Mr Darcy is currently in the area.'

'Oh, yes, he is. Is he not a handsome and charming man?'

'Charming? I had heard that he is quite arrogant…'

'Oh, no, Lieutenant. You must have heard about a different Mr Darcy. Mr Darcy of Pemberley is utterly charming. A little quiet, maybe, but a perfectly amiable gentleman,' gushed Mrs Long.

'It must have been a different gentleman,' conceded a confused Wickham. Darcy, charming? What was the world coming to? There had to be a reason.
~~~

Before he had a chance to enquire further, Mrs Long confided, 'maybe I should not say so, but I believe Mr Darcy is sweet on Miss Elizabeth. He spends much of his time at Brook Hall. I suppose it could be one of the other girls, but he always dances first with Miss Elizabeth.'

Well, well, well, it looked like Darcy and Miss Elizabeth may be an item. There was scope for revenge if that was true.

After all, Darcy's pride would not allow him to associate himself with a disgraced family. No matter how much he might be smitten.

~~~oo0Ooo~~~

During the ride home, Elizabeth passed the time relating her conversation with Lieutenant Wickham.

'I gather you did not believe the Lieutenant?' asked Mrs Mortimer.

'Mama, you know Mr Darcy. Do you truly believe he would act in a dishonourable fashion? I certainly do not. I only wonder why Mr Wickham would relate such a story.'

'Perhaps I am cynical, but I would assume that such a tale of woe garners sympathy from foolish young women. And such sympathy could lead to a wish to comfort the gentleman…'

'You believe he is a practiced seducer.' Elizabeth stated rather than asked. When Mrs Mortimer agreed, Lizzy suggested, 'I suppose we had better inform Mr Darcy about Lieutenant Wickham's calumny.'

~~~oo0Ooo~~~

21 Warning

Lady Lucas and Charlotte called at Brook Hall, to share some news. While some people might consider it gossip, in this case Lady Lucas was motivated by concern.

After a few minutes of polite conversation with Mrs Mortimer and all her daughters while they enjoyed their tea, Lady Lucas came to the reason for her visit.

'Mrs Mortimer, I have some very disturbing news. It concerns Emily Evans, one of the maids at the Long's estate.'

'I have not heard anything about her, but I have been home all day...'

Lady Lucas sighed. 'It seems she was sent on an errand late yesterday afternoon. When she did not return, they sent their servants out looking for her. She was found this morning... The poor child was dead.'

The lady took another sip of tea to steady herself. 'What I have to relate is shocking. I do not know if I should do so in front of your daughters...'

Mrs Mortimer looked thoughtfully at the sisters before making a decision. 'Girls, I leave it up to you. Based on this warning, we know something bad has happened to Emily. If you feel that you would prefer not to hear the details, please leave now.'

The sisters exchanged glances. Kitty, who was the gentlest of the girls and had the most vivid imagination, swallowed convulsively. 'I do not wish to hear what has happened, but I believe that I should. Since Lady Lucas does not normally spread gossip, for her to come to us bodes ill. I think we need to hear it.'

'Very well said, Kitty. Do you agree with your sister?' she asked the other girls. 'You may leave if you wish.'

When the sisters declined to leave, Mrs Mortimer turned to Lady Lucas. 'Please go on, Lady Lucas.'

'Emily was found in the woods, a short way off the path to Meryton. She was barely recognisable, and she had been most violently interfered with.' Lady Lucas related with a grim expression.

'The harpies and the men will claim that she was at fault, but I knew the girl. She counted but four and ten summers and she was extremely shy. Even John, who is kindness itself, could never get her so much as to raise her eyes to him, when he visited the Longs.'

All the ladies were horrified at the recounting. 'Who would have done such a thing to the child?' exclaimed Jane, who had turned white.

'We do not know for certain, but there was some red thread near where her body was found. The exact shade of a militia uniform.'

'One of the militia men? But they are supposed to protect people,' exclaimed Mary.

Charlotte at last spoke up. 'We cannot be certain. That thread may have been there for days. And we cannot even establish from whose uniform it may have come. After all, coats get damaged all the time during training. I doubt there is a single uniform in pristine condition.'

'But you are concerned it may be one of them.' Mrs Mortimer stated rather than asked.

'We have never had such an occurrence before the militia arrived. Sir William has conferred with Colonel Forster, but the man was not exactly helpful. He tried to make out that the poor child *asked for it*,' huffed Lady Lucas.

'As you said, men generally blame the misdeeds of men on women. It is dreadfully unfair, but there is nothing we can do about that.'

'We can do nothing about the men's attitudes, but we can take precautions. I came here to warn you that there is an animal out there, or potentially several, and women are not safe. Please do not go out alone,' she looked meaningfully at Elizabeth.

'We will be careful.'

Lydia sighed. 'It is too bad. The officers look rather handsome in their regimentals. But if one of them murdered Emily, I suppose it would be better not to associate with any of them.'

'Lydia,' chided Mrs Mortimer.

'I know, Aunt Stephanie. *Soldiers, or even officers are not suitable husband material. Apart from that, I am too young to even consider marriage,*' she quoted. 'But they *do* look rather dashing.'

Lydia was irrepressible as always, but Mrs Mortimer realised that the girl was using humour to disguise her upset. She just shook her head at Lydia.

Lady Lucas and Charlotte took their leave shortly afterwards, to call on other neighbours to spread the warning.

~~~ooO0oo~~~

The atmosphere in the parlour at Brook Hall was subdued after their departure. Mrs Mortimer considered all the options and came to a decision.

'Girls, until this is cleared up or until the militia leaves, none of you are to go out on your own. If you leave the estate, you will always take a footman with you. Is that clear.'

The girls reluctantly agreed.

'There is one more thing, from now on, you will also go armed. Mary, Kitty, Lydia, I know you do not like knives but you all have learned how to shoot. I did not buy all those pocket pistols just to have them sitting in the cupboard. You will each carry at least two.'

She then addressed Jane and Elizabeth. 'While I know that you are competent edged weapons, they are difficult to carry unobtrusively. Therefore, I want you to carried guns as well. It gives you greater options.'

'By the bye. I meant for all of you to not even leave the house unarmed. While I do not think anyone would be foolish enough to try and attack you on our own grounds, I prefer you to take precautions which turn out not to be needed, rather than have you end up like Emily Evans.'
~~~

At that reminder, even Elizabeth, who had been inclined to argue about unnecessary precautions, agreed to abide by Mrs Mortimer's edict.

~~~ooO0oo~~~

The day had been grey and overcast until the early afternoon when the heavens opened up.

A few minutes later, a rather damp Mr Darcy was announced by Mr Kirby.

'I am sorry, Mrs Mortimer, ladies, I did not mean to barge in and inconvenience you, but I did not expect the rain to start so early. Since I was three miles from Netherfield and only half a mile from here, I was hoping to beg shelter off you till the storm passes.'

'Mr Darcy, there is no need to apologise, you are always welcome,' offered Mrs Mortimer. 'Come sit by the fire and dry off.'

'This may help,' murmured Mr Kirby who had returned with a towel.

Darcy gratefully accepted the towel and used it to good purpose.

When he sat down in the chair closest to the fire, Elizabeth handed him a cup of tea. 'I put in extra sugar. You may need it.'

When Elizabeth sat down again, she fidgeted a little, and then suggested, 'Mama, now that Mr Darcy is here do you think we should tell him about our new acquaintance?'

'Since you are the one, he spoke to the most, I believe you should be the one to tell the story.'

Darcy watched the interchange with curiosity. When he had come in, he had been to disturbed to notice, but now that he started to relax, it seemed to him there was a strained atmosphere in the room.

'Pray tell, how does a new acquaintance of yours affect me?'

'Mr Darcy, two days ago we attended a card party at the Long Estate. Mrs Long is very sociable, and she often invites friends and acquaintances for a pleasant evening of cards and conversation. Mama, my sisters and myself had been invited, as well as a few other families and several officers from the militia. The officers included a new Lieutenant, who had only recently joined. A Lieutenant Wickham.'
~~~

Elizabeth paused in her narrative and noted the startled expression on Darcy's face. 'Is his name George Wickham perchance?'

'It is indeed and he claims to know you. Based on your reaction you know him as well.'

Darcy became very guarded, wondering what lies Wickham had told this time and how much he had been believed. 'I do know him. He is the son of our former steward and my father's godson.'

'So he told me. He also told me some folderol about you denying him a living which your father meant for him to have.'

'Folderol?' Darcy was stunned. It appeared that for once Wickham may have been unsuccessful. 'You are both right and wrong. If I might explain?'

'We were hoping that you would, Mr Darcy. While we do not believe you to be dishonourable, it is advisable for us to have the facts to refute the lie, should he attempt to spread it amongst our friends.'

'Just so. Yes, my father wanted Wickham to have the living, *if* he became ordained. But Wickham did not wish to take ordination, instead he requested the value of the living as a lumpsum, so that he could study law. I was very happy to pay him the requested three thousand pounds, since I knew he would be completely unsuited as a clergyman. His habits and morals are reprehensible.'

Darcy fortified himself with another sip of tea before continuing. 'Two years later the incumbent died, and the living became available. At that point Wickham returned and demanded the living, having squandered the money he had received for it. Naturally, I denied him the living. He went away swearing revenge.'

'What a clever scoundrel,' exclaimed Elizabeth. 'He mixes just enough truth with his lie to make the whole believable.'

'But you did not believe him. An occurrence which is almost unheard of. What gave him away?'

'He besmirched your honour.' Elizabeth grinned at him. 'Mr Darcy, you are not perfect, since there is no such thing as a perfect human being. But I know that you are an honourable man. If you denied him the living, then you must have had a good reason to do so. Therefore, Lieutenant Wickham must have been lying.'

'Thank you, Miss Elizabeth, for your faith in me.'

Mrs Mortimer had listened thoughtfully. She now had a question of her own. 'Mr Darcy, you said that Mr Wickham's habits and morals are reprehensible. Would you elaborate?'

Darcy fidgeted uncomfortably wondering how to respond to that question.

'Mr Darcy, I have a reason for asking this question. Please do not be afraid to shock us by being blunt.'

Darcy became suspicious. 'Something has happened.' It was a statement, not a question.

Mrs Mortimer nodded. 'Please, tell us.'

'Very well. Wickham leaves debts wherever he goes, he is a gambler and a womaniser. While I do not condone that kind of behaviour I would not object as long as he confined himself to professionals. But he also seduces young women. He is exceedingly charming when he wishes to be, but sometimes when seduction does not work, he has been known to... ah... use force.'

'And the women keep quiet because society blames them, instead of the rake.' Mrs Mortimer completed the statement.

'Just so. It is patently unfair, but that is the way it is.'

'Mr Darcy, tell me honestly. Do you think Wickham would kill?'

'To the best of my knowledge... not deliberately. Unless it was me, and he was certain he could get away unscathed and unsuspected. But you said something has happened. What was it?'

'A young maid was found this morning in the woods. She had been violated and killed.'

'Red thread, possibly from a militia uniform was found nearby,' added Elizabeth.

'Could it have been Wickham?'

'It is possible, but unlikely, based on my knowledge of him. In any case, I expect it would be impossible to prove.'

'We have already come to the same conclusion.

'What about Colonel Forster?' asked Darcy.

'He is of no help. According to him, the girl asked for it, whereas we know for a fact that she was an exceedingly shy young girl and certainly did not ask to be killed.'

Darcy deliberated for a few minutes. 'I need to send a message to London to my cousin Colonel Fitzwilliam, although I expect the message will need to be forwarded to wherever he is at the moment. Even though he is in the Regulars, he might be able to suggest how to get Colonel Forster to take the situation seriously.'

'If you would like to prepare your missive in my study, I will show you the way.'

Darcy accepted and prepared a note to his cousin, briefly explaining the circumstances and asking his advice.

By the time he finished, Mrs Mortimer had arranged for a courier to take the message to London.

When Darcy returned to the parlour, the atmosphere seemed to have returned to normal. The ladies were working on various projects and quietly chatting.

Mrs Mortimer welcomed him with a smile and invited him to join them.

When he was seated by the fire again, Darcy wondered how to broach the subject.

Lydia, who was watching the various emotions chasing over his features, suggested, 'Mr Darcy, please save yourself the trouble of composing an elegant speech. Simply tell us what is on your mind. I feel certain that we will be able to understand plain English.'

That irreverent quip startled a chuckle out of Darcy. 'Thank you, Miss Lydia. I shall do my best.'

He became serious again. 'I am concerned for the wellbeing of all you ladies. I was trying to work out how to ask you all to stay indoors until Wickham, or whoever is responsible, is dealt with.'

'Mr Darcy, it could be months until the responsible person is *dealt with*, as you say. I would go out of my mind if I cannot get outdoors on a regular basis. Even a few days of rain make me... unsettled,' protested Elizabeth.

'Irritable, short-tempered, impossible to live with...' murmured Lydia just loud enough to be heard.

Elizabeth laughed. 'Yes, that too. So you see, Mr Darcy, staying indoors is not an option. But we have discussed this situation already and will take suitable precautions.'

When Darcy still looked ready to argue, Mrs Mortimer interjected, 'Mr Darcy, I am fully aware of the misfortunes that can befall young ladies, and I have done my best to ensure that my daughters are safe. They have learned how to defend themselves.'

Darcy opened his mouth to refute Mrs Mortimer when Jane spoke up. 'Mr Darcy, do you perchance remember that Lord Neville had an accident three years ago?'

Darcy looked puzzled as he tried to remember. 'Y-e-s, I believe I heard that he broke his ankle.'

'He did not break his ankle... I broke it for him when he was trying to compromise me in the middle of Gunther's,' declared Jane.

'You did *what*?'

'I kicked his ankle and broke it. Then I pretended he had become ill, which was why it looked like I was holding him up, rather than he was trying to grab me and take liberties.'

'But you are so...'

'Gentle, demure, sweet, ladylike?'

Darcy nodded in shock.

'I am all those things, but I will not let some rake take advantage of me. I am not a victim.'

'Obviously not. My apologies, Miss Mortimer. I meant no offense.' He gave up. This was a battle he was not going to win.

Soon after, most of the girls excused themselves to engage in other tasks.

Darcy waited out the storm in the comfort of the parlour, in the now more relaxed company of Mrs Mortimer and Elizabeth.

Over the next few days, Mrs Mortimer spread the warning about Mr Wickham's habits to the community

<div align="center">~~~oo0Ooo~~~</div>

22 Compromise

Caroline Bingley was getting desperate. Mr Darcy had lately been paying a great deal of attention to Miss Elizabeth.

At this rate, she could miss out on the prize she had set her cap on. She suspected that it was only days before Mr Darcy would ask for a courtship with the chit. Then Caroline would never be Mistress of Pemberley.

Unless she could take matters into her own hands.

~~~ooO0oo~~~

It was after midnight when her maid Lucy reported that the gentlemen had gone to their rooms.

Caroline waited another hour to ensure Darcy would be fast asleep. Clad in her best silk nightgown and peignoir she quietly opened her door and ensured the hallway was empty.

She carefully walked along the hall to the guest-wing, keeping out of the light of the few lamps as much as possible. At Darcy's room she stopped to listen at the door. The only sound emanating from the room was a soft snore.

Caroline smiled to herself, everything was going to plan. She carefully turned the handle and almost sighed in relief when the door opened soundlessly.

She had been afraid that Mr Darcy might have enough sense to lock his door. It was almost a shame to betray that much trust, but he was not giving her a choice. She, Caroline Bingley, daughter of a lowly tradesman, was going to be the next Mistress of Pemberley, one of the most beautiful, and not to forget biggest and richest, estates in the country.

Caroline quietly slipped into the room and carefully closed the door behind her. She waited a moment for her eyes to adjust. The only light
~~~

in the room came from a few embers in the fireplace. Since she knew the layout of the room, it was enough.

She stealthily moved towards the bed, carefully feeling with her hands and bare feet for any unexpected obstacles. There were none.

By now her eyes had adjusted sufficiently that she could see that the bed curtains were open and the large body of a man was on the other side of the large bed. The dark hair stood out against the white pillow case, making his position easy to identify.

Caroline smiled as she loosened the sash of her peignoir and dropped it to the floor. She then lifted the blankets and gently slipped into the bed.

Once under the covers she realised that she had become chilled in her flimsy attire. She therefore took a few minutes to warm up. After all she did not want to startle Mr Darcy out of his sleep by a freezing presence in his bed.

She needed to be warm and welcoming if he roused.

Unfortunately, the lateness of the hour, and the gradually returning warmth, proved to be soporific. She drifted off to sleep without noticing that the man in bed with her had turned over, and encountering a warm body next to his had drawn her into a close embrace. All without waking up.

Both occupants of the bed slept exceedingly well with the reassuring warmth of another body next to them.

~~~ooO0Ooo~~~

Caroline woke due to the light of curtains being drawn. She felt wonderfully relaxed and well rested. She smiled to herself to feel the warm body at her back and the arm draped over her side, holding her close.

She let out a contented sigh, startling the footman who was drawing back the curtains on the second window.

Now that they had an audience, as well as an independent witness, Caroline knew it was time to play her role.
~~~

She put on a shocked expression before turning to the man, after all she had just been caught in Mr Darcy's bed.

As she turned over to face the footman, she also saw the face of her sleeping companion, and let out a scream.

Now she did not have to pretend to be shocked, she truly was confused, angry and embarrassed.

Her scream had woken up the man, who opened his eyes, and upon seeing Miss Bingley, grinned lasciviously. 'Good morning, lovely lady. Did you sleep well?'

Caroline was trying to scramble out of bed, but the arm which had been so comforting only a few minutes ago, was now an immovable obstacle to her escape.

'Who are you? And what are you doing in my bed?' she screamed.

'Corporal Bennings, at your service. And this is my bed. I suppose it is Mr Darcy's, but he said for me to use it since I was dead on my feet when we got here late last night.' He shrugged, which was quite an achievement since he was propped up on one elbow. It also made Caroline aware that he was not wearing a nightshirt.

'I was just about asleep on my feet when we got here, otherwise I am sure I would have risen to the occasion.' He suddenly grinned. 'But I am awake now...'

He started to pull her closer. 'It was good of the Colonel to arrange for some entertainment for me.'

'Take your hands off me, you...' cried Caroline. 'I am not a harlot. I am Miss Bingley.'

Bennings looked startled, and then started laughing as understanding set in. 'You are Charles Bingley's sister and this is Darcy's bed. We were all wondering how long it would take for you to lose your patience and try to sneak into his bed.'

He laughed uproariously while Caroline tore free of his grasp and scrambled out of bed. She noticed that the footman had beaten a hasty retreat.

She scooped up her peignoir and put it on. As she was tying the sash, Bennings had a final word for her.

'Miss Bingley, a word of advice. Do not try this again. Nobody would ever believe that Mr Darcy would have invited you into his room, let alone his bed. It is common knowledge that you disgust him and he can barely stand the sight of you.'

Caroline had not thought she could be more embarrassed than to wake up next to a strange man. Yet the Corporal's words, so casually uttered, made her blush even more.

Had she been truly so blind as not to see that Mr Darcy had no interest in her? Was she so caught up in her ambition to be Mistress of Pemberley that she had wilfully ignored his attempts to avoid her?

No, it could not be. What would a lowly Corporal, totally unconnected to Mr Darcy, know about how the gentleman felt.

And in the end, it did not matter how Darcy felt. He was a gentleman and would do his duty, when found in a compromising situation with a lady.

It never occurred to Caroline that nobody regarded her as a lady.

~~~ooO0Ooo~~~

Since he was awake, Corporal Bennings got up stiffly and dressed for the day. When he was presentable, he found a footman to direct him to the dining room, where he found Colonel Fitzwilliam and Mr Darcy.

Bennings assembled a plate of food and joined them at the table, where he started eating with relish.

The others had just started breakfast, and Mr Darcy was waiting impatiently for his cousin to finish his first cup of coffee to provide an explanation for his unexpected arrival.

At last Richard Fitzwilliam put down his cup.

Darcy said with exasperation, 'I waited long enough. Last night I respected that you were too tired to speak coherently. Now you have had your coffee, I would like to know why you are here. Not that I am unhappy to see you, but I thought you were still in Spain.'

'Bennings and I returned to London two days ago. Yesterday morning your letters caught up with me. When you mentioned Wickham, I had to come. That scoundrel has been running around lose for much too
~~~

long.' He grinned maliciously. 'Since Wickham appears to be sniffing around a lady whom you are interested in, I thought this time you would let me kill him. Apart from that, I simply must meet the woman who has dragged you out of your hermitage.'

The Colonel noticed the speculative look Darcy directed at the Corporal. 'Before you ask, Bennings is my batman and at the last engagement in Spain, he deliberately took a wound aimed at me. He needs to rest and recuperate, somewhere with good food, clean sheets and pleasant company.'

Bennings murmured, 'it is not as bad as all that.'

Fitzwilliam gave him a quelling look. 'It would be if I had received that kind of a wound.'

The Corporal shrugged with a satisfied smile. 'I am not complaining. The company here is certainly… charming.'

'Apart from my cousin, you have not met anybody yet. And Darcy usually does not go out of his way to be charming.'

'He let me have his bed last night.' Bennings' smile deepened. 'And you are wrong about not meeting anyone else. I think I met our hostess this morning.'

Darcy, who knew Caroline's habit of sleeping late, was surprised into asking, 'where did you meet Miss Bingley?'

'In your bed.'

Bennings chuckled at the stunned look on the cousins' faces.

'In my bed?' Darcy gasped.

'In Darcy's bed?' came a shocked voice from behind Bennings. Bingley had just entered the dining room and her the last part of the conversation.

Darcy introduced Bennings to their host, and explained. 'They arrived while I was having a nightcap after you had gone to bed last night.'

'We had some problems on the road, otherwise we would have been here in time for dinner. Bennings was in bad shape when we arrived, so Darce offered him the use of his bed, since it was the only guestroom which was made up and there was already a fire going in the room. Mrs Hill was not expecting an extra guest, and because Darce did not want to put her to the trouble of making up more than one room in the middle of the night, he bunked with me.'

The Corporal was embarrassed when he heard the last part of the explanation. 'I am sorry, Sir. If I had realised that you would have to share a room with the Colonel, I would never have accepted your generous offer.'

Darcy shrugged, trying to deflect the praise. 'You needed to sleep, and it is no hardship to spend time with my favourite cousin. Except of course that he snores...'

Bingley was less concerned by the fact that he had an unexpected houseguest than the comment about his sister. 'Are you saying that you spent the night with my sister?'

'I do not know about the night, but she was in bed with me when I woke up this morning. Seems she was going to try for a spot of compromise. I can tell you she was not best pleased to find me in Mr Darcy's stead.'

'She would have been even less pleased if I had been in my own bed last night,' muttered Darcy.

Bingley was disturbed, but was hoping there was a mistake in the identity of the woman. 'Are you certain that it was my sister, not a maid who had come to keep you company?'

'She introduced herself as Miss Bingley, when I suggested the same thing as you did just now. I suppose you could ask the footman who saw her...'

Bingley's shoulders slumped. 'That will not be necessary.' He looked speculatively at the Corporal. 'Would you do the gentlemanly thing and marry her? She has a dowry of twenty thousand pounds...'

'Luckily, I am not a gentleman. I am sorry, Mr Bingley, but while your sister is a good-looking woman, her vicious tongue and poor manners are well known, and I have no desire to be saddled with her.'

Bingley smiled sadly. 'I know how you feel, I too would like to be shot of her, but unfortunately she is family and still my responsibility.' He turned to Darcy. 'I suppose you are grateful that your considerate nature spared you from Caroline.'

Darcy looked uncomfortable, but Colonel Fitzwilliam answered for him. 'Bingley, from what I hear, Darcy's reputation would suffer more if he married your sister, than if she had been found in his bed this morning by half the Ton.'

Darcy agreed with the others. 'I am sorry, Bingley, but I agree with the Corporal. No man with sense wants a vicious gossip for a wife unless he is desperate for money. I think you had better cut her lose before she embarrasses you again, because I do not believe you can find her a husband, and be rid of her in that way.'

Their host was silent for a minute before he replied with a sigh, 'I must think on what to do...'

<div style="text-align:center">~~~oo0Ooo~~~</div>

Miss Bingley, having regained her composure after returning to her room, decided to pretend that the incident did not happen. After all, even if that man did mention her indiscretion, she was convinced that no one would give credence to such a story.

She dressed and went down to break her fast. She arrived at the partially open dining room door just in time to hear her brother ask, 'Are you certain that it was my sister, not a maid who had come to keep you company?' She allowed herself a small smirk. It was as she expected. Her brother did not believe that she could behave in such a way.

Miss Bingley took a moment to gather her dignity about herself to refute the man's claim, when she heard her brother offer her as a wife to that man. The shock rooted her to the spot. Charles was asking this nobody to marry her and even mentioned her dowry as an incentive?

How dare he. She was about to storm into the room and blast her brother for his presumption, when Corporal Bennings declined the offer.

Now Caroline did not know whether to be relieved or offended. She certainly had no wish to marry that man, but to be turned down in such a manner was humiliating. Worse was to come, when her brother agreed with the man.

The Colonel's and Darcy's comments put the final nail into her self-esteem. She turned and rushed back to her room, where she broke into tears.

Caroline Bingley at last believed that she would never be Mrs Darcy, Mistress of Pemberley.

~~~oo0Ooo~~~
~~~

23 Advanced Education

Miss Bingley claimed to have a dreadful headache and remained in her room all day. Mrs Hurst was suffering from morning sickness, and her husband hovered to lend any assistance he could.

Bennings, having been told to make himself comfortable, settled into the library with a book to keep him company by the fire. He was happy to comply with the suggestion since the weather still looked uncertain.

Which left the three gentlemen on their own to please themselves. It pleased them to visit their neighbours at Brook Hall.

Mr Kirby admitted them and left them in the library, while he informed the ladies of the visitors.

They had only waited for a minute or two when they suddenly heard metal scraping on metal. Darcy and Bingley did not pay much attention to the sound, but Colonel Fitzwilliam was all too familiar with it.

'There is a fight going on,' he exclaimed as he rushed out of the room. He stopped for a moment to determine the direction of the sound, before running towards the back of the house, followed by Darcy and Bingley.

When they arrived at the glass panelled doors to the ballroom, the Colonel could see what appeared to be a young, pockmarked man viciously attacking a young lady. To his amazement the young lady was also wielding a sabre and giving a good account of herself. Despite being several inches shorter than her attacker, she was holding her own.

He was drawing his own sabre and was opening the door, when Darcy arrived.

The young woman noticed their entrance, and instead of distracting her attacker to give the Colonel a chance to subdue him, she shouted, 'stop,' and whirled to face him.

At the same time the attacker also turned to face the men, and stepped in front of the young lady in a protective attitude.

The sudden change in position stopped the Colonel, and with a chagrined look he stopped and partly lowered his weapon.

Darcy found his voice, 'Miss Elizabeth, are you well?'

The young woman answered with a bright smile, 'I am perfectly well, Mr Darcy. Thank you for asking. I presume the Colonel is a friend of yours?'

Colonel Fitzwilliam asked cautiously, 'I presume this was a training bout?'

'Indeed, it was.' Elizabeth place a gentle restraining hand on Miss Martin's sword arm. 'I believe the danger is over, Miss Martin.'

Whereupon Miss Martin sheathed her own sword, and accepted the sabre from Elizabeth.

The Colonel followed suit and sheathed his weapon. He turned to Darcy, 'Cousin, would you do me the honour of introducing me to this remarkable lady?'

Darcy introduced his cousin, and Elizabeth reciprocated by introducing Julia Martin. 'Mr Darcy, Colonel Fitzwilliam, Mr Bingley,' Bingley had arrived behind his friends, 'I would like to introduce to you our arms-mistress and my good friend, Miss Martin.'

Darcy and Bingley acknowledged the introduction politely. The Colonel asked, 'Miss Julia Martin? It must be. I do not believe there could be two Miss Martin's with such formidable skills. I have served with your cousin.'

'Yes, Colonel Fitzwilliam, Cousin Peter has mentioned you on a number of occasions. He speaks very highly of your abilities.'

'I must admit, when Sergeant Martin spoke about your abilities, I thought he was exaggerating. I see I was wrong.'

'Miss Elizabeth, I hope you do not think me patronising when I say that I have rarely seen such an excellent bout. Although I am surprised to see you using a sabre, I would have thought foil would be easier on someone with your stature.'

'If you had come on a different day, it might have been foil or epee.' Elizabeth smirked.

'You are a lady with many talents and exceptionally skilled. Most men whom I know would be hesitant to spar without at least some protection, even when using blunted practice blades,' Richard offered respectfully.

'What makes you think our blades were blunted?'

'You were using live blades?' exclaimed Darcy in horror.

As Elizabeth shrugged, Colonel Fitzwilliam held out his hand to Miss Martin, who understood the gesture and with a smirk handed him Elizabeth's weapon, hilt first.

He tested the edge carefully, and handed the sabre back to Miss Martin. 'Live blades,' he confirmed.

Darcy swallowed convulsively. 'I think I need a drink.'

'Shall we go to the library and I will ring for tea,' offered Elizabeth politely. After taking another look at Darcy, she suggested, 'or maybe something stronger.'

'Yes, please,' croaked Darcy and offered his arm to Elizabeth. Bingley followed them out of the room.

Miss Martin stored the weapons and was surprised to find Colonel Fitzwilliam waiting for her. He offered her his arm and asked, 'shall we join the others?'

Flattered by the courtesy, Julia took his arm and accompanied him to the library.

~~~ooO0Ooo~~~

'I suppose it all started when I was eight years old and wanted to be a pirate,' explained Elizabeth. They were seated in the library. Tea had been served and the gentleman had been provided with snifters of brandy.

Darcy was particularly grateful for the burning sensation, which took away the chill he had felt when he thought Elizabeth to be in danger.

'A pirate, eh,' chuckled the Colonel. 'Why not a law-abiding soldier?'
~~~

'Because the army does not allow women in its ranks, which I believe is very short-sighted of them. At least outlaws are not bound by stuffy rules and prejudices.'

Richard laughed. 'You have a point. Although I have never before seen a lady fight like I witnessed earlier, I know a number of women who are excellent strategists, and would make great generals. My own mother included. Although if you ever mention that I said so, I will of course deny it.'

'I suppose I used to envy boys who were not only allowed, but encouraged to do and learn exciting things. My father had allowed me to read whatever I wanted to, and he had started to teach me Greek so that I could read his favourite book, The Iliad, in the original.'

'Mrs Bennet tolerated my reading, since her husband allowed it, but when I wanted to do the kind of physical things like all the boys in the neighbourhood, she objected strenuously.'

Elizabeth sighed. 'I suppose Mrs Bennet felt like a mother hen who was trying to raise a duckling.'

'I think it was more like a mother hen trying to raise a wildcat,' Mrs Mortimer laughed from the doorway.

The gentlemen rose at her entrance, and offered greetings. Darcy introduced his cousin, who looked at the lady searchingly. 'I am sorry to be staring, but you look familiar. I have the feeling we have met somewhere before, but I cannot place the occasion.'

Darcy smirked at his cousin. 'Try casting your mind back twenty years, at Matlock... and it involved a tree...'

'That was you? You must allow me to tell you that I greatly admired you. It was then that I determined that I would only marry a woman who could climb a tree. I considered that the pinnacle of a lady's accomplishments.' He grinned. 'And I still do.'

'Careful, Colonel Fitzwilliam, I have five daughters and each and every one of them knows how to climb a tree.'

'All of them?'

'Every single one.'

'Darcy, you should have told me about these wonders earlier. I would have come weeks ago if I had but known.'

'I did not know myself until just now. With the exception of our hostess of course.'

By then the other sisters had been informed of the visitors, and were now filing into the library.

Mrs Mortimer performed the introductions and everyone took a seat.

'Miss Elizabeth was telling us how it came about that she acquired such great skill at fencing.'

'I am afraid that was my fault. As Elizabeth said, Mrs Bennet was unhappy to have three daughters whom she did not understand. And those same three daughters were unhappy about not being understood. So, I adopted them. Since Elizabeth wanted to learn to fence, I taught her the basics. When she improved, I hired other teachers for her.'

'Eight years ago, Mrs Mortimer hired me to teach the girls how to take care of themselves,' Miss Martin added.

'What do you mean by taking care of themselves?'

'It is highly unlikely that any one man will ever be able to force his attentions on any of these ladies. If he tries, he will be... in severe pain, if he survives.'

'We also know how to shoot,' Lydia declared proudly.

'You would shoot someone?' Bingley asked, horrified.

'I hope I never have to find out,' Lydia answered seriously.

Colonel Fitzwilliam looked around the room at all these pleasant and smiling young women, and hoped he would be around to witness if any man foolish enough to tangle with these ladies received his comeuppance.

<p style="text-align:center">~~~ooo0Ooo~~~</p>

'Charles, I would like to speak to you,' Caroline Bingley told her brother when he returned from Brook Hall.

Bingley sighed. He had had a lovely, although confusing, morning with the Mortimer ladies. He really did not want to have his mood spoiled by an argument with his sister, but seeing the determined look, he decided to get the confrontation over with.

'Very well, come to the study with me,' he agreed tiredly.

They had barely sat down when Miss Bingley demanded, 'Charles, I would like you to release my dowry to me.'

This request was the last thing Bingley had expected. Therefore, he just asked, 'why?'

'Because I have realised that I will never find a husband in this country. The men I am interested in have no interest in me, and any man who is interested in marrying me is only interested in my dowry. And he is usually still a tradesman, who is looked down upon by members of the first circles.'

She shrugged. 'As you heard the other day, I made myself the laughing stock of the Ton, and do not try to deny it,' she said when her brother looked like he wanted to object. 'Our father meant well when he sent me to that seminary. But I became too ambitious and I reached too high. It has been brought home to me that I need to find a different level of society.'

'But I will not marry a tradesman in this country. I am tired of being looked down on by the Ton. I want to be respected for myself. I want to go where my background is irrelevant. I want to go to the new world to make a new life for myself. That is why I need you to release my dowry to me.'

Bingley had listened in growing amazement. This was a side to his sister he had not seen before. But as she continued speaking with such passion, he realised that Caroline had a point. At least from her perspective.

'I shall miss you,' he said without thinking.

Miss Bingley looked startled and lost some of her tension. 'I shall miss you too. But you do understand why I have to leave and you will release my dowry?'

'Yes, to both if that is what you truly want.'

'It is what I need.'

'Very well. When would you like to leave?'

'The sooner the better. I would like to leave first thing tomorrow. Louisa can be your hostess if you wish to stay.'

When Bingley looked uncomfortable, she said, 'and, Charles… I hope you and Miss Mortimer will be very happy.'

'Thank you, Caroline. I will give you letters for our solicitor and for the bank to take with you.'

'Thank you, Charles.' Caroline rose, and after giving her brother a kiss on the cheek, went to her room to see to her packing.

Her brother remained in his study, contemplating the changes in his sister. After this morning's discussions about her behaviour and reputation, he had determined to confront her and demand that she behave with more decorum and consideration. Caroline's choice to leave the country had taken the wind out of his sails.

Now he was beset by conflicting emotions. Relief, at not having to the force the issue, and deflation that his strong stance had been rendered unnecessary. He regretted that he had not learnt his lesson earlier.

Miss Bingley managed to leave just before the weather closed in for several days of rain.

<div align="center">~~~ooO0Ooo~~~</div>

24 Final Exams

The weather cleared up at last. Elizabeth was eager to get out of the house. As much as she loved her family, being cooped up with them for several days without a chance to get outdoors, strained her limited patience.

She dressed with care to ensure she would be both comfortable and safe in all situations. She added her warm pelisse and was ready for her ramble.

On her way out, she encountered Jane and Kitty who were also determined to make use of the weather by going for a stroll.

'Where are you planning on going,' Elizabeth enquired of Jane.

'We thought we would go as far as the foot of Oakham Mount.'

Elizabeth beamed at the other girls. 'Shall we meet there when I return from the top and we can walk home together?'

'That sounds like a splendid idea.'

'I shall see you there in about an hour. Do you have everything you need?' Elizabeth looked pointedly at Jane's pelisse which matched her own.

'Yes, I am prepared for anything. Do not worry so. You are getting to be as bad as Mother,' Jane chided.

'Mayhap we should call you Mother Hen,' laughed Kitty.

'Maybe you should,' laughed Elizabeth as she set off at a brisk walk, leaving the other two girls to proceed at a slower pace.

She almost ran all the way to Oakham Mount. When she reached the top only half an hour later, she was breathing heavily. It had been good to be able to stretch her legs without worrying if the others could keep up with her.

She dropped onto her favourite rock and stretched her legs out in front of her.

Elizabeth reflected that it was good that few people came to this spot. They might have been scandalised if they had seen the breeches and Hessians she had concealed under her pelisse.

While dresses and skirts were pretty and feminine, but when she wanted to be able to move unencumbered, Elizabeth still wore her breeches on occasions. It felt good to be able to move freely.

She spent some time enjoying the view while musing on the reasons for different modes of dress for men and women.

She amused herself imagining several men of her acquaintance wearing a dress. When she pictured Sir William Lucas in Miss Bingley's favourite outfit, she broke into a fit of giggles. She decided that the colour and the feathers would not suit the gentleman's complexion.

The laughter startled her out of her reflections, and Elizabeth realised that it was time she returned to the foot of the hill to meet her sisters.

She was almost at the meeting place, when she thought it would be fun to surprise the girls by sneaking up on them from a direction they did not expect.

She left the path and quietly approached the intersection of paths which led off to Brook Hall, Netherfield and Longbourn, when she heard a female shriek.

A few moments later, she heard Jane's voice demanding, 'let her go.'

~~~ooO0Ooo~~~

Bingley, Darcy and Fitzwilliam also took the opportunity of the improved weather to go for a ride before calling at Brook Hall.

The had checked out the lower fields to ensure that there was no flooding after all the rain, and found that the area was draining quite well. By the time they finished the inspection, it was late enough that they could call on the ladies.

They had just passed Oakham Mount when they heard a shot.
~~~

Bingley looked puzzled, 'I have not heard that anyone would be out hunting today.'

Fitzwilliam informed him, 'that was no rifle. That shot was fired from a pistol.' He looked around. 'I think it came from that direction.'

He kicked his horse into a canter. Darcy and Bingley caught up with him when Bingley asked, 'what is the rush?'

'No one hunts with a pistol.'

They burst through the edge of trees at the intersection of paths when they saw one soldier in a militia uniform crumpled on the ground, with a gore spattered Kitty on her knees beside him, hiding her face in her hands, and sobbing hysterically.

Two other soldiers were rushing towards Miss Jane Mortimer who was standing her ground holding two pistols trained at the men.

The next moment Miss Elizabeth stepped out from behind a tree and shouted, 'you should know that both her pistols are still loaded,' as she waved one pistol in the air while pointing the other at the men.

George Wickham shouted back, 'I do not think your sister will shoot and you have only one shot left.'

'Yes, but I will shoot you first,' replied Elizabeth coolly. 'And my sister might surprise your friend by pulling the trigger after all. I admit, her aim is not as good as mine and instead of killing him, she might just geld him.'

'I recommend gelding both of them,' called Colonel Fitzwilliam. He and his friends had slowed down when they saw the situation was mostly under control, and he had no wish to startle any of the participants into precipitate action.

Wickham whirled at the sound of his voice. 'Fitzwilliam,' he gasped, the colour draining from his face.

'One and the same,' drawled the Colonel in a nonchalant manner. Inside he was furious that his sabre was useless at this distance, and if he fired his pistol while mounted, he risked hitting one of the ladies who were beyond Wickham.

'It looks like your charm did not work on these ladies. What happened? Were you again refusing to take no for an answer?'

Fitzwilliam approached slowly. Darcy and Bingley allowed him to lead.

'Careful, Fitzwilliam. I do not think that Darcy would like it if it got out that the woman, whom he is interested in, is a slut,' Wickham blustered. Threatening a lady's reputation had always been an effective means to escape punishment.

Tinkling laughter behind Wickham startled him. In his anxiety over the Colonel, he had forgotten that the lady he just insulted was behind him… with a loaded gun… and she had just killed Lieutenant Cooper.

Darcy had been terrified for the sisters when they arrived. Wickham's words made him furious. He was considering attacking the man barehanded, when the laughter stopped him.

'Lieutenant Wickham, you forget, there is a very simple way to stop a rumour from being spread.' Elizabeth waited for Wickham to respond. When he simply looked puzzled, she added, 'kill it at the source.'

Fitzwilliam bowed to Elizabeth in deepest respect. He grinned at Wickham. 'Or kill the source. Dead men tell no tales…'

For the first time in his life Wickham was truly frightened. While Fitzwilliam got angry and kept threatening him, Darcy had always stopped his cousin from applying a permanent solution. But this gently bred young lady was calmly telling him that she was prepared to kill him. And considering she had already shot Cooper…

He looked around trying to find an escape, when he spotted the youngest sister still kneeling on the ground, only three steps away.

Before anyone could stop him, he was in motion, thinking to use Kitty as a hostage. When he bent down to grab her arm while drawing a knife, his intentions were clear to her sisters.

For Elizabeth time slowed down. All her focus was on the man who was threatening her most vulnerable sister's life. She took careful aim.

Two shots rang out simultaneously. Wickham had but a moment to realise that he had misjudged the ladies, before he collapsed next to his dead friend, to be examined by his final judge.

Denny, thinking that all the attention was off him, started to back into the surrounding trees, when he heard a peremptory command to stop.

'I still have one shot,' declared a grim-faced Jane.

At that point Denny capitulated, mentally cursing Wickham for coming up with this disastrous idea.

~~~ooO0oo~~~

As soon as Denny was restrained by Colonel Fitzwilliam, the sisters rushed to Kitty, embracing her and trying to comfort the sobbing girl.

Elizabeth's mind was in a whirl. She had to get Kitty home as quickly as possible. 'Can you stand?' she asked.

Kitty nodded and struggled to her feet with the assistance of her sisters.

'Take my horse,' offered Fitzwilliam. 'I will stay here and look after things. Send a cart to take them back to the camp.'

The Colonel shortened the stirrups and led his horse to Elizabeth. 'I presume you know how to ride astride.'

Lizzy gave him a lopsided grin. 'I am even dressed for it,' she said as she mounted.

'Let me assist you,' Fitzwilliam offered to Kitty. But the girl flinched in panic at the sight of the red uniform.

'I will do it,' declared Bingley, who had been almost forgotten by the others. 'If you will allow me, Miss Catherine...' he said gently to the trembling girl.

The courtesy and the gentle tone helped to reassure Kitty, and she whispered, 'thank you.'

Bingley gently lifted her and placed her before Elizabeth, who held her sister to herself with one arm, while she took hold of the reins with the other hand.

Bingley remounted his own horse, 'I will escort you if I may.'
~~~

Darcy had hoped to escort the ladies himself, but he realised that Bingley's non-threatening presence would be better for the traumatised sister. Instead he offered the reins of Hermes to Miss Mortimer.

'I suspect you would like to accompany your sisters.'

He was rewarded with a brilliant smile. 'Thank you, Mr Darcy. You are most kind.'

Once Jane was in the saddle, it did not take long to return to Brook Hall. As soon as they were out of sight of the clearing, Kitty started to relax a little in the embrace of her sister.

By the time they arrived at the house, Kitty had regained her composure enough to walk to her room with her sisters in attendance.

On their way to Kitty's room, Elizabeth called for a bath to be prepared and hot sweet tea to be delivered.

Bingley trailed behind and reported what he knew about the occurrence to a concerned Mrs Mortimer.

<p style="text-align:center">~~~oo0Ooo~~~</p>

25 Repercussions

Darcy and Fitzwilliam waited at the cross-roads. The Colonel had ensured that Denny could not get free, before drawing his cousin away for a private discussion.

He looked searchingly at Darcy. 'How do you feel about what you just witnessed.'

Darcy shrugged. 'Ambivalent, I suppose. Wickham used to be my friend, but I despised the man he had become. While I am sorry it has come to this, part of me is glad that he is dead and cannot hurt anyone again. Especially Georgiana and Elizabeth.'

'That is not what I meant, Cousin.' Fitzwilliam was surprised that Darcy had solely focused on the dead man, but not how he had come to his unlamented death.

When Darcy looked at him with incomprehension, he said, 'you just watched the lady, with whom you are enamoured, kill a man. Has that not even registered?'

'She just did what she had to do to protect her sister.'

'You do not have a problem with a woman who is prepared to kill?'

'Richard, she was defending family,' replied Darcy hotly. 'You may get on your high horse and call her unwomanly for that, but she has only risen in my estimation.'

'What makes you think I think badly of the lady? I have the greatest respect for both ladies. In fact, I am all admiration for the way they dealt with the situation. You seem to forget I am a soldier. I have seen death before. Although I am surprised at your reaction. I did not think you had it in you.'

Darcy was mollified at his cousin's words. 'I suppose you expected me to react like most men of our acquaintance. They want their women to be meek and mild and submissive. To be agreeable and never question their judgement.'

Richard chuckled. 'Cousin, it seems that we are more alike than I thought. I like a woman with fire and spirit, who will stand up to me when she thinks that I am in the wrong. I despise all those fawning, spineless debutants and heiresses which my mother insists on introducing to me.'

Darcy smiled fondly. 'That is what I like about Miss Elizabeth. While she is kind and considerate, she will not acquiesce to something she believes is wrong.'

He shook his head in wonderment. 'The surprise today was Miss Mortimer. She is always quiet and gentle and serene. I did not think she had it in her to be so fierce.' While Darcy had not forgotten about Lord Neville's ankle, there was a big difference between kicking a man in the ankle or shooting him.

Richard sighed. 'It is a pity that Bingley is enamoured with her...'

Darcy gave Richard a questioning look when he stopped.

The Colonel shrugged. 'When I first saw her, being polite and gentle and controlled, I thought that she and Bingley would suit admirably. While she is an handsome woman, her demeanour did not inspire much respect in me. Now though...'

'Now that you saw her shoot a man, you have changed your mind about her. You are now interested.'

'It is irrelevant, I do not poach.'

Darcy smirked. 'You were apparently too busy watching the action. You did not notice the look of horror on Bingley's face. He is a gentle soul, and I doubt he will be able to look at Miss Mortimer and not remember her actions.'

'You think...' Richard smiled hopefully.

'Yes, I think he is having second thoughts.'

<p style="text-align:center">~~~ooo0ooo~~~</p>

Charles Bingley was having not only second, but also third and fourth thoughts about the angel with whom he was in love. Or at least, he had thought he was in love with her.

Now he was not so certain.

Miss Mortimer had seemed sweet and gentle and demure. Not the cold, calculating and fierce woman he had seen less than an hour ago.

If she had held a flaming sword rather than a pistol, he would not have been surprised. She had been the very picture of an avenging angel.

While intellectually he could understand that she had been defending her sister, his heart and his gut did not agree.

How could he live with a woman who could do such a horrendous thing?

It shamed him to admit that he could not have done what she did. He could not have harmed a man even in defence of his family. He might have been able to land a blow, but to kill? His stomach churned even as he contemplated such a hypothetical action.

He hoped that Miss Kitty would soon recover. She had been properly horrified and distraught at the events that had occurred in her defence.

He had been gratified that, when she had flinched from the sight of Colonel Fitzwilliam's uniform, she had accepted his own help to lift her onto the horse.

But it was not enough. On the ride back to the house, Bingley had wanted to be the one to hold her and comfort her. He had wanted to be the one to whom she turned for comfort.

He suddenly realised what he was thinking. Could he truly be so inconstant as to change his affections from one sister to another in an instant?

On further consideration, Bingley had to admit to himself that he was falling in and out of love on a regular basis. He had thought that his feelings for Miss Mortimer were different. Yet here he was again changing his affections.

What was he to do?

Considering that Miss Catherine had just had a major shock, she would probably not be interested in any man for some time. That would give him the time he needed to discover the nature and strength of his own feelings.

Yes, he would wait and see what might happen.

~~~oo0Ooo~~~

Soon a cart arrived with their horses tied to the back. 'Good, someone was thinking,' the Colonel approved.

'Do you want me to come with you to see Colonel Forster?' enquired Darcy.

'No, I can deal with him easily on my own. You go and see to your lady. I suspect she worries about your reaction. You need to reassure her.'

Darcy waited while the bodies were loaded onto the cart and covered with a blanket. Then Denny was lifted in, and the cart, followed by the Colonel took off for the camp.

With a wave at his cousin, Darcy turned Hermes towards Brook Hall.

~~~oo0Ooo~~~

Darcy arrived at the house and was greeted by Mr Kirby. 'Mrs Mortimer sends her apologies, Sir. The house is all at sixes and sevens at the moment. I am to tell you that Mr Bingley is in the parlour.'

'What about Miss Elizabeth?'

'She is in the library.'

'Would it be too much to ask if I could see her?'

Mr Kirby gave him a thoughtful look, before he nodded. 'I think that would be helpful. I will leave the door open and a footman on call. Please follow me.'

Mr Kirby announced Mr Darcy, who entered the library to find Elizabeth curled up on a sofa in front of the fire. She had changed into an old comfortable dress and she was hugging a shawl tightly about her.

Elizabeth looked up at him with haunted eyes. 'Have you come to say goodbye?' she asked.

Darcy moved to sit beside her on the sofa. 'No, Miss Elizabeth. I have come to see how you are and to tell you how impressed I was with your marksmanship.' He smiled at her astonished expression.

When she just stared at him, he asked, 'how do you fare? Please tell me honestly.'

'After we settled Kitty, I lost my breakfast. So did Jane. Mother is with Kitty. Mary and Lydia are busy telling Jane how wonderful she is. They were telling me the same thing, but I needed some peace and quiet to come to terms with what I did.'

She looked at her fingers which worried the fringe of her shawl. Darcy waited patiently for her to gather her thoughts and speak again.

'Today I killed two men. The bible says "thou shalt not kill". Part of me feels guilty for what I have done, but another part of me rejoices that because of my actions, my sister is safe. Bruised and upset, but safe.'

She suddenly looked up and met Darcy's eyes. 'Is it wrong of me to feel proud that I killed those men?'

'Those men attacked your sister. Yes, I think you should be proud that you saved her. If Wickham and his friends had not attacked, they would be alive. It is their own fault that they are dead. If you had not shot them, they would have harmed your sister and gone on to harm other women.'

Darcy realised that Elizabeth had not thought of that aspect. 'You should be proud for saving not only your sister, but several, or possibly several dozen other women, who would have suffered injury and dishonour at their hands. You know that society is cruel. It blames a woman for being the victim. They even go so far as to extend that dishonour to the rest of the family.'

Darcy gently disentangled one of Elizabeth's hands from the shawl and raised it to his lips. 'Today you saved not only Miss Catherine, but all your sisters and yourself. I have the greatest admiration for you.'

Tears were streaming down Elizabeth's cheek as she gave a tremulous smile. 'I was worried that my actions had driven you away. Only a rare man would not be horrified at what I have done.'

'Miss Elizabeth, the only thing to drive me away is for you to say you do not wish to see me again. Otherwise nothing short of death will keep me away.'

He heard her breath hitch and saw that she looked uncertainly. 'Shall we speak of that in a few days, when you have fully regained your composure? I would very much like to do so.'

'In a few days. Yes, please.'

'What I meant to say before I was diverted, I grew up on an estate. Sometimes it is necessary to kill a rabid dog or any other animal that has become a danger to people,' explained Darcy.

'A man is not an animal.'

'That makes it worse. He should know better than to harm others.'

Elizabeth thought about his words. They felt right. Yes, killing for no good reason was wrong. Yet the defence of family was a good reason. She nodded to herself. Yes, she could live with that. She might have nightmares for a time, but she could live with those as well.

Her smile became a little lighter. 'Thank you, Mr Darcy. You have greatly relieved my mind.'

~~~oo0Ooo~~~

Meanwhile Kitty had had a bath and copious amounts of sweet tea. Now that she was clean again and her gory clothes had been removed from her sight, she started to calm down and take notice of her surroundings.

She was in her room, wearing a clean shift and a clean robe, and was being held by Mrs Mortimer.

When she raised her head, Mrs Mortimer smiled at her and said, 'I think you are starting to feel better.'

'I do. What happened? I remember rushing ahead when I saw some flowers that were a perfect composition for me to paint, while Jane adjusted a boot-lace. But then Lieutenant Cooper stepped out from the trees, grabbing me and saying he would...' Kitty stopped. The words that the man had used were not something she wanted to repeat.
~~~

'You do not have to tell me now, Kitty. You have had a shock. Lizzy and Jane brought you home after they took care of the situation. But I have sent for Sir William Lucas, and you will have to make a statement to him. Do you think you can do that?'

'Will you be with me?'

'Of course, I will. And anybody else you want to be there.'

'Can I rest a little longer?'

'Yes, you can rest as long as you need. Will you be well enough if I send Mrs Taylor to you. I need to go and see Jane.'

'Is something wrong with Jane? Did those men hurt her?'

'No, they did not hurt her, but she shot one of them and is rather upset at the moment.'

'Did she shoot Lieutenant Cooper?' Kitty flinched as she remembered the shot and being splattered with...

'No, Lizzy did. Jane severely wounded Lieutenant Wickham.'

'Why did she shoot him? I vaguely remember him arguing with someone, but he was not hurting me.'

Mrs Mortimer was reluctant to speak about the information imparted by Lizzy and Jane. Kitty noticed her hesitation, and demanded, 'tell me. It cannot be worse than what I have suffered.'

'Lieutenant Wickham was threatening to kill you...'

'Is that why Jane shot him?'

'Yes, she did. Jane's shot wounded him severely, but Lizzy also fired and her shot killed him. He cannot threaten you again.'

'Jane and Lizzy must feel horrible at the moment. You must go to them. I will be fine...' encouraged Kitty. 'Please tell Jane and Lizzy that I am grateful...'

Mrs Mortimer tightened her hug for a moment. 'I know you will be fine again soon. And so, will your sisters.' At least Mrs Mortimer hoped they would be.

~~~ooo0ooo~~~
~~~

26 Confrontation

Mrs Mortimer walked into pandemonium when she entered Jane's room. Mary and Lydia, as well as Miss Julia Martin were congratulating Jane on being brave, while Jane argued that she was a horrible person.

Mrs Mortimer listened for a moment before she firmly said, 'enough.'

Although she had not raised her voice, the sisters and Miss Martin fell silent.

'You should know that Kitty is starting to recover and she asked me to convey her thanks to you and Lizzy.'

Jane swallowed convulsively. 'I killed a man…'

'You wounded him. Lizzy killed him. Keep in mind that he was threatening to kill your sister. Personally, I prefer Lieutenant Wickham to be dead than Kitty. Especially as he would have been free to rape other women.' Mrs Mortimer deliberately did not use euphemisms. She needed to shock Jane out of her funk. 'And I suspect that trio was responsible for Emily Evans.'

It seemed to work. Jane lost the frantic look which Mrs Mortimer suspected was the outward sign of her mental flagellation. She went to Jane and drew her into an embrace. 'I want to add my thanks for your actions in keeping Kitty safe.'

The hug and the words released the floodgates of Jane's emotions. She clung to her guardian and sobbed out her anxiety, guilt and fear.

Jane was calming down when Mrs Kirby quietly entered the room. 'I am sorry to interrupt, but Sir William Lucas has arrived as you requested. He is waiting in the drawing-room.'

'Please tell him that I will be with him presently. Could you also find Lizzy and ask her to join Sir William?'

Jane was pulling herself together and wiping her face with a handkerchief Mary handed her. 'I will be fine shortly. Please, there is no need to wait for me,' she said with a hint of a smile.

'I think you had better join us as well when you are up to it…'

Jane nodded. 'I will be there as soon as I have freshened up.'

~~~ooO0oo~~~

Sir William Lucas was worriedly pacing in the drawing room when Mrs Mortimer entered. 'Are you well, dear lady? Your footman said there had been an incident at Brook Hall, and that someone was dead, but he had no details.'

'I am well, Sir William. Thank you for coming. I do not yet know the full story myself, but Jane, Elizabeth and Kitty were attacked by three officers of the militia, and as I understand it, Lizzy accounted for two of them. Mr Bingley, Mr Darcy and Colonel Fitzwilliam came onto the scene and captured the third man. Mr Bingley escorted the girls home and Colonel Fitzwilliam was going to return the man and the bodies to the camp.'

'What a shocking occurrence,' exclaimed Sir William. 'I have recently been made aware that some of the officers were not acting like gentlemen ought, but attacking your daughters on your property…'

'They were led by Lieutenant Wickham, a scoundrel with a history of racking up debts, gambling and womanising,' Mr Darcy said as he entered the room with Elizabeth on his arm, and had heard the comment.

'Lieutenant Wickham? That charming young man? Surely not,' protested Sir William. 'Although, come to think of it, my wife said something about him the other day.' He harrumphed, 'I admit, perhaps I was not paying as much attention as I should…'

'Thanks to intelligence provided by Mr Darcy, we have been warning mothers of daughters as well as shopkeepers about his habits.'

'I am afraid today's attack may have been aimed at me. He would have blamed me for cutting off his credit and his easy access to young ladies. He would also have been aware that I greatly admire Miss
~~~

Elizabeth. I suspect he was seeking revenge on me, by attacking her and her sisters.'

~~~ooO0Ooo~~~

Jane had joined them and tea had been provided when there was a commotion in the entry. Before the butler had a chance to announce them, Colonel Forster, flanked by Captains Carter and Tetlow burst into the room. Colonel Fitzwilliam followed a moment later, after a quick word to Mr Kirby.

Forster looked around the room and declared, 'Mr Darcy, I arrest you for the wilful murder of Lieutenant Wickham.'

'Colonel Forster, you labour under a misapprehension. Did not Colonel Fitzwilliam tell you? I shot Lieutenant Wickham when he attacked my sister.' Elizabeth stood up and placed herself between the irate Colonel and his intended victim.

'Yes, he told me that fanciful fabrication. But everyone knows that Mr Darcy was jealous of Wickham and always hounding him. Blackening his name and withholding what was rightfully his.' Forster dismissed her claims. He was obviously not interested in facts when they disagreed with his opinion. 'Now step out of my way so that I can arrest the true culprit.'

Sir William Lucas, who under normal circumstances was an amiable and relaxed man, was getting irate. 'You, Sir, have no jurisdiction over civilians, and since you cannot even keep the men in your command under control, I would not entrust you even with my dog.'

Mrs Mortimer added, 'Considering that three of your men attacked three of my daughters on our own property, I do not believe any woman is safe around your men. I will give instructions for all my neighbours, and especially the women, to go armed until you and your men have quit the area.'

'How dare you claim that my men would behave in such a despicable fashion. It is perfectly clear that Mr Darcy conspired to kill Lieutenant Wickham out of jealousy.'

'What proof have you that Mr Darcy had any reason to be jealous of Lieutenant Wickham? After all, it is Mr Darcy who has the position and
~~~

the wealth. Whereas Lieutenant Wickham has nothing other than a reputation as a wastrel, a gambler and a womaniser.'

'Mr Darcy, out of jealousy, denied Wickham the living to which he was entitled.'

'A living can only be given to a clergyman. Wickham refused to take orders. Instead he asked for, and was given, three thousand pounds in lieu of the living.'

'You have no proof of that claim. Wickham told me that you would say anything to make him look bad.'

'As a matter of fact, I have a contract, signed by Wickham in front of three unimpeachable witnesses that he renounced any claim on the living in lieu of three thousand pounds.'

'I would like to see that contract… if it even exists. I believe you would say anything to shift the blame onto a dead man. Even going so far as to claim that two young ladies shot my officers.' Forster snorted dismissively. 'Ladies have too delicate a constitution to handle weapons. And if by some miracle they learned how to fire a gun, they would miss by a mile.'

'Colonel Forster, would you please step outside for a few minutes,' Elizabeth asked sweetly, desperately controlling her temper at the patronising way this oaf spoke.

'Why?'

'I would like to show you something, Sir,' replied Elizabeth, as she turned and headed for the door.

'I have not finished here yet,' protested Forster.

'It will take but a minute, and it will clarify the situation,' said Elizabeth over her shoulder. As she put on her pelisse, which Mr Kirby handed to her, she requested quietly, 'get Miss Martin to bring my pistols.'

The others followed Elizabeth, which forced Colonel Forster to join them. She led the way around the side of the house to the area set up as a firing range. There were several targets as well as two scarecrows set up at the back.

After checking the wind direction, Elizabeth instructed one of the footmen who had followed the group, 'tie a handkerchief to the head of the right-hand scarecrow, and another to the body of the left-hand one.'

Both Darcy and Fitzwilliam guessed the purpose of the request and each reached into his coat and extracted a pristine square of linen, which they handed to the footman, ensuring that Colonel Forster could see that the kerchiefs were pristine.

'Lydia, you are about the same height as Kitty. Would you please stand slightly to the right of the right-hand scarecrow?' Elizabeth requested of her youngest sister.

The girl grinned with excitement and took her position.

'What are you doing?' asked Forster impatiently.

'Proving a point about the delicate constitution of ladies.'

Julia, who had just arrived, opened the case she was carrying.

To the amazement of Forster and his men, Elizabeth took out the guns and expertly loaded them.

'Watch and learn,' she instructed.

Lizzy raised the first gun and took careful aim at the head of the scarecrow next to Lydia, and pulled the trigger. She immediately raised the second gun in her left hand and fired at the second target.

She handed the pistols back to Julia before she turned to Colonel Forster.

'Colonel, would you please inspect the targets?'

Forster walked up to the scarecrows, followed by the assembled company.

Lydia was inspecting the target next to her. 'Nice shooting, Lizzy,' she said casually.

Forster looked at the handkerchief in disbelief. It sported a bullet hole at the exact height of where a temple would be. 'You could have killed your sister,' he exclaimed in horror.

'Only if I had missed.'

'What kind of a woman are you?

'One who is an excellent shot and one who is prepared to defend her family. Not a delicate fainting damsel in distress.'

'Do you always go armed?'

'Since you and your men have arrived, yes. We trust our neighbours, but we do not trust you or your men. With good reason it turned out.'

Mrs Mortimer, who had been content to let Elizabeth make her point, took control of the situation. 'Now that you have seen what my daughter can do, shall we step back inside where it is warm.'

They returned to the drawing-room to find that Kitty had come to tell her part of the story. She was accompanied by Mrs Taylor, who held her hand.

Forster was still having trouble accepting the guilt of his men, and was determined to prove Darcy the villain. 'Lieutenant Wickham's body had two bullet holes.'

'The body shot was mine,' declared Jane. 'But I am not the markswoman that my sister is. She went for the more difficult target.'

'For which I am eternally grateful.' Kitty joined the conversation.

'I do not believe we have been introduced.'

'I am the intended victim.' Kitty removed the shawl she had wrapped around her neck and shoulders. The livid bruises on her neck and her upper arms stood out against her pale skin, making the Colonel stare in consternation. 'My men did that?'

'Indeed, they did. They also threatened to take their pleasure of me. They seemed to be particularly excited because I was unwilling. The fact that you would allow such behaviour from your men to go unchecked, quite frankly disgusts me.'

'You are quite certain it was Lieutenant Cooper who did this? Not Mr Darcy?

'Colonel, I may not yet be out in society, but I can tell the difference between an officer of the militia and a gentleman. These bruises were inflicted by an officer.'

'Colonel Fitzwilliam is an officer, and due to your distress, you might have mistaken him...'

'Colonel Forster, any more scurrilous accusations like that from you, and I will have to discuss them with you tomorrow at dawn...' growled Richard.

Kitty glared at Forster. 'Colonel Fitzwilliam is a gentleman who would never attack a lady. And when we encountered your officers, I was not distressed. Surprised, yes, to find them on our land... but not distressed. I was perfectly capable of recognising Lieutenants Denny, Cooper and Wickham,' declared Kitty, furious that the odious man would question her perception.

Forster, opposed at every turn by the women in this strange household, was getting frustrated.

'How much is Darcy paying you to lie for him?' he exploded.

Sir William Lucas drew himself up to his full height. 'How dare you slander the ladies,' he thundered at the seething officer. 'You are a disgrace to the uniform you wear. You are living proof why the militia are not considered to be real soldiers. I am only pleased that you are not in the regulars. Such singular stupidity and prejudice as you display would surely lose us the war with France.'

Forster grabbed the hilt of his sword and drew it. 'How dare you,' he shouted.

As he was about to lunge at Sir William, he was momentarily distracted by a sword flying through the air, accompanied by a shouted, 'Lizzy'.

The sword was caught by Elizabeth, who had been standing next to Sir William. A moment later she stepped in front of the gentleman and parried Forster's lunge. Sir William was being dragged away by Kitty, to give Elizabeth room to manoeuvre.

At being thwarted yet again, Forster was lost to all reason. He attacked Elizabeth in a blind fury. Lizzy, although superbly trained, had not the strength to completely withstand such a berserk attack.

She was slowly being driven back.

<p style="text-align:center">~~~ooo0ooo~~~</p>

27 Aftermath

Colonel Forster collapsed at Elizabeth's feet.

When Lizzy looked up from the felled man in surprise, she saw Lydia, proudly brandishing a silver coffee pot, grinning at her.

When she looked around, concerned about the reactions of Forster's men, she saw Captains Carter and Tetlow being firmly restrained by Colonel Fitzwilliam and several footmen.

Fitzwilliam sighed in relief. Since he had been too far away to intercept the Colonel, he had taken a chance, tackling Captain Carter rather than Colonel Forster. But having seen Elizabeth's skill with a blade, he thought it better to keep the other officers off her back, and allow her to take care of Forster. He had not expected Forster to go berserk the way he did. However, another Mortimer sister had stepped up to save the day.

Seeing that everything was secure, Lizzy lowered her weapon. She smiled faintly as Miss Martin approached her with her hand outstretched to relieve her of the sword. 'Sorry to put you on the spot, Miss Elizabeth, but I was too far away to be of help.'

'While I appreciate your confidence in me, I would prefer never having to repeat this experience,' Elizabeth replied in a tired voice. Now that the danger was over, reaction set in, and she started to tremble.

Mr Darcy stepped up to her side and gently supported her to the nearest sofa, where she gratefully collapsed.

<div align="center">~~~ooO0Ooo~~~</div>

The next few minutes were a flurry of activity. Colonel Forster was disarmed and secured. The Captains were also disarmed, but while they assured their captors that they had no intention of causing trouble, they were placed on chairs at the side of the room and remained under guard by the footmen.

Sir William announced that he was placing Colonel Forster under arrest for attempted murder, although he suspected that the man was mentally unstable and belonged in Bedlam.

The sisters crowded around Elizabeth, displacing Darcy, who, although reluctant, gave way graciously.

~~~ooo0Ooo~~~

'Where do you keep the contract which Wickham signed?' asked Colonel Fitzwilliam.

'I keep a copy at Pemberley...' replied Darcy.

'Drat, that is a long ride, but I suppose I must,' grumbled Fitzwilliam.

Darcy smiled. 'Another copy is at our family solicitor's in London.'

'Why did you not say so in the first place?'

'Because you interrupted... again.'

'Well then. You had better give me a note for Thompson, so that I can collect it while I am in London reporting to my superiors and put in a complaint with the militia.'

Captain Carter interjected, 'do you truly have a signed contract that Wickham renounced the Living for a sum of money?'

'I do. I also have receipts for the debts that I bought from the merchants at Lambton and in a few other places. As well as statements from three men, whose daughters Wickham forcibly interfered with. In case you a wondering, those women are dead. Two died in childbirth and the third killed herself because she could not live with the shame.'

'I did not think he needed to force any women. He was all charming and personable. But if this is true, it puts today's events in a different light.'

'And that son of a... mumble... still owes me money,' Tetlow now complained.

'That is why Wickham managed to squander four thousand pounds in just two years. He was a very bad gambler.'

Carter's shoulders slumped. 'I am sorry that Colonel Forster was so unreasonable. I do not understand how Wickham was able to make him
~~~

believe as strongly as he did.' He shook his head. 'I admit, I believed Wickham too, but I am prepared to listen to reason, if someone can offer proof.'

He shrugged his shoulders. 'I must confess I was also sceptical when you told us that Miss Elizabeth killed Wickham and Cooper. I did not think a gently bred lady was capable of doing so. But after her performance with the guns, and when that slip of a girl held of Forster, who is a big man and was in a blind fury, that makes me inclined to believe you.'

Colonel Fitzwilliam suggested, 'did you ever consider that Pemberley is not entailed? Darcy's father could have left it to whomever he wanted. Darcy, not Wickham, has inherited the position, the estate and the money. Wickham gambled away his inheritance and has nothing. Why should Darcy be jealous of Wickham?'

Carter looked at Fitzwilliam. 'I suspect the Colonel did not wish to be told he was wrong by an officer of the regulars. He has an issue with real soldiers, many of whom look down on the militia.'

'I thought as much. But Sir William was correct. He is too stupid and prejudiced to be allowed to command men.'

'Yes, Sir. Do you wish us to remain here while you get proof? I am afraid you will need it to convince some of the other men. They are all baying for Mr Darcy's blood.'

Mrs Mortimer recommended, 'I suggest you send a note to the camp to say that the Colonel has gone to London to press charges. But do not specify which Colonel.'

Carter grinned at the suggestion. 'Pity you are not in command of our unit.'

<div style="text-align:center">~~~ooOOoo~~~</div>

Soon Colonel Fitzwilliam and two footmen from Brook Hall were on their way to London. They arrived in time to see the solicitor, who handed over the contract when Fitzwilliam presented Darcy's note.

Considering the lateness of the hour, Colonel Fitzwilliam decided to spend the night at Matlock House.

As it happened his parents were spending an evening at home without company.

'Richard, this is a pleasant surprise. To what do we owe the pleasure of your company?' his father enquired, when the Colonel joined his parents after refreshing himself and changing for dinner.

'Would you believe some fool Colonel of the militia tried to arrest Darcy for the murder of Wickham?'

'Darcy killed Wickham at last?'

'No, he did not, and neither did I. Wickham, who had joined the militia, and another militia officer were killed while attacking a young woman. Darcy, Bingley and I happened to come upon the scene. When I returned the bodies to their camp, that fatheaded Militia Colonel decided that Darcy killed Wickham out of jealousy, since Wickham had been spreading his lies again.'

His parents were all astonishment at the news, and insisted on hearing a full account. Richard obliged them, and had the satisfaction of seeing the incredulity on their faces when he revealed that the men had been shot by Miss Elizabeth. His father was properly horrified at the aftermath, while Lady Matlock became thoughtful.

After he had finished relating his reasons for being in town, she asked, 'you were in Meryton, you said?'

When Richard confirmed the location, Lady Matlock grinned. 'You called the young lady Miss Elizabeth, but you did not identify her further. Shall I give you her full name?' When Richard nodded, she said triumphantly, 'Elizabeth Rose Mortimer.'

Now it was Richards turn to be surprised. 'How do you know?'

'Mrs Stephanie Mortimer is an old friend of mine.'

'Mrs Mortimer? I seem to remember you inviting a Mrs Mortimer and her two daughters to a ball once. What was it, two or three years ago?' Lord Matlock asked his wife.

'It was three years ago. Your memory is excellent. But you always remember handsome women,' Lady Matlock teased her husband.

'I certainly always remember the one I was lucky enough to marry.'

Lord Matlock turned to his son. 'I presume you want an impartial investigator to look into Colonel Forster's antics?' At Richards confirmation he suggested, 'I can arrange that for you if you like. I know just who to speak to.'

The rest of the evening was spent in pleasant conversation, although Lady Matlock did notice that the name of Jane Mortimer came up on several occasions. Maybe there was hope for her son yet.

~~~ooO0Ooo~~~

The next morning, while everyone at Brook Hall was waiting for Fitzwilliam's return, Bingley used the opportunity to speak to Jane.

He had guided her to two chairs removed from the rest of the party, to provide them with some privacy.

'Miss Mortimer, yesterday I saw a side of you I had not expected,' he began his rehearsed speech.

'I am ashamed to admit it, but you quite frankly terrify me. I found it extremely confronting that you could shoot a man. Yes, I know it was in the defence of your sister, and I am exceedingly grateful that you did so. I am also not proud of the fact that I doubt that I could have done so in your place.'

'To have a friend who is capable of defending her family is a privilege, but the fact remains that I am completely intimidated by you. You are a wonderful lady, intelligent, beautiful and courageous, and I am in awe of you...'

'But you have no wish to be associated more closely,' Jane gently finished the sentence for him when he hesitated. She had expected this after seeing his reaction the day before, but it still hurt.

'I am sorry, but there it is... I simply cannot countenance a wife who is so much more than I am. I suppose it is small minded of me...'

'Say no more, Mr Bingley. I quite understand. When I started to learn to look after myself, I had a long discussion with Mrs Mortimer and Miss Martin about the impact this ability might have on gentlemen. I accepted then that most gentlemen prefer to be the stronger partner in a relationship. The best I can hope for is an equal, who is comfortable with a woman who is his equal.'
~~~

'Like Darcy and Miss Elizabeth.'

'Exactly.'

'Darcy has always been my mentor. He is much stronger than I am, even though he does not make an issue of that fact.' Bingley sighed. 'I am afraid that I have to learn to be my own man before I can consider marriage. As I am, I would be a disappointment to my wife.'

'Unless you choose a woman who likes to have her own way…'

'You mean like my sister…? I have considered that I have been surrounded by people whom I let manage me. Now I need to learn new habits.'

'I wish you well in your very worthwhile endeavour, Mr Bingley.'

~~~oo0Ooo~~~

By noon, Colonel Fitzwilliam was on his way back to Meryton in the company of several investigating officers of both the Regulars and the Militia. The man in charge was Major Jarrett.

When he met up with the officers, the Colonel spotted a familiar face. 'Sergeant Martin, it has been a long time.'

'That it has. It must be three years or more.'

'How is your leg?'

'Much better. While it is not quite good enough for battle, thanks to your recommendation, I got this nice cushy job at headquarters. Except, of course, when I get dragged out on a job.'

Once on their way, Colonel Fitzwilliam explained the situation in detail. There was a significant amount of disbelief from most of the officers, until the sergeant laughed. 'Is Miss Julia Martin still at Brook Hall?'

'Yes, she is.'

'She is my cousin, and I trained her in fighting, when she got so badly scarred that no man wanted to marry her. If she taught the young ladies, then I believe every word you said about what they can do.'

After this recommendation, the officers were inclined to see for themselves, rather than dismiss the story out of hand.
~~~

They arrived at Brook Hall just in time for tea. Richard had sent an express ahead and they were expected.

Mrs Mortimer, anxious to get the situation cleared up as expeditiously as possible, had invited Sir William Lucas to join them again. Darcy and Bingley had stayed overnight to ensure no hotheads from the militia could waylay them.

In addition to her daughters, even Miss Martin and Captains Carter and Tetlow were present.

After introductions were made, Mrs Mortimer invited the officers to join them for tea, while everyone gave their account of the happenings of the previous day. Kitty removed the scarf she was wearing, allowing the men to see the bruises she had sustained.

Darcy produced the contract and the other documents which Richard had picked up from Darcy house that morning.

'Where is Colonel Forster now?' enquired Major Jarrett.

'We had to lock him into a cellar. He seems to have lost his mind,' answered Captain Carter. 'He keeps shouting that he will kill Miss Elizabeth for opposing him.'

'He has an exceedingly low opinion of women's abilities and is incensed that I did not bow to his superiority, and allowed him to kill Sir William,' Elizabeth explained.

'I would like to see him for myself,' announced Major Jarrett.

'Mr Kirby will show you the way,' agreed Mrs Mortimer. 'I believe it would be easier if no women are present at the interview.'

Major Jarrett, accompanied by several of his men, and escorted by the same number of footmen went to interview Colonel Forster.

They returned but a few minutes later.

Jarrett looked troubled. 'I have never seen a man so disturbed. I am inclined to believe your account, but I need to verify that Miss Elizabeth is as capable as you claim. I would appreciate a demonstration of the lady's abilities on the morrow.'

'By all means, Major,' agreed Mrs Mortimer. 'It is a relief to deal with an officer who has an open mind.'

Shortly afterwards, the soldiers left with Colonel Forster, who was restrained and bundled into the carriage.

Everyone at Brook Hall heaved a huge sigh of relief to see the last of him.

~~~oo0Ooo~~~

The following afternoon, the investigators returned for the promised demonstration.

Elizabeth once again used the scarecrow targets, although, since Major Jarrett and his officers were not hostile, the way Colonel Forster had been, she avoided the theatrics of having one of her sisters standing next to the target. Her shots were as accurate as they had been on the last display, which satisfied the officers.

They adjourned to the drawing-room to discuss the outcome of their investigation.

'When we arrived at the camp, we questioned Lieutenant Denny, who had not been placed under arrest by Colonel Forster. Initially he tried to deny any wrongdoing, but eventually he admitted that Lieutenant Wickham wanted to settle a score with Mr Darcy, by ruining preferably Miss Elizabeth, or one of her sisters, if they could not get hold of her.'

Major Jarrett focused on Elizabeth. 'Since Denny confirmed that Miss Elizabeth shot Cooper when he was hurting Miss Catherine and refused to stop, she was justified in taking the actions she did. The same goes for when Wickham went for Miss Catherine with a knife. No charges will be brought against Miss Elizabeth Mortimer.'

'What will happen to Lieutenant Denny?' asked Sir William who was again present to ensure that the military did not overstep their jurisdiction.

'Since he was complicit in the attack on gentlewomen, he will be transported to Botany Bay.

'That leaves Colonel Forster. He attempted to kill me, and only the quick actions by Miss Elizabeth and Miss Lydia saved my life. I want him to be brought up on charges for attempted murder.'
~~~

'Sir William, Colonel Forster's mind has become unhinged. He keeps ranting that he wishes to kill Miss Elizabeth for defying him.' Major Jarrett looked uncomfortable when he continued. 'That is not all he is ranting about. He also said that he should mete out the same punishment to Miss Elizabeth that he meted out to someone named Emily for her defiance. I could not get him to say what punishment he was referring to. But it sounded...' he trailed off.

Sir William looked horrified. 'I suspect he referred to Emily Evans, a young girl who was violated and killed last week.'

Major Jarrett nodded. 'I am sad to say that I am not surprised. When I went to see Mrs Forster to advise her that her husband had been arrested, she begged me to keep him away from her. By the looks of her, she is barely more than a child and has suffered abuse.'

Sir William offered, 'I will send my wife to Mrs Forster. Lady Lucas will know how to help the young woman.'

'Thank you, Sir William. That would be most helpful.' The Major looked around the room. 'Based on the information you have provided to me, I now know how to deal with Colonel Forster.'

The following day the residents of Brook Hall and Lucas Lodge were informed that Colonel Forster had suffered a fatal accident while cleaning his gun.

<p style="text-align:center">~~~oo0Ooo~~~</p>

28 Understanding

Sunday morning dawned bright and clear, making the last few days seem like an unpleasant dream. It seemed impossible that dark things could happen when the world looked bathed in sunshine.

Mrs Mortimer and her daughters, accompanied by Mrs Taylor and Miss Martin, attended services to give thanks for their safe deliverance from the troubles of the previous week. The reactions of the ladies varied depending on each of their personalities.

Jane was not as sanguine about shooting Wickham as she made out to be. While she appreciated that everyone was telling her that she had only wounded him, she suspected that the wound would have killed him eventually. But since she could not have been certain that Lizzy could pull the trigger a second time, she had decided to act. Now she had to live with the consequences.

These consequences included the loss of Mr Bingley. Prior to these events, he had been charming, attentive and interested in her and her opinions, not just her beauty. She had enjoyed his company and felt that she was falling in love with him. It had hurt when he told her that she terrified him, and it had taken all her courage to appear composed and accept his withdrawal with outward serenity. She wondered if there was another man as strong as Mr Darcy, who had not been put off by her sister's actions.

Elizabeth was tired. The last few nights she had been haunted by nightmares, seeing the faces of the men she had shot. The fact that she could kill troubled her, but Mr Darcy's support helped her deal with the situation, at least when she was awake. During the night when she could not sleep, she would remember the words *nothing short of death will keep me away* and feel comforted.

Since she had met Mr Darcy and come to know him, she found that she liked him a great deal. She had enjoyed their discussions and even their arguments. Elizabeth was amazed at his acceptance of her.

Nothing seemed to faze him, neither her intelligence nor her physical pursuits.

And even the events of this week were not enough to drive him away, as she had feared might happen. Instead, he had supported her and helped her come to terms with her actions. All those qualities combined were exceedingly attractive, and almost without realising, she had come to love him. Now she hoped that she had not misunderstood his words, and that he felt the same way about herself.

Kitty had had some very difficult days. The fact that despite her training she had done nothing to defend herself troubled her deeply. The sudden attack had shocked her, and she had frozen, unable to move or even think. She was grateful that her sisters had come to her rescue, but she felt she should have done something to make the rescue unnecessary.

Miss Martin had been of great help, telling Kitty that her reaction to the situation, both at the time and since was completely normal. Very few people could actively react to danger, when it meant hurting someone. Miss Martin also told her that her sisters had been able to react because they had not been the target of the attack. They had time to evaluate the situation.

The constant reassurance, and her sisters telling her that they did not blame her in the least, was starting to reduce the guilt she felt.

Lydia, on the other hand, was very proud of herself for having dealt with Colonel Forster. The bubbly girl enjoyed the praise that her quick thinking and decisive action had engendered.

She was concerned about her sisters' reaction to the events, and had tried to cheer them up... with mixed success. While the sisters appreciated her well-meaning efforts, her cheer and optimism did, at times, grate on their nerves.

Mary was grateful that her sisters were safe. She had had the least involvement in the actions, for which she was thankful. Since then she had supported her sisters with a calming presence, her willingness to listen, and occasionally a shoulder to cry on.

Mrs Mortimer, like Mary, was grateful that her girls were safe. In the days since, she, together with Miss Martin, Mrs Taylor and Mary, had tried to ensure that the girls would always have someone they could lean on. She was pleased to see that the girls were on their way to slowly but surely recover their equilibrium.

~~~oo00oo~~~

The party from Netherfield was also present.

Mr Darcy was concerned that Miss Elizabeth looked tired, but his cousin had reassured him that her reaction was perfectly normal and that her nightmares would ease in time, especially with the support Darcy and her family were giving her.

Elizabeth had often surprised him due to her unconventional education, but he realised that it perfectly suited her personality. And he loved that personality. She was intelligent, strong, vivacious and active, and he appreciated all those traits.

Now Darcy hoped that Miss Elizabeth would soon be recovered sufficiently for the discussion he longed to have with her. Ever since the assembly, just over a month ago, when they met officially, he had come to know her. His feelings for her had grown from the initial liking, to a love he had not expected to ever feel.

Colonel Fitzwilliam's thoughts were also on a lady. He had not had much opportunity to get to know Miss Mortimer, especially since he discovered the hidden side of her, but he was hoping to remain in the area and remedy that situation. He hoped that it might lead to a situation where he could trade his first love, the army, for a new one.

Charles Bingley was rather subdued. He had done a considerable amount of soul-searching over the last few days, and did not particularly like what he found. He had always considered his amiability as a strength. Now he had discovered that it was a weakness, which had allowed everyone, not only his sister, to make him bend to their wishes. He was at last determined to learn to make his own decisions, while still remaining true to his basic nature.

~~~oo00oo~~~

After the service, Mrs Mortimer informed the gentleman that they planned on a quiet day to rest from the strains and stresses of the week, but hoped that the gentleman would be free the following day and join them for dinner.

Although disappointed that they could not spend time with the ladies today, the gentlemen assured Mrs Mortimer that they would be delighted to accept her invitation.

~~~oo0Ooo~~~

Darcy and Fitzwilliam were eager to get to Brook Hall as early as courtesy allowed.

Bingley, although not as motivated, was pleased to go along with them. He had realised that what he had felt for Miss Catherine immediately after the attack was simply concern for the young girl, but had been accentuated by his reaction to the event which he had just witnessed. Now he was glad to go and ascertain that she was well on the road to recovery.

When they arrived, Darcy was informed by Mrs Mortimer that Elizabeth and Lydia were in the garden. Since he could hardly wait to see Elizabeth again, he immediately requested permission to join them. When Mrs Mortimer gave him leave to do so, he did not wait to listen what else she tried to tell him.

~~~oo0Ooo~~~

Darcy strode along the path and had just come around a corner when he was greeted by a most unwelcome sight. He stopped and stared in horror. There was Elizabeth, his Elizabeth, in the arms of a man and she did not look like it was against her will. The man was moderately tall and well built, with pleasant features.

Elizabeth was hugging the stranger, and he seemed to be whispering something in her ear which elicited a peal of laughter from her.

As Darcy watched with a sinking feeling in his stomach, Elizabeth rose onto her toes and kissed the man on the cheek. She then stepped back and took his arm to lead him into the house.

He was lost in thought when he heard Lydia's cheerful voice, 'Good afternoon, Mr Darcy. It is good to see you. You are just in time to meet our cousin. Our real cousin, not one of our courtesy cousins.'

Darcy, who was caught off guard and still reeling from seeing Elizabeth, was confused. 'Real cousin, courtesy cousin? I am afraid I do not understand, Miss Lydia.'

'It is simple, William is our real cousin, as his father and our father were related. The others are Mrs Mortimer's grandsons, or more accurately her husband's grandsons from his first marriage.'

'Since you are Mrs Mortimer's daughter, but those cousins you mention are actually her grandsons, that would make them your nephews, not your cousins.'

'True, but I refuse to call a man twice my age, nephew. For goodness sakes, Patrick is two and thirty, while I am not even six and ten. It would be even worse if he called me aunt. That would make me feel positively ancient. And I am not even out yet,' huffed Lydia.

'So, the cousin who is visiting is William?'

'William Collins, yes. We have not seen him in ages, and he is the nicest young man. He came to live with us for a while when his father died.'

During this dialog Lydia had guided Darcy into the house, and he came face to face with Miss Elizabeth and William Collins.

~~~ooo0Ooo~~~

Elizabeth's face lit up when she saw Darcy entering the parlour. 'Mr Darcy, my cousin has just arrived for a visit. We have not seen him since he left at Easter to take up his new position.'

Darcy, due to his earlier shock was still bewildered, but seeing the welcome in Elizabeth's expression, reassured him that he had probably observed a family reunion rather than anything else.

'Mr Darcy, may I introduce my cousin, Mr William Collins. He is the new vicar at Hunsford. Cousin William, this is Mr Darcy, of Pemberley in Derbyshire. He is a nephew to Lady Catherine de Bourgh.'

Darcy recovered enough to respond, 'I am pleased to make your acquaintance, Mr Collins.'

'The pleasure is all mine, Sir. I have heard so much about you. Lady Catherine speaks of you… frequently.' William grinned at Darcy.

'Do I gather from your expression that my aunt still insists that I would marry my cousin?' Darcy returned the grin of the pleasant young man. His earlier misgivings were being allayed by the open friendliness.
~~~

'She does, indeed. Although Miss de Bourgh seems to have a very different opinion...'

'My cousin and I have discussed the issue, and while I love my cousin as family, neither of us has a wish to be wed. At least not to each other.'

'I have heard the lady state this on a number of occasions, but Lady Catherine appears immune to any opinion but her own.'

Darcy chuckled. 'Mr Collins, please forgive me if I say that you are not the kind of man that I would expect my aunt to favour as her parson.'

'You think I am not obsequious enough for her liking?'

When Darcy looked discomfited, it was William's turn to laugh. 'I must admit to a small deception. A friend of mine was interviewed by Lady Catherine and rejected for being too forthright. Since he knew that I was also looking for a position, he sent me a letter and advised on the proper approach to the Lady.'

'Lady Catherine seemed pleased by my abject admiration of her wisdom and granted me the living. She is most put out at present because the living is for life and she cannot withdraw it. Only the bishop can remove me, but only for not performing my duties adequately.'

Darcy could not help himself, he laughed outright at Mr Collins' stratagem.

'I am convinced that the people of Hunsford are deeply in your debt and forever grateful.'

'I must admit, attendance of Sunday Service has improved in recent months...'

They chatted a little longer, until Darcy could not wait any more. He suggested that since there was still time before dinner and the afternoon was relatively warm, a stroll in the garden might be pleasant.

~~~oo0Ooo~~~
~~~

29 Graduation

All the sisters except Kitty agreed, since she still needed to change for dinner, and soon the gentlemen from Netherfield and William Collins escorted them outside. While Bingley and Collins stayed with Mary and Lydia, Fitzwilliam offered his arm to Jane, and Darcy, with Elizabeth on his arm strolled off in a different direction.

When Darcy, who was still trying to gather his thoughts after his earlier upset, remained quiet for too long, Elizabeth asked cautiously, 'is something the matter, Mr Darcy?'

'I am sorry for being so quiet, Miss Elizabeth. When I came today, I was hoping to speak to you, but when I arrived you were in the garden. I came outside to find you, and happened to see you just as you were greeting your cousin.' Darcy shrugged and smiled uncomfortably.

'You thought...'

'I did not know who he was and I was afraid that I was too late.'

All Elizabeth could say was 'Oh.' Would Mr Darcy decide that she had behaved indecorously and was now disappointed with her? Elizabeth felt pained at the thought.

'I felt devastated which only confirmed to me what I have known for some time now.'

Darcy stopped and turned to face Elizabeth. 'I am completely and irrevocably in love with you, and nothing would make me happier than if you agreed to become my wife.' He anxiously watched her expression.

He loved her and wanted to marry her! Even though the sun was starting to set, the smile on Elizabeth's face seemed to light up the garden.

'Mr Darcy, I love you too, and yes, I will marry you.'

Darcy's smile mirrored Elizabeth's when he raised her hands to his lips, and simply said, 'thank you.'

After a small eternity staring into each other's eyes, Elizabeth looked around and not seeing their companions, asked, 'are you not going to kiss me, Mr Darcy?'

His eyes widened momentarily in surprise, before he enthusiastically complied with her suggestion.

When they came up for air, he said, 'my name is Fitzwilliam, but my family call me William. I would like it very much if you used that name.'

'That will be a little confusing at the moment, William, but I feel certain that we will cope. I hope you will call me Elizabeth or Lizzy.'

'Thank you, Elizabeth.' He smiled at her in contentment. 'Shall we go and speak to your mother?'

'Yes, I think we should,' Elizabeth agreed, since that kiss had awakened feelings in her that she thought best not to encourage just yet. But it seemed to her that only the fact that she was holding William's arm stopped her from floating away as they walked back to the house.

<div style="text-align:center">~~~ooO0oo~~~</div>

Colonel Fitzwilliam was escorting Miss Mortimer just out of earshot of the foursome trailing behind them.

Jane was quiet, wondering what she could say to this gentleman, when he opened the conversation in a surprising manner, 'please, Miss Mortimer, do not judge Mr Bingley too harshly. He is a gentle soul and has never truly had to deal with the realities of life.'

'I do not blame him, Colonel. I know what I did is not the sort of thing a gently bred young lady is supposed to do. Out of all my acquaintances, Mr Darcy appears to be the only man who can deal with what Lizzy did,' she admitted sadly, not looking at him.

'I also admire how you and Miss Elizabeth defended your sister.'

Jane raised her head in startlement and for the first time truly looked at the Colonel. He wore a slight smile which seemed to be encouraging.

'You do? You do not think me to be some savage?'

'Not at all, Miss Mortimer. You seem to forget that I am a soldier, I have seen death countless times. Much of it unnecessary. But what you did was necessary and it takes an exceedingly strong person to take such an action.'

I can guarantee you that Wickham would have harmed Miss Catherine, if you had not stopped him. You did not know if Miss Elizabeth would have the courage to pull the trigger a second time. Based on my experience, I am amazed that she was able to do so. You acted appropriately in the defence of your sister, and I admire you for it.'

He let the words sink in before he continued. 'I must admit, that before that incident I thought you were a lovely well-bred young lady, like so many others. To be brutally honest, I thought you insipid.'

Fitzwilliam smiled apologetically as Jane gasped. 'Then I saw you defend your sister. You were strong and steady and unflinching. At that point I changed my mind about you and envied Bingley. Propitiously for me, he chose to quit the field.'

Jane stared at the Colonel in disbelief. 'Mr Bingley chose to withdraw his attention because of what I did, but you *like* me because of what I did?'

'I do indeed, Miss Mortimer. I think you would suit me very well indeed. If you would allow, I would like to court you, for you to find out if I could possibly suit you.'

'Colonel Fitzwilliam, I… I do not know what to say… I did not expect this… not after what happened last week…'

'Miss Mortimer, I am not insisting for you to make a decision this minute. If you would like to think about it for a day or two, I can wait. Now that I have found you, I am in no hurry.' He smiled at her.

Jane suddenly realised that with that relaxed smile, he was rather attractive. While he was not classically handsome like his cousin, his more craggy features were still very easy on the eye.

'If you would like to come for tea on Wednesday, I will give you my answer then, if that is agreeable to you?' she suggested.

Fitzwilliam beamed at Jane. 'Very agreeable, indeed.'

~~~ooO0Ooo~~~

Elizabeth and Darcy were the first to return to the parlour where Mrs Mortimer sat, reading a book, while Kitty was still upstairs, changing for dinner.

She looked up when the couple entered, and to her it was immediately obvious that they entered as a couple.

She cocked her head to one side, smiled mischievously and asked, 'what took you so long?'

Darcy looked around and suggested mildly, 'we are the first ones returned from the walk.'

'I was not speaking about your walk...' She gave their linked arms a significant look.

Darcy looked down and realised what Mrs Mortimer had seen. He smiled and bowed in acknowledgment. 'Mrs Mortimer, will you do me the honour and grant me Miss Elizabeth's hand in marriage?'

'Elizabeth, do you wish to be Mr Darcy's wife?'

'Yes, please, Mama.'

'Very well, Mr Darcy you have my permission to marry Elizabeth, but only if, as someone once said, you take the rest of her as well.'

After a moment's confusion, Darcy grimaced. 'And I thought my sense of humour was bad.'

'So, how soon do you wish to get married?'

Darcy looked at Elizabeth, who smiled enthusiastically. 'Soon?' he asked with a broad smile.

'As soon as possible,' Elizabeth agreed.

'The soonest you can get married is the ninth of December, if we have the first banns read next Sunday,' suggested Mrs Mortimer.

'Would the ninth of December suit you, my love?' asked Darcy.

'It would suit me admirably,' agreed Elizabeth.

~~~ooO0Ooo~~~

The following day Mrs Mortimer requested Darcy's and Elizabeth's presence in her study to discuss the list of wedding guests.

The first name he added to the list was Georgiana.

'My sister will be excited when she receives the news, although I doubt that she will be surprised.' Darcy smiled at Elizabeth. 'Your name featured quite regularly in my letters to her.'

'Why not send for your sister now, and give her a chance to meet Elizabeth and the other girls before the wedding. We would be delighted to have her stay with us now and after the wedding,' offered Mrs Mortimer. 'It will also give you a chance to have time for yourselves after the wedding...'

'I do not wish to impose on you...'

'Nonsense, I am simply trading one daughter for another.' Mrs Mortimer teased. 'Since you are stealing one of my daughters, the least you can do is to provide a replacement.'

Darcy found Mrs Mortimer's manner of extending an invitation delightfully unusual. He glanced at Elizabeth, who nodded with a pleased smile. 'Thank you. I will send for her today. She could be here by the weekend.'

'That is perfect timing. She will be in time to hear the first banns read.

~~~ooo0Ooo~~~

At last the weather cooperated, drying out the roads, and making it possible for Georgiana and her companion, Mrs Annesley to arrive late on Friday afternoon.

Since they had sent a messenger ahead, Darcy was at Brook Hall to welcome his sister.

While Georgiana was thrilled that her brother had found a woman to marry for mutual love, she was nervous about being a guest in the house of a stranger. The nervousness did not survive the warm welcome from Mrs Mortimer, and the enthusiastic reception by Elizabeth and her sisters.
~~~

When she joined her brother after refreshing herself and changing for dinner, Georgiana was slightly bewildered by the sheer number of women in the house, each of whom was determined to make her feel welcome.

'Compared to the girls I met at that school, Lizzy and her sisters are rather unconventional, but, oh, so much nicer,' she enthused. 'I am so very happy for you to have found her.'

'Not half as happy as I am,' Darcy replied.

~~~oo0Ooo~~~

The banns had been read in Meryton and in Lambton three Sundays in a row without any objections.

Darcy had informed his uncle and aunt of his upcoming marriage while he was in London arranging for the settlement papers. Lord and Lady Matlock were delighted at the news and forgot to mention the information to Lady Catherine, but asked to be invited to the wedding.

William Collins had returned to Hunsford. Since Lady Catherine was in a snit about his latest sermon, she refused him an audience. Which meant that he had no opportunity to mention that one of his cousins was marrying Mr Darcy. Of course, it was pure coincidence that he had chosen such a controversial sermon.

Darcy asked his cousin to stand up with him as his best man.

Since Jane had agreed to a courtship with Colonel Fitzwilliam, Elizabeth asked her to be the bridesmaid.

All the preparations had been accomplished. The wedding dress was finished and Elizabeth's trousseau was complete and packed.

The wedding guests had arrived. Everything was done.

~~~oo0Ooo~~~

The day of the wedding had arrived. The only unconventional aspect was that the bride was being given away by her mother.

Mrs Mortimer walked proudly into the church with Elizabeth on her arm. When they reached the front of the church, she kissed Elizabeth's cheek before she passed her daughter's hand to a beaming Darcy.

The wedding ceremony was simple and over quickly.

Once they signed the register, Miss Elizabeth Mortimer had graduated to be Mrs Fitzwilliam Darcy.

~~~ooO0Ooo~~~

Mrs Bennet sat quietly weeping at the back of the church.

The daughter, whom she had disliked the most because she considered her unmarriageable, due to being too bookish, too unladylike, too much of a hoyden, was the first daughter to get married.

And to such a man. He was tall and very handsome, and he was rumoured to have ten thousand pounds a year and owned half of Derbyshire. How had this plain and ill-dressed girl captured such an outstanding gentleman?

Although, Elizabeth did look rather well today. If only she had better taste in clothes. There was still barely any lace on her dress.

And yet, Elizabeth was getting married, while Jane, her most beautiful daughter was only the bridesmaid.

The world was surely becoming quite incomprehensible and determined to vex her.

~~~ooO0Ooo~~~

The End

Maybe...